FIELD OF DUST

FIELD OF DUST

BASED ON A TRUE STORY

ANGELA JEAN YOUNG

The Book Guild Ltd

First published in Great Britain in 2017 by
The Book Guild Ltd
9 Priory Business Park
Wistow Road, Kibworth
Leicestershire, LE8 0RX
Freephone: 0800 999 2982
www.bookguild.co.uk
Email: info@bookguild.co.uk
Twitter: @bookguild

This is a work of historical fiction based on fact. The key characters were members of
Angela Jean Young's family, others real people central to their lives. Every effort
has been made to preserve the integrity of those referred to in the text.
Otherwise, any resemblance to actual persons is purely coincidental.

Typeset in Minion Pro

Printed and bound in Great Britain by 4edge Limited

ISBN 978 1912083 169

British Library Cataloguing in Publication Data.
A catalogue record for this book is available from the British Library.

Printed on FSC accredited paper

To the memory of Florence Gant.

I remembered the time when the village of Northfleet consisted of a few houses on the shore, together with those on the hill above, where then there was a little village green, now alas! only a field of dust.

The Reverend Frederick Southgate
Vicar of St. Botolph's, Northfleet, 1884

1

'Come on, Floss, your mam won't be out for ages yet… it'll all be over if we don't hurry up.'

Jessie Larkin sounded really fed up with her friend. Several times that afternoon, she'd been back to the same spot outside The Huggens Arms where Florence Grant was standing under the hanging lamp. Shivering with the damp riverside air permeating her threadbare pinafore, no amount of gory detail could tempt her away from that spot. Flossie knew better than to disobey her mother.

'It'll be worth a clip round the ear, I promise,' pleaded Jess. 'Our Arthur reckons he could see dozens of bloated bodies. Henry Luck's been keeping a tally. We had to hold our noses when the barge went by the first time. Piled high, it was. There's bound to be loads more by now, my pa says. They're coming up early with the sewage.'

It was all too much to bear. Flossie dropped the balls of cement clinker she'd been idly smashing to dust against the pub wall and ran off after Jessie. After all, there was a good chance she'd be back before her mother's money ran out. If it bought her more than five gins, Mary Grant wouldn't remember that she'd left her daughter outside the pub anyway.

The girls clambered onto the slippery landing stage at Robin's Creek and joined the throng of excited children perched on the end, so as to get the best view round the bend of the river.

'Look,' shouted Henry, pointing with a piece of rotting driftwood. 'There's more. Cor blimey, they looks like they're about to burst.' Pushing his cap sideways he puffed out his cheeks in demonstration. The other kids laughed, the girls squealing as their favourite jester teetered precariously close to the edge.

'Don't be falling in,' shrieked Maisy Turner, 'or you'll end up like one of them.'

The children were hardened to seeing dead bodies floating in the Thames. Travelling downstream on the tide, they would often get wedged under moored vessels in Northfleet Harbour and remain stuck there for days, the putrid smell finally giving them away. It happened all the time. The bustling London docks were dangerous places to work – a docker misplacing a step with a heavy load could disappear without trace. All too frequently the bodies of frail women would be hooked out of the river, their haunted faces revealing the desperation that led them to suicide. Waterloo Bridge wasn't known as the 'Bridge of Sighs' for nothing.

But this was different. Henry had been keeping a tally on the side wall. So far *two hundred* had been chalked up, fifty of them children. For hours he and half his school class had watched, transfixed by the gruesome sight of tiny bodies dressed in their Sunday best bobbing past the bottom of College Road, their bloated parents rising and falling around them.

'I'd better be going,' Maisy Turner said reluctantly. 'My tea'll be ready.' Some of the others followed her up the slope, carefully picking their way round piles of rotting seaweed and kicking up cement dust to hide the blobs of tar on their boots so their mothers wouldn't notice.

'I'm not going anywhere,' Henry shouted. 'Bevan's *Spry*'ll be back soon. Not missing that for all the tea in China. She's brand new.' With that he plonked himself down on a rusty mooring bollard and gazed out across the misty river, searching for the brown sails of the empty Thames barge. Its crew had been coming and going for days, dragging unfortunate victims of the disaster out of the disgusting water. Built for transporting barrels of cement, this was a dreadful first assignment for the vessel and its crew.

It had been a week like no other. Rumours were rife about the demise of the paddle steamer *SS Princess Alice*. Flossie had heard no end of different versions of the tragedy. It was hard to take in because, only six days earlier, on Tuesday 3rd September 1878, she and Jessie had been standing by the smart pier gates – as they usually did after finishing their chores – watching the happy hundreds exiting the tunnel leading from the famous Rosherville Pleasure Gardens to pile aboard the doomed wooden pleasure boat. There was always a chance someone would throw away a programme, or better still, discard a hastily bought souvenir as they rushed through. It was a pleasantly warm evening and the girls stayed until the very last person boarded the packed vessel.

The *Alice* was making a routine 'moonlight trip' from Northfleet to Swan Pier near London Bridge. Hundreds of Londoners had paid around two shillings for the return fare to visit the gardens. Close to Woolwich town she collided with the collier *Bywell Castle*, splitting her in two just behind her starboard paddle wheel. The lightly built *Alice* didn't stand a chance against a ship that was four times bigger. It took her less than five minutes to sink to the bottom of the river. A hundred or so were rescued, clinging to bits of flotsam, but 650 lost their lives.

Flossie wept when she heard her father reading out the horrifying details from the local paper:

3

'Soon policemen and watermen were seen, by the feeble light, bearing ghastly objects into the offices of the Steam Packet Company. A boat consignment of the dead contained mostly little children, whose light bodies and ample drapery had kept them afloat even while they were smothered in the festering Thames. A row of little innocents, plump and pretty, well-dressed children, all dead and cold, some with life's ruddy tinge still in their cheeks and lips, the lips from which the merry prattle had gone forever. It was a spectacle to move the most hardened official and dwell forever in his dreams.'

Stories quickly circulated about the paddle steamer being overcrowded and not properly manned, as well as reports that the pilot of the *Bywell Castle* had failed to realise the danger soon enough. Everybody was blaming everybody else. One thing was certain, though: this part of the river was one of the most polluted in the country. Industrial waste and raw sewage were frequently pumped directly into it. Not only did this contribute to the high death toll of those who went into the river, but it caused sunken corpses to rise to the surface after only six days, rather than the usual nine.

'Here it comes!' Henry yelled, leaping off the bollard just in time to see the small mizzen sail being raised to help the flat-bottomed barge swing round into the harbour.

Arthur had been right, there were still an awful lot of corpses floating in the murky water and the smell was dreadful. The sound of the tiller being pushed over signalled the massive vessel coming about. Henry eagerly grabbed at the rope being hurled ashore, but it was so heavy, it knocked him over. The girls gasped as they watched it slither into the river and the barge lurch on the tide. Some of the boys dashed to help pull the sodden rope back up just as a deckhand leapt ashore, effortlessly dragging it out of the water and twirling it expertly round the bollard.

Trying hard to regain his composure, Henry banged his cap against the harbour wall, creating a cloud of cement dust that was so dense it made them all cough and rub their eyes.

'I could have done that, I know about knots,' he said unconvincingly, the boast making little impression on his dwindling audience. 'My grandpa used to make rigging for Pitcher's in the old days. His shipyard built Navy gunboats. Had sixty-eight-pounder cannons, they did.'

The children had heard all it before, and as the last few turned to leave, Henry tried a final tack: 'My Uncle Tom's taking me up Woolwich later when his shift's over. On the *train*. Won't be the first time for me, of course. Any of you lot ever been on a train?'

Jessie raised her eyebrows at Flossie. Henry was such a braggart. Only a few of the kids from around The Creek had ever been on a train. The closest they ever got to one was watching from the bridge above the chalk cutting as the puffing giants forged their way to and from Gravesend. Flossie knew only too well what it meant to go home peppered with coal smut on her clothes – invariably a good slap on the backs of her legs.

'What's up Woolwich, then?' Albert Bull replied inquisitively.

'Bit of the *Alice*,' Henry shouted back, pleased that at least someone had responded, even if it was only his steadfast best friend. 'The paddle wheel. It's beached, so we have to go while the tide's out. Tell you all about it tomorrow.' With that he skittered off along the jetty and disappeared around the corner, heading for his cottage in Dock Row, with loyal Albert, as always, trailing along behind.

'Think I'll go to school tomorrow,' said Jessie as they picked the seaweed off their boots outside The Huggens Arms. 'The class will be excited when they hear what we've seen. Will you be coming?'

'Depends if my mam'll let me,' Flossie replied dejectedly. 'There's the lodgers' washing to do.' Unlike her friend, Flossie would willingly have gone to school far more often, if allowed.

'Well, it looks like she hasn't found you missing. You could hear her singing a mile off. Do you want me to wait with you? No telling what she'll be like when she sees daylight now.' Jessie put her arm protectively around her friend's shoulder.

'No point in both of us getting what's coming,' Flossie sighed, resigned to her fate.

The girls had been friends from the minute they'd laid eyes on one another. Both lived in The Creek or 'The Crick' as it was called by the locals, here on the Kent side of the River Thames. Originally just a few dwellings constructed around boatbuilding yards, the street had gradually expanded after a local man, James Parker, set up his Roman cement business there. Twenty-five years later, better quality Portland cement had taken over. Cheap to make and highly profitable, it was now in mass production with nine cement factories operating in Northfleet. Each one needed a vast army of men, whose main requirements were sufficient brawn and endurance to stand up to the heavy labour required.

The Creek by this time was a bustling row of forty-six 'cottages', three alehouses and a grocer's shop, each dwelling bulging at the seams with large families and lodgers. Jessie lived at number 7, between The New Blue Anchor and The Huggens Arms. Flossie was further along at number 30, next door to The Hope. Despite it being Mary Grant's true local, Charlie Baker, the long-suffering licensee, had finally told her never to darken his door again.

'I do not wish for such blasphemy to be heard by my eight offspring,' he had made clear to her as she was finally ejected. So The Hope had to be given a wide berth – especially when the pub's Irish lodgers – the two Patricks, Murphy and Delaney – were in charge. It didn't do to mess with them, that was for sure.

Along with her ma and pa and siblings, Jessie had been born in The Creek. This wasn't the case with Flossie. Her memories were a bit hazy, but she vaguely remembered travelling with her younger sister Lottie, when she was about four, from a place called Ipswich. All she could recall was clinging on to her father for dear life amid all the pushing and shoving, being crammed into a cold, uncomfortable carriage and engulfed in choking smoke as it thundered out of the station. She'd been on a train all right, but it wasn't something she was going to share with Henry Luck. She couldn't recall any other details and there was never any talk of the past in her house. Children learned the hard way not to ask too many questions.

The sun was low in the sky before a dishevelled Mary staggered out of the public bar, her thick, wiry hair shedding the pins that had secured it in a bun. Squinting at the fading light, she beckoned to her daughter for support. With the drunken woman leaning heavily on her as they lurched down The Creek, Flossie battled to keep them both upright. Spotting Bessie Turner scrubbing the step of number 19, Mary pushed Flossie aside and wobbled across the granite chippings into the middle of the street. With hands on hips, she uttered some kind of profanity before almost falling backwards into a huge hole full of mud.

'Don't you go shouting the odds at me, Mary Grant,' Bessie screeched, pushing herself up from the boot scraper and hurling the carbolic soap into her metal bucket. 'You should be at home cooking your husband's supper. Whistle's about to blow, you know that.'

Poking her head out the door to see what the commotion was all about, Maisy Turner sheltered behind her mother's skirts on witnessing the state Mary was in. It was all too common an occurrence. Raising her eyebrows at Flossie, Maisy retreated into the house, coarse dripping still smeared around her mouth.

Flossie had just managed to get her mother inside their own front door as the whistle finally blew. A chorus of whistles, actually, from the half-dozen cement factories all within earshot. Luckily, her sister Lottie had already laid out the few meagre scraps from the pantry for their meal, and so between them they were able to prop their mother up in her chair, hair restored to a semblance of order, before their father's familiar footsteps were heard outside the window.

The end of the working day was quite an event. Mothers would rush to drag their children off the street as dozens of men criss-crossed The Creek from all directions, cement dust cascading from their caps and shoulders. The same scene could be witnessed in all the surrounding streets and alleys. With bodies too tired to linger and throats too parched to speak, they'd quickly disappear behind their front doors. In no time the street would be deserted again, leaving a trail of footprints in the thick new layer of grey dust. It was a sight to behold. Blink and you'd miss it.

Like so many itinerant workers, Samuel Grant had heard about the need for men in the burgeoning Northfleet factories whilst struggling to make a living in Ipswich. He, Mary, Flossie and Lottie had arrived with virtually no money and little idea of what they would find. That was five years ago. The Knight, Bevan & Sturge factory, which came right up to the end of The Creek and towered over their rented house, had offered him a job on the spot. Still in his twenties and thankfully fit and strong, he was put to work unloading blue clay from barges arriving at the wharf. Dug from the marshy banks of the Medway, sometimes eight feet thick, Sam had to use a spade to cut it up – much like butter in a grocer's shop – and then load it onto wagons pulled by powerful horses. It was back-breaking work and he worked every shift going, yet rarely had any money left in the coffers. Mary saw to that, in The Huggens Arms.

Holding open the front door for the three lodgers who worked alongside him, Sam kicked off his well-worn hobnailed boots and threw his cloth cap onto a wooden stool in the corner of the kitchen. The other men followed suit. Flossie filled a tin bowl with warm water from the range and she and Lottie watched as they washed their hands and faces, their pallor gradually returning to a healthy pink. Desperate to tell her tale of bodies and bonnets in the Thames, Flossie knew she'd have to wait until they were all seated around the table and tucking into their much-needed bread and smoked bacon. She just had to hope her mother didn't wake up and start holding forth.

Later, the girls carried the washing bowl across the pebbles and emptied the powder-grey water into the river, there being no fresh water available. They were used to having to do it. Rapid building had resulted in cesspits being dug within feet of the wells. The previous year, ten months had passed without any water at all while everyone argued about the water being contaminated and who was going to pay to put it right. They had been forced to fill their buckets from wells belonging to the landlord's other tenants, a fair walk away.

As she washed out the last dollops of cement, Flossie caught sight of old Annie Devonshire from number 35, making her way towards them, waving her stick.

'Don't you be putting those hands o' yours into the river unless you go tempting fate, young Flossie,' she shouted, her voice full of concern as she pointed to the dirty brown liquid swishing around in the bowl. 'This is what finished off those poor creatures what fell off the boat. Been this way since the Great Stink.'

Annie had lived in The Creek for over fifty years and knew better than anyone about the river and its horrors.

'What was the Great Stink?' Lottie enquired innocently as they headed back together towards their houses.

'That was what it became known as,' Annie replied, propping herself up on her stick. 'Happened about twenty years ago. We had the hottest summer I've ever known and the sewage on the riverbanks was cooking in the scorching sun. Result was a stench as disgusting as can ever be imagined. Whole city came to a standstill. Even the powers that be in Westminster covered their noses with their kerchiefs. They tried dousing Parliament's curtains in a mixture of chloride and lime, but it didn't help, so when everyone stopped working that was the last straw. Something had to be done about the filth, and quick.'

'So what happened?' Lottie asked excitedly.

'That's when they started building all the sewers and the big pumping stations up London way, my dearie. But all that did was push their muck down here. Terrible, it was. My Joseph declared he'd rather be on the high seas than this fetid river. Mind you, it was good news for our sons working at the cement mills. All those new sewers, bridges, canals, docks, piers and the like kept men in jobs. What's more, Portland's strength stole the show at the Great Exhibition.'

Realising that they had been out longer than they should have been, Flossie motioned to Lottie to make their way back home. Waving goodbye to Annie, the girls heard Henry Luck and Albert Bull's voices close by.

'Tide's gone out,' Henry yelled as they raced past. 'Reckon there'll be stuff from the *Alice* washed up on Botany Bay. Marsh mud might have hardened a bit by now. Come on!'

'Can't, we'll get into too much of a mess,' Flossie shouted back. 'Mam'll murder us if we get our stockings ruined.'

'You'll miss all the fun, then,' Henry added with a conspiratorial glint in his eye.

As word of the adventure spread, children started appearing from front doors and back alleys. Some adults joined in too, no doubt hoping to find coins or jewellery. But it was when the Grants' young lodgers tagged along as well that Flossie changed her mind. Her father had headed off to The Huggens and her mother was snoring in the chair, so even if she had to drag Lottie along with her, it was better than being stuck at home.

As the girls skipped down Galley Hill, cement dust from White's factory swirled round them in the breeze. A hum of excitement was coming from Botany Bay. Thirty or so people were already digging in the mud, some with spades, but most just with their hands.

'Looks like we're too late, they've beaten us to it,' Albert grumbled, nodding in the direction of Arthur Larkin, who was waving something in the air.

'Well, I'll be blowed,' said Henry, spitting on the shingle in annoyance as he watched Arthur wipe the runny mud off a pocket watch onto his sleeve.

As far as the eye could see, the squelchy mud was slowly giving up its hidden treasures. Women plunged their finds into buckets of river water to check their worth. Flossie was relieved to see Jessie, but started to feel uneasy when a tussle over a brooch looked like it was about to turn nasty.

Things got even worse when Susannah Lydon, a lunatic from the private Manor House asylum, staggered down the hill. Finding a muddy straw bonnet, no doubt once decorated with lace and silk flowers, she stuck the black, stodgy mess on her head and tied the ribbons under her chin. It was a comical sight as a mixture of mud and slime ran down her face and front. Beaming from ear to ear, she revealed teeth the same colour as the hat. Several of the young men were circling her, poking fun, and when she uncovered a purse with her boot, they were quick to snatch it off her. Throwing it between them, they mimicked and jeered as Susannah lurched helplessly at them.

Just when it was becoming unruly, a blood-curdling scream

stopped everyone in their tracks. Flossie grabbed hold of her sister and moved closer to Jessie. The scavenging halted and people gathered.

'It's an arm!' shouted Patrick Murphy.

It was true. Sticking out of the mud was someone's hand and wrist. The smell hit Flossie before she'd had time to take it all in.

'Reckon it's a woman. Don't look real. Pongs bloody real enough, though. Pass me a spade and I'll dig the rest out.'

Curiosity soon got the better of the crowd, most of them holding their noses as they stared at the body. Some grabbed sticks and prodded it, checking for jewellery, causing swarms of flies to hover overhead. Flossie covered her little sister's eyes and dragged her away. It wasn't something someone so young should have to witness.

For once the scullery was empty. Thankfully, Mary had gone to bed. As Flossie was clearing the place up and warming some milk on the stove for her sister, her father returned, dried mud spattered all over his breeches.

'I hear you got a bit of a shock, then,' he said, lighting the oil lamps. After brushing off the worst of the grime, he sat himself down in the corner chair and beckoned the girls to sit on his lap. This was the time that they both loved. He smelt strongly of sweet beer and tobacco, which wasn't unpleasant. Wrapping his sturdy arms around them, they each held a rough hand, Lottie inspecting the deep cracks filled with clay.

'Our lodgers come in The Huggens talking about that poor woman's body. No one had much idea about what to do with it. Luckily old Tom Handley's still got his fishing boat, so we wrapped it up in a canvas and rowed it over to Tilbury Fort. It's five shillings a body, you know. They're laid out side by side waiting to be moved to Woolwich. More than a hundred, but there's no hope of telling who they are.'

The girls held on even more tightly. Their pa was a hero.

'I think that should put an end to messing about with them poor lost souls, eh, girls, what do you reckon?'

Lottie was already asleep. Flossie buried her head in her father's jacket and closed her eyes. At last she felt safe. Little did she know that what she had witnessed would go down in history as the greatest loss of life of any shipping disaster on the River Thames.

2

Flossie had guessed right. She wasn't able to join her best friend heading for the national school the next morning. Mary's hangover meant she had to help with the washing. She envied Jessie, in her smart smock, making her way along the back alley. Truth was, with or without the washing, there often wasn't tuppence to pay for a week's schooling.

Sighing as she spotted the meagre amount of laundry soap left on the draining board, Flossie prepared herself for a visit to Jenkins the grocer before the day's work could start.

'Get him to cut a pennyworth off the large block,' Mary shouted as she stumbled around, collecting up discarded shirts and combinations. 'Two ounces of Reckitt's Paris Blue, too. Take a thruppenny bit off the table.'

Everyone did their washing on a Monday. That way it would all be dried, pressed, aired, folded and put away long before Sunday, the day of rest and clean clothes. For washerwomen like Mary, washday had to carry over to Tuesday and even Wednesday if the rain was heavy. *At least the sun's trying to break through*, Flossie thought to herself. *Might dry this lot off by nightfall.*

Thankfully, with so many men in The Creek wearing flannel

shirts in filthy working conditions, Mary didn't have to look far for employment. The only way for parents to make ends meet when they had numerous mouths to feed was to offer board and lodgings, so most dwellings had three or four single young men sharing a room. It was not surprising that with them coming from far and wide in search of labouring work, the area had become a hotchpotch of religious worship, customs and accents.

But there were scant pickings to be had washing clothes, and every penny counted. It didn't do to succumb to temptation and trespass onto another washerwoman's 'patch'. Mary found this out to her cost when she strayed too far touting for business and crossed Bessie Turner. Ever since, the two women had kept a constant eye on one another's washing lines, and were rarely civil, particularly after Mary had paid a visit to The Huggens.

John O'Connell, Edmond O'Leary and Joe Ollerenshaw, the young men living in the Grants' front room, were only too happy to get their clothes washed for a thruppenny bit a week. Experience had taught them to pay Samuel for their rent and board, yet the money still seemed to end up quenching Mary's thirst.

'I get in arrears,' she screamed at her husband one day after George Jenkins refused to give her milk and cheese on credit, ''cause you don't give me enough for the housekeeping.' Sam was used to being savaged in this way, but knew she'd spend *all* her time in The Huggens if he gave in to her wiles.

A slab of lye soap now to hand, Flossie immersed the dirty washing in a half-barrel of hot water. The smell of wood ash and melting lard made her retch, but she did her best to stir and beat the clothing with a dolly stick made from rejected staves found in the cooper's yard. Thankfully, leaving it to soak meant she had a chance to get her mother to drink a restorative mug of ginger beer.

'Essential for extinguishing the fiery thirst brought on by a tendency to over-imbibe,' was how Sylvester Lee, the local costermonger, had put it to Mary whilst tempting her to buy his home-made elixir. 'Penny, with a farthing back on the bottle. Guaranteed to please.'

Sylvester and his wife, Priscilla, lived in a caravan on the shore, selling an array of goods including jellied eels, pickled whelks, cough lozenges, peppermint water and ginger beer from an overladen donkey cart. He would tour the streets wearing a tall, dented black hat and a white neckerchief, playing a hurdy-gurdy, with a white-headed capuchin monkey that danced as it held out a child's cap for money. Unfortunately the monkey was vicious and had bitten Maisy Turner badly. Flossie usually ran inside when she heard Sylvester's melodious tunes approaching.

Back in the yard, mother and daughter scrubbed collars and cuffs on a washboard, working together to drag the sodden clothes to the other half of the barrel for rinsing. Here they would be treated with a dose of blueing to disguise the grey, and potato gratings for starch. Half the morning would be over by the time they went into battle with the mangle. Turning the handle to force the garments through was exhausting and the rising steam made their matching auburn hair turn to frizz. Finally, Mary, with Flossie and Lottie passing up the pegs, hung everything out on a series of ropes that criss-crossed the yard. It was ill-advised to leave it out for too long, though; cement dust was always in the air and could soon turn the washing grey and stiff.

By contrast to the weekly working-class washdays in The Creek, the custom of one huge wash every so many weeks still occurred in the big houses where the cement-mill owners lived. The middle classes took pride in having enough linen to manage without washing frequently. You were thought poor if you had a weekly washday. A visiting washerwoman would come in to undertake the 'great wash'. The little interim 'slop-washes' of things that had to be laundered in between times would be done by the housemaids.

Agnes Avery from Thorpeness was a housemaid at Hive House, owned by Mr and Mrs John Knight, who had three children. Mrs Knight also employed a cook and nursemaid, but no one to help Agnes with their great wash. Having a husband of standing, employing over six hundred men, it definitely didn't do to be seen to be washing linen too frequently, so it was decided they could last six weeks before a washerwoman was needed.

'I've got my hands full, slop-washing,' Agnes admitted as she showed Mary the washroom and offered her the job. Mary's mouth dropped open on seeing that the washroom was in its own building and not part of the scullery, and that the kitchens and butler's pantry took up most of the basement. Agnes wondered what she would have made of the rest of the place, were she to be allowed upstairs.

Hive House, parkland and orchard originally extended from the High Street down to the river. The house itself was three-storeyed with an imposing entrance hall, library, drawing room, dining room and ten bedrooms, all enclosed within walled gardens. It had its own carriage house and stables as well. Thomas Sturge had purchased the estate of eleven and a half acres and in 1853 built the Knight, Bevan & Sturge cement mill on part of the land. New streets of terraced houses were constructed close by to accommodate his workforce.

'Luck of the Irish, me being in the fishmonger's and meeting that Agnes Avery,' Mary told Flossie, revelling in her news. 'There we were, talking about the mackerel on the slab being caught in Suffolk, and, lo and behold, it turns out we both come from near there. Got me the job. So long as I remain temperate and mind me 'P's and 'Q's, I'll get three whole shillings for two days' work.'

Flossie laughed at her mother's mock posh accent and curtsey, but knew there was little chance of seeing any of the extra money.

For weeks after the *Princess Alice* disaster, bodies were still being retrieved. A large number were found trapped inside the hull when its two halves were finally raised to the surface. Soldiers were sent to help dockers like James and Tom Luck deal with the dead – so many that much of Woolwich dockyard was needed to handle the emergency. Stories circulated about crowds of dazed and anxious people shuffling down lines of corpses, looking for loved ones. As soon as a body was identified, it was coffined and promptly buried. Long processions of army wagons could be seen carrying the dead to Woolwich cemetery. On the 21st September, 120 unidentified victims were buried there in a mass grave.

At the inquest, people gave remarkable accounts of what had happened. One lucky survivor, who was standing on the bow of the paddle steamer as it was severed, told how it rose into the air before slowly sinking, miraculously enabling him to step across onto the deck of the collier. After thirty days of deliberations, during which a hundred witnesses were interviewed, the coroner delivered a verdict of death by misadventure.

The post-mortem may have been over, but there were still rich pickings to be had downriver. As the tide ebbed and flowed, mud larks could be regularly seen making their way along the shoreline to Northfleet. These river-scavengers usually only worked the stretch from Vauxhall Bridge to Woolwich, but news of the *Alice* had brought them out in force. The children of The Creek were shocked to see such poor creatures silently wading up to their middles through the mud. They were all ages, from mere children to pitiable, decrepit old men and women, bent over double, crawling among the barges at the wharves and jetties clad in nothing more than rags, their emaciated bodies grimed with the foul soil of the river. Paddling and groping for small pieces of coal, bone, wood, rope and old iron – in fact anything of value to fill their baskets – their torn garments stiffened up like boards as they sorted through their paltry treasure on the riverbank.

Henry Luck and Albert Bull were sitting on the landing stage, watching with a mixture of wonder and disgust when a creature raised itself up from the shallows beneath. Completely covered in mud and vile-smelling, it was just recognisable as a small, half-naked boy, who slithered alongside them with a toothless grin. Henry sat, transfixed, as Albert tried to make out what the boy was saying.

'Me gets a penny fer a buckit of iron, ha'penny fer one pound of wet rope, free farvings if it be dry and one penny fer free pounds of bones,' the child gabbled excitedly. 'Copper nails be the best, four pennies a pound.'

Mesmerised by the banter, they listened in awe to tales of boys leaving the riverbank only when the water was up to their armpits, scraping the mud from their trousers and then frequenting the cab-stands where a farthing or two could be made opening cab doors, or holding gentlemen's horses. It seemed barely conceivable that a boy, who looked no older than them, could live on a couple of coppers a day (though, by all accounts, his present haul would bring in nearer eight). The child had never attended the ragged school, even though he was supposed to, and had spent seven days inside a house of correction for sweeping an empty coal barge and selling the pickings on for a penny a pot.

He said he preferred it there to mud larking as he'd been given a coat and shoes to wear. Although he hadn't had much to eat, 'I never went to bed 'ungry as I oftens had to do at liberty. Might try it on again come winter,' he added with a muddy grin, 'so's not to be obliged to go into the cold, wet mud of a morning.'

But the best bit was saved till last. 'When river's icy, I be a pure-finder. I get eight pence a bucket. Don't take me long to fill up, wiv the streets bein' full of it, but I 'ave to sort it. Some places wonnit dry and limy-lookin', uvvers more sticky.'

Pure, the boy explained to a bewildered Albert, was dogs' dung, and was sold to the numerous tanneries in Bermondsey due to its cleansing and purifying properties. Some pure-finders had 'good connections' and were granted permission to cleanse kennels. They made a fair living supplying to regular clients. Those who didn't had to drag their buckets around the thirty tanning yards, touting their wares.

Albert found a furry jelly bean stuck at the bottom of his pocket and offered it to the boy, who grinned, grabbed it and disappeared into the mist with the rest of his silent army, back to their haunts in the riverside alleys of London.

Some weeks later, Sam took Flossie to Woolwich cemetery. They walked silently between the four rows of graves and headstones, some named, others marking groups of unidentified people from places like Barking and Erith. Nearby was the joint grave of the captain of the *Princess Alice* and three members of his family who had drowned with him on that terrible day. A large ornamental marble cross later stood as a memorial to the tragedy. It carried the inscription: *Erected by a national sixpenny subscription to which more than 23,000 persons contributed.*

'Stay out of The Huggens today,' Sam told Mary as he stepped gingerly over the ashes she was scraping out the range. 'If you want to go with me tonight, you stay sober...'

Mary grunted without looking up and tossed the fragments back into the grate, her hands and nails as black as the coals. Having already disposed of her earnings, there was no choice *but* to abstain.

That evening the Grants were set to attend Bevan's newly opened Factory Club on the High Street. Built at the expense of the mill owner, Thomas Bevan, in honour of his eldest son Robert's coming of age, it boasted room for nine hundred workers and recreational facilities such as billiards and bagatelle. Personally, Sam thought it altogether too grand with its white rendered frontage, classical pillars and decorative ironwork, but he admired the skilfully crafted Portland cement statues.

A blast from the cement company's whistles made Mary jump. 'Go on, be on your way or you'll be late for work,' she snarled.

Sam grabbed his cap from the stool, opened the door and dashed off down The Creek. To avoid being a latecomer you had to jostle your way through the narrow alley, every man aware he had to be at the factory steps before the whistles stopped. No one wanted their pay docked for being late.

Packed together like sardines, getting through the alley took forever. Sam considered why he felt so melancholy. Everything seemed such a struggle these days, not helped by Mary's drinking and her vile temper. What had gone wrong? Everyone in The Crick knew what she was like and he cringed at the thought of how she might embarrass him in front of his foreman tonight. Heaven knows what she would look like, too – mutton dressed as lamb, most probably. It never used to be that way.

The truth was that Sam was young and inexperienced when he met Mary. His mother died when he was very small, leaving her children to be brought up in Stanway Workhouse near Colchester. Unable to make a living in the fields, his father had been incarcerated there ever since. Sam often woke up dripping with sweat, still imagining he could hear the sound of the heavy bell-chain scraping across the stone floor. He could never forget the hunger pangs he'd experienced while queuing for his rations alongside three hundred other inmates.

Job prospects were good in Ipswich, so it made sense to head there after he was released. With little money, he took up lodgings close to the prison – so close he could hear the convicts exercising in the yard and glimpse the top of the gallows behind the castellated walls. The cottages in his row were barely nine feet apart and the stench of human excrement was intolerable. He vowed to get away as soon as he was able.

Once in employment, and with a few spare coppers in his pocket, he started to get to know the local hostelries. That's when he encountered Mary. Immediately attracted by her vivacity and flamboyance, he found her assured manner irresistible. It didn't take long before he had fallen head over heels for her and they were making plans to leave. Little did he know then what a fickle nature she had, and what he was letting himself in for. With hindsight, he would never have left Ipswich with her. She had changed so much and become cold and distant. She seemed ungrateful for all he had done to make life better for her and the girls.

Shuffling through Bevan's gate, the deafening rumbling and grinding brought him back to reality. Lowering his head to stop the swirling dust getting into his eyes, he sighed deeply and disappeared into the factory.

Mary cursed as she scrubbed under her fingernails with Sam's stiff bristle brush. Resenting his attitude to her drinking, she wondered what else he could expect after bringing her to such a miserable place. Ipswich was far livelier and she was used to having fun, so was it any surprise she had become depressed with the monotony of her life in Northfleet?

Shrugging her shoulders, she headed upstairs into the cold, damp bedroom. Unable to turn the clock back, no matter how much care she took over her ablutions it was obvious Sam no longer found her attractive. Not that that stopped him from having his way with her whenever he chose. Staring at her reflection in the long, silvered mirror, she ran her hand over her thickening waist and heavy belly. The corset which had given her a desirable hourglass figure lay discarded on the chair. She was going to have to tell him soon. Tonight, perhaps. After a drink or two at the club, he might not be too displeased.

This was the third time she'd fallen in less than two years, desperate to make up for the disappointment of losing their first boy, James Samuel. Born in The Creek, he was almost one year old and just walking when he was taken by scarlet fever. Within a period of four short weeks the family had been greeted by Reverend Southgate at St. Botolph's for both his baptism and his burial. One minute they were cheerfully gathered around the small font, the next they stood, distraught, as the tiny wooden coffin was carried past them and placed before the altar.

The preceding weeks had been terrible. They watched as his tiny body was engulfed with abscesses and a brutal red rash which no amount of cool water would ease. Flossie had run to fetch the doctor when little James' skin starting peeling, but there was nothing to be done. Children died all too regularly, only half reaching their first birthday. That year scarlet fever was just one of many diseases that raged through The Creek. The Baileys, next door, had lost two children to it, a third mercifully recovering, although now deaf.

Finding herself pregnant again soon after James Samuel's death kept Mary strong, but she went to pieces completely when another son was stillborn. Drowning her sorrows in gin, the next pregnancy ended in an early miscarriage. She felt like she had been in mourning almost all the time since leaving Ipswich, and fleetingly wondered if she was being punished. No, Northfleet was to blame for her troubles, so who could blame her for seeking solace in drink?

Buttoning up the side of her clean black skirt was a trial. The cheap fabric pulled and stretched. At the back of the cupboard she found a fancy, though heavily crumpled, blouse and carried it downstairs to where the iron was heating up on the range. Whatever happened, she was determined to make a good impression at the club.

Aware that her complexion and skin were no longer clear and soft – as she fancied Lillie Langtry's might be – a dab of powder and rouge were applied, which made all the difference. The next challenge was to tame her freshly washed, wild red hair. Twisting the curls into a braided bun and fixing it to the side of her head with the aid of several pins, she satisfied herself that she looked suitably restrained for such an occasion. Finally, retrieving her best Sunday bonnet from the top of the closet, she carefully removed the brown-paper wrapping, which was thick with dust, and smiled on seeing that the deep-piled scarlet chenille with wide matching ribbons looked as good as new. On unfolding and straightening the snippets of netting and the large, dyed pigeon feathers protruding from the top, the bonnet doubled in height.

'This'll cause a stir when we enter the Factory Club,' she said, tying the ribbons under her chin. 'One in the eye for *you*, Bessie Turner.'

On his return home Sam was heartened to find that Mary had kept off the drink all day and had, instead, spent time on her appearance. The dishevelled wreck he usually encountered after work had been transformed. Even the hat, which had seen better days, looked perfect and reminded him of their early days together.

Bessie Turner's eyes did pop out when she caught sight of Mary walking in on Sam's arm, the theatrical bonnet was hard to miss. Most of Bevan's factory wives knew her well, too, so none welcomed them to their tables. Sam was relieved to spot their lodgers, Joe Ollerenshaw and John O'Connell, sitting with their young lady friends. They couldn't really refuse, so shuffled round to make room. Thankfully, Mary showed great restraint, managing to keep her alcohol intake down to a respectable level.

The evening passed without incident, both of them finding it surprisingly enjoyable. The men even managed to get in a game or two of billiards whilst the women chatted.

Mary picked the moment carefully to break her news. Catching Sam midway through his fourth beer, his senses were numbed enough for the information to wash over him without much reaction. Through the haze, only one thing was crystal clear to him: that, God willing, this time they might be lucky. Mary might produce a healthy son who would fill her with happiness and make everything better for all of them.

3

'It's no good arguing with the tallyman, Mary. You've tried hoodwinking him before,' Kate Bailey chastised her neighbour after she complained, yet again, about her entry in the tally book. 'So stop cussing and help me get some supper for our little ones. You've likely harvested less than usual now you're carrying.'

Kate had got her three boys with her in the hop fields, and they were hungry. Conceding defeat, Mary grudgingly accepted the pay on offer and threw her stick into the pile with such force that it caused an avalanche. The women and children had finished their day's hop picking and, as dusk fell, were queueing for the tallyman to measure their quantity of bushels. He had two sticks, a long one from which a shorter stick was cut. He kept the longer piece and the worker the shorter. The two pieces were then placed together and a notch scored across both for every five bushels picked. When the notches tallied, payment was made. There could be no argument. Each worker had a page in a book where the tally was recorded.

Returning wearily to their makeshift home, Kate and Mary took turns carrying Lottie. The day's toil produced only eight pence a bushel, and that was conditional on there being no leaves, so care had to be taken when stripping the bines. At least they had enough for a hot meal round the campfire – providing they could stay awake to eat it.

The early autumn sunshine and fresh air had given Flossie rosy cheeks and left her feeling quite light-headed. She and the Bailey boys had been mimicking the stilt-walkers as they stepped nimbly between the rows of bines, cutting the top strings to enable the hops to drop to the ground. The boys pretended to trip and topple on stiffened legs and had Flossie in stitches. It had been a while since she'd felt such merriment.

The hordes of hop pickers had arrived on the first weekend in September to hear the local clergyman give his blessing for the forthcoming harvest.

'With more acres under cultivation and new wires spanning the hop bines,' he informed them, 'the yield will be improved, providing better earnings for all!'

While the adults cheered, the children raced through narrow alleys created by the bines growing overhead. Out of the sun, the dark tunnels were magical.

The season lasted throughout the month when a migrating army of over sixty thousand people – mostly women and children – invaded Kent. Known as 'the jamboree of the wandering tribes', the wild, unrestrained lifestyle they experienced drew gypsies from every part of southern England, who joined forces with the Irish poor and occupants of London's lodging houses and workhouses.

Factory work slowed in the summer on account of the heat, and it was mainly women who suffered from the corresponding lack of employment. Allen & Hanburys' patent medicines, in Bethnal Green, sacked a quarter of the girls every summer, as did Bryant & May – it turned out that matchgirls' nimble fingers proved highly profitable when hop picking. Ironers and laundresses were thrown out of work when the middle classes went off on holiday, and the tailoring trade, whose business slumped at the end of the London season, was similarly affected. So the social mix of females in the fields was a sight to behold.

Those who couldn't afford the hop-pickers' special fares on the railways traipsed on foot from London. Sometimes entire families of 'trampers' set off a whole month before the harvest started. A ragged procession of poverty-stricken humanity, carrying their possessions and animals, left the slums and the fog behind only to find themselves encamped in squalid and overcrowded conditions in the fields. Provision for seasonal workers was virtually non-existent and the meagre Hopper huts provided by the farmers filled up quickly. Brick-built, with corrugated iron sheets for roofing, they were hardly palatial, but at least offered some protection against the elements. Barns, stables, cattle sheds and pigsties would all be crammed to bursting, leaving the majority to sleep outside underneath roughly constructed canvas shelters, or simply in the fields like the cattle.

Mary and Kate went hopping in the fields around the village of Southfleet. Only two miles from home, it was close enough for a weekend undertaking, so they carried their home-made shelter and straw bedding to and fro. William Bailey ferried them in his horse and cart, much to the delight of the children, who squealed with joy every time Dobbin dropped his dung en route. Flossie loved Dobbin and often visited him, tied up on his own bit of wasteland when he wasn't working. He had seen better days and had a touch of mange, but was still strong and appreciated the odd scrumped apple when it was on offer. Having spent his working life on farmland off Bow Street, Dobbin was all that was left of William and Kate Bailey's old way of life amid green fields, cherry orchards and meadows spreading out as far as the eye could see. All that was gone now. Bow Street had become Northfleet High Street, One Tree Lane had become College Road and the surrounding landscape had changed beyond recognition.

William sometimes went out in Tom Handley's rowboat so he could see the transformation from the river. Extensive wharfages and docks now forged out from the once-picturesque riverbank, with ugly warehouses and storerooms behind them. Further to the rear were dozens of immense drying kilns and tanks, erected on ground from which chalk had been quarried. It was a sobering reminder of how he and Dobbin came to be scraping a meagre living as a rag-and-bone man.

It was still cool as they set off shortly after dawn on the last weekend in the hop fields. Dobbin struggled with his load on the hills, William urging his old horse on with a 'C'mon, boy' and a tap on his hindquarters. By the time they reached the open fields and tempting, fruit-laden orchards, the sun had warmed them and the surrounding countryside.

Passing a heavy wrought-iron gate, a magnificent house could be glimpsed, partially obscured behind tangled creepers, tall sunflowers and hollyhocks. Lying back and listening to the leaves rustling in the breeze, Flossie realised she'd never been anywhere so peaceful. It was a far cry from the cacophony they endured in The Creek.

But all good things have to come to an end. Keeping the children happy wasn't easy. At one point Lottie burst into uncontrollable tears after her deep pink velvet Alice band caught on a low branch and fell into a muddy gully. The Bailey boys roared with laughter until Kate boxed the ears of her eldest and pushed him out of the cart to retrieve the soggy adornment. It wasn't enough to placate Lottie, however. When Flossie offered up her own navy-blue bow, Lottie snatched it and threw it over the side into the mud. How a child so angelic much of the time could become so insufferable was beyond comprehension. Eventually, after a few harsh words from their mother, the sobbing gave way to sulking and peace was restored for the rest of the journey.

Everyone was pleased when they finally arrived at their

rough-and-ready temporary home and Kate and Mary hastily warmed up a potato stew in the fading light. A large crowd of Londoners were setting up camp close by. Flossie and Lottie couldn't help staring at them. They looked like slum-dwellers: shabbily dressed, decrepit old women with rotting teeth, smoking rank baccy out of cutties – short pipes that burned red-hot and, so it was said, kept your nose warm. All around them were thick-necked, low-browed hobbledehoys in greasy cords and threadbare pea jackets. One of them came close, flapping his arms and clucking like a chicken, frightening Lottie and making her grip her older sister's hand tightly.

'I think he must be an imbecile,' Flossie whispered.

The youngsters couldn't wait to join in the revelry after their meal. Paraffin lamps were carried out of the huts and placed on the hop bins. Campfires, once banked up, added a rosy glow to the chilled air. Forming a circle, gypsy men struck up on fiddles and hornpipes, stamping their feet to the beat. Old women in headscarves began to howl and clap in encouragement. Suddenly, as if from nowhere, a swarm of small children, delirious with excitement, jumped into the ring, weaving in and out the musicians. Young girls followed them, their skirts held aloft, dancing the polka.

'How pretty they are,' Mary said to Kate as they watched the agile East End factory girls spinning around.

'Foul-tongued and all,' Kate replied. 'Rival anything you'll hear in Billingsgate.'

It was true. Even the Irish girls, with their high morals, could shock when they opened their mouths.

Finding it getting altogether too raucous, Kate decided it was time to round up the children for bed. She turned to Mary, but she was gone.

'Now there's a surprise,' she mumbled.

Mary had a habit of disappearing, leaving Kate to watch over their brood. She wouldn't be gone long, just long enough for a tipple outside one of the nearby alehouses. It was strictly off-sales, all the alehouses carrying signs saying *No Dogs, Gypsies or Hoppers*. It was the same at the church; its magnificent iron-studded oak doors firmly locked during hop picking to discourage young men, such as Kate's sons, from disturbing the ancient marble tombs of knights of old.

'I'm glad you're back, Floss,' Jessie confessed as they stared wistfully at the costumes in the draper's window. 'It's been lonely of a Saturday since you've been hopping.' The girls were out for a late evening stroll along the High Street, something they loved to do together. It was already dark and their heavy shawls offered a welcome protection against the chill air.

Shopkeepers stayed open late on Saturdays for the womenfolk to buy the Sunday dinner after pay-time, so it was extremely busy and everyone had a need to see what was on offer. Part of the street was illuminated by the intense white light of the new gas lamps, the rest by the smoky red flame of the old-fashioned grease lamps. Some shops invented their own lighting effects, which the girls found thrilling. Inside Lincoln's the Chemist, candlelight flickered through cleverly arranged bundles of firewood and garden sieves, which, when reflected off a sparkling ground-glass globe, gave the feeling of being in an Aladdin's cave. At James Fox the Grocer's, a fresh supply of watercress was illuminated by candles sticking out of old swedes and turnips.

On opposite sides of the street the fishmonger and butcher competed with each other to see who could out-yell whom.

'Three a penny, Yarmouth bloaters. Beautiful whelks, a penny a lot.'

'Buy my bags o' mystery, it's only me what knows what's in 'em.'

Holding up salted, fried sprats and strings of sausages, they exhorted their customers to buy as their young assistants darted amongst them eagerly displaying their wares by the light of brown-paper flares. The air was full of tiny specks of soot which smudged on touching, yet somehow it all just added to the excitement of the evening.

From somewhere nearby, Flossie could hear a familiar refrain. 'Hot chestnuts, penny a score!' Spotting the handcart with its crimson fire glowing inside a brazier, she opened her palm to reveal the few coins she'd been holding on to tightly and nudged her friend.

'C'mon, Jess – *hot chestnuts!*'

Heading home down College Road, they were glad of their woollen mittens as they tossed the chestnuts up and down to cool them. Flossie had Jess in stitches with her tales of what she had seen whilst hopping.

'I wish I could've been there with you,' Jessie sighed. But they both knew that was unlikely ever to happen. Her father, George Larkin, worked for Robins. Sam was at Bevan's. They didn't mix as the two cement factories didn't see eye to eye.

The mistrust had been building for years, ever since Knight, Bevan & Sturge opened up right next door to the well-established Robins in The Creek. The rivalry had become fierce, leading to a riot, which the local newspaper was quick to report:

A barge loaded with bricks tied up at high tide next to the public landing stage slipway. Bricks were being unloaded onto a horse-drawn cart before being hauled the four hundred or so yards to the site of Thomas Sturge's new cement works, when the horse, on being released from the cart shafts, lost its footing on the slippery surface and fell into the water. As Sturge's men were scrambling to retrieve the poor beast, the works bell of Robins & Cox cement factory – opposite the slipway – rang and sixty men emerged from the gates. On seeing their competitors ranged along the slipway ramp, all hell broke loose.

Some of the men got onto the barge to try and stop the unloading, and fights broke out. Subsequently seven of the men were arrested.

Nathaniel Larkin, Jess' grandfather, had been one of Robins' men defending 'their territory'. He was found guilty of assault and fined five shillings, though he reckoned he'd got off lightly. If the jury hadn't been sympathetic, they would have transported him to the colonies.

Of course, Samuel Grant had known nothing of this when he first arrived from Ipswich looking for labouring work. Grateful for the job offered to him at Bevan's, he soon realised that not everyone was happy about the cement factories encroaching upon the surrounding villages.

The materials used in making Portland cement in North Kent came from mud and clay deposits along the Medway and white chalk dug from the ground locally. After mixing with water, the slurry was dried to form a slip, which was then burned off with coke in kilns to form clinker. Unfortunately, during the burning process noxious gases were emitted, which caused some members of the local gentry to complain about the foul air. When the Gostling cement works announced plans to build more kilns, there was vigorous opposition, led by the Reverend Southgate, on the grounds that the factory was much closer to the village than the others and the resulting pollution presented a danger to people's health. So, in a bid to avoid a costly court case and compensation, Gostling increased the intended height of his new brick chimney from 100 feet to 220 feet. At the official 'topping-off' ceremony on the 2nd October 1873, a young worker was hoisted up the inside of the chimney on a bosun's chair to fix a flag on top. As he stepped out onto the scaffolding, the chimney gave way, bursting out at the side, sending masonry cascading down onto the onlookers below.

Sam heard the rumble first, followed by the crash, and it

sent a chill down his spine. All the workers around him stopped shovelling and stood rooted to the spot as the reverberations echoed across the river. Within seconds, factory whistles from near and far began blowing.

'Half the new chimney's collapsed,' someone shouted. Downing tools, the men surged towards the Undershore.

On reaching Gallopers Wharf, Sam and Joe Ollerenshaw fought their way through gritty dust and fallen bricks until they could hear Gostling's men scrambling around in the rubble looking for their mates. When the body of the boy who had fallen to his death was retrieved from the top of a kiln, the true scale of the disaster unfolded. Six more workers were dead, buried under the debris. Many others were injured.

Alehouse talk laid the blame for the disaster squarely at Reverend Southgate's door.

'If he hadn't complained,' people said, 'Gostling would have kept the chimney to a safe height and no one would have been killed.'

Four days after the tragedy, waiting solemnly outside The Royal Charlotte public house at the top of Dock Row, Sam swallowed hard as the coffins of Cornelius Bruce, Charles Tremain, Thomas Yates and John Allen came into view, carried on the shoulders of their fellow workers. Bevan's had given their employees an hour off to pay their respects. Joining the procession of families and friends, Sam walked slowly to the church lych-gate where the body of John Allen was placed in a shillibeer carriage and taken on to the Roman Catholic church.

St. Botolph's was besieged by crowds of locals, many keen to know if the Reverend Southgate was going to conduct the service. Sam stood by the Huggens Memorial, idly studying the state of the church's crumbling stonework. It was late afternoon and the sun was already going down.

'Cornelius was my brother's lodger,' a voice from behind him said quietly. It was the docker, Tom Luck, whose company

Sam had enjoyed over a pint or two in The Huggens. 'He was a widower, not yet forty. Left behind three little ones.' Turning round, Sam saw that Tom had his young nephew, Henry, alongside him.

'They bunk up with me and my brother,' Henry confirmed. 'Me ma's kept them at home today. They're too young to understand.'

Sam had to smile at that grown-up remark, Henry being only five years of age himself.

'Lord knows what will happen to them now,' sighed Tom. 'Workhouse, in all probability. Did you hear they can't find a next of kin for the Catholic? John Allen's not his real name, by all accounts. Turns out he's a deserter from the army.'

They stood patiently until the heavy oak church doors opened and the Reverend Southgate emerged carrying a large lantern to lead the pallbearers to the freshly dug grave where the three men were to be buried together.

'He's got some nerve, I'll say that for him,' Tom whispered as the crowd fell silent. Sam nodded in agreement.

When wealthy residents, led by a local JP, sought to have White's cement works at Galley Hill closed by court action a few months later, tempers boiled over. Incensed by what they considered an attempt to deprive them of their livelihoods, White's labourers decided to demonstrate. Workers from neighbouring factories, men working on the river and shopkeepers fearing loss of income joined them. The cry went out that the 'great unpaid' were aiming to close all the cement works in the area. After all, they had nothing to lose from the closures. For the thousands of workers and their families, though, the threat to jobs was very real.

Excitement mounted as the procession came into view in a blaze of torchlight, at the head of which was a white horse adorned with blue ribbons. Flossie and Henry waved frantically as Sam and Tom Luck passed by, holding up banners saying *Cement forever!* People carrying loaves of bread on sticks made their way along the gaily decorated High Street. Stopping on the hill, they swelled the crowd already massing in front of the hastily erected hustings. The Greenhithe Brass Band struck up, lifting everyone's spirits on the cold autumn afternoon, before various speakers, including dignitaries who opposed the closure plan, took the stand.

The crowd roared its appreciation when promises to keep White's open were given, then broke into wild applause as one of their own held up a loaf in one hand, shouting, 'See this? Our *daily bread*. Without work we'll starve!'

The thrill of having seen her father marching alongside men like Tom Luck, who'd come in support of the five thousand-strong cement workers, was something that neither Flossie, nor Henry, would ever forget.

4

The rest of the year was bleak for Flossie. The warm sunshine that had enveloped her in the hop fields felt like a distant memory as winter's grip tightened. Thick fog rolled in across the river, merging seamlessly with the choking cement dust, so you could no longer see Tilbury on the other side. The Thames was dangerous at the best of times, but especially so when an impenetrable layer of fog clung steadfastly to the marshes. Barges and lighters on the overcrowded waterway had to blast their horns to be heard over the remorseless din of the surrounding factories.

The smog made everyone weary. It was only when you were sent to the butchers at the top of the cliffs, or on a Sunday when the family climbed the hill up to the church, that there was some welcome relief from it. Babies cried all day and night, unaware that rubbing their sore eyes made them sting all the more. Tempers were short and fists quick to fly. Fred Coulter from number 22 got taken away by two policemen one night after losing a fight in The Hope and then taking it out on his landlady.

'Pity he didn't have a wife to belt,' John O'Connell scoffed as he tucked into his bread and bloaters at the Grants' tea table. 'Wouldn't have been arrested then.'

Mary visibly winced, knowing what he was saying was true. Marriage wasn't all it was cut out to be. For a woman, her identity virtually ceased to exist. By law she became the property of her husband and she was expected to obey and support him at all times. Their children belonged to him, as did any property and money that she brought into the house. Married women often had to suffer abuse from drunken or violent husbands, the option of divorce being virtually impossible both legally and practically.

Standing on her usual spot outside The Huggens, shawl sodden and the braid from her pigtails slowly slipping, Flossie's thick hair descended into an unruly mess down her back despite its liberal coating of Rowlands' Macassar Oil. She could hear familiar voices down near the water, and wandered over to have a look. A group of children were watching something going on beneath the slipway as men rolled barrels of cement down onto a vessel that was all but invisible in the murk.

Suddenly, with a howl, two ghostly faces caked in chalk, with sooty black rings around their eyes, leapt out from the darkness, rattling and clanking the mooring chains, their eerie noises scattering the children in all directions. Flossie gasped and then laughed as she caught sight of Henry Luck and Albert Bull looming out of the fog, wrapped in tattered sheets, shrieking with delight at their achievement.

'We've got the ague,' Henry squealed. 'Watch out, it's catching.'

'No they haven't,' Flossie shouted crossly as the boys chased around, making some of the younger children cry. 'Hardly anyone's caught the ague since the cement came.'

It was true. The ague – malarial fever, once prevalent in the Northfleet marshes – hadn't troubled the Creek-dwellers for some time, but the fear was still there.

'You and Jess going souling tonight, Floss?' Henry yelled,

aware that he now had her undivided attention. 'The Dock Row soulers are meeting the Crick soulers by the old bottle kiln.'

Having been considered too young to go souling on last All Hallows Eve – something that still rankled her – Flossie nodded appreciatively, flattered at finally being asked, even if it was by Henry Luck, who knew she didn't like him calling her 'Floss'.

Henry's older brother, Edward, was lighting and sharing out flares just as Flossie and Jessie arrived for the rendezvous.

'Have you brought one?' he asked, eyes darting, searching for a flame.

The girls shook their heads.

'Oh well, you'll have to make do with this.' A pathetic piece of driftwood with a candle tied each side at the top was handed over. 'Just watch out for dripping wax. Don't blame me if it gets on your boots.'

Edward could be even more obnoxious than Henry as far as Flossie was concerned.

'You wouldn't know,' he continued superciliously, 'that it's our tradition to form a circle round the old Beehive with our torches, to show our respect and all that.'

Manhandling Flossie into a space against the crumbling red bricks, he then jumped up onto an upturned crate and launched into a speech about how the beehive-shaped kiln was where William Aspdin first made Portland cement in Northfleet, and built a twenty-foot-high wall around the site of the renamed Robins & Aspdin's factory, to keep the invention a secret. It was all too complicated for Flossie, so she daydreamed until she felt Jessie tugging at her sleeve. Both girls raised their eyebrows, knowing that this was more about Edward having just secured a job at Robins, now he was twelve, than anything to do with tradition.

Flossie had seen him of late, stamping the *Three Kilns* label on cement bags in Robins' yard – that was when he wasn't running to and from The Hope fetching beer for the gang filling them. He left a trail of cement dust several inches thick.

'I'm getting a penny for every hundred I stamp,' he'd shouted, clearly pleased with himself.

As the lecture ended, everyone held their torches aloft, forming a circle of flames round the crumbling kiln. Flossie had to admit it looked spectacular in the twilight.

Well wrapped up, the motley gang eventually set off, following Albert with his large hurricane lamp. The girls giggled in anticipation. This was going to be an adventure indeed. Standing outside The Plough Inn, they debated where to start. From previous experience, they all knew there was no point in walking down the drive of Grove House, or bothering the elderly ladies in the Huggens College alms houses, but the chaplain's vicarage certainly seemed worthy of a visit. Albert led the tribe up Grove Road to the tradesman's entrance. Tentatively opening the small wooden door in the brick wall, the children filed in one by one. As she entered, Flossie could just make out around four dozen pleasant-looking dwellings and a graceful spire surrounded by immaculate lawns and gardens. It was a haven of peace and tranquillity.

'Look over here,' shouted Henry, pointing towards the massive wrought-iron gates in front of the alms houses. 'It's John Huggens sitting on an armchair, and there's a plaque underneath.'

The sun was disappearing fast, so Albert rushed over and lifted his lamp to throw light on the ornamental arch with a statue on the top.

'Says he was the Good Samaritan and all that.'

'Not for the likes of old people like Annie Devonshire,' Jessie said, rather more loudly than she meant to. 'Make a perfect home for her, but she ain't high-and-mighty enough for Huggens.'

It was true. Huggens' philanthropy wouldn't stretch to Annie. His homes were built for educated, middle-class ladies who found themselves in 'reduced circumstances', not the lower orders.

'Come on!' yelled Edward Luck. 'Let's get on with what we came for.'

The group shuffled across the chaplain's courtyard and huddled together by the kitchen door, then, prompted by their leader, burst into song:

"A soul, a soul, a soul cake!
Please, good missus, a soul cake!
An apple, a pear, a plum or a cherry
Any good thing to make us all merry
One for Peter, two for Paul, three for Him who made us all."

It didn't take long before a burly, red-faced housekeeper appeared with a wicker basket full of warm, enticing cakes. 'Here, share 'em out. Keep the basket in case you strike lucky again. I don't need no prayers saying for me, so be off with you.'

They didn't need telling twice, so off they set again. Sticking to Warwick Place and York Terrace, the alleyways they knew best, the children thrilled to the sights and sounds of Soul Night and the intoxicating aromas wafting from their burgeoning basket. As they started to sing outside Jessie's house, the door opened and all were hit by the overpowering aroma of spice. Nell Larkin's soul cakes were bursting with currants and raisins, with marzipan across the top – as good an offering for the dead as you were likely to get anywhere.

'Eat up,' Edward shouted, passing the delicious morsels round. 'Remember, each cake eaten is another soul released from Purgatory.' Flossie and Jessie didn't like the sound of that, but it didn't hinder their enjoyment.

At the end of November Mary lost the baby she had been carrying. The labour started far too early and progressed with alarming speed, leaving Sam in no doubt that the child would not survive. Flossie was sent next door to get Kate Bailey and her eldest daughter to help Mary through the worst and to clean up afterwards. Sam scurried the girls out when the screaming got bad and then made himself scarce.

Mary took it badly when she found out that the tiny scrap had been another longed-for boy, and frightened the girls with her ramblings. Kate was reluctant to leave as Mary became weak and delirious with such a heavy loss of blood, and sent Sam to get the doctor. There was just enough money to pay for the prescribed iron tablets, but after that they had to rely on a cure-all tonic from Sylvester Lee and regular bowls of nourishing broth proffered by neighbours.

The house fell silent as Mary slept most of the time and the lodgers were encouraged to seek out the welcoming warmth of The Huggens Arms. For Flossie, it was a miserable time having to look after Lottie and their mother. Though she was used to doing the weekly wash and putting food on the table when Mary was inebriated, cleaning out the range was hard work for someone so young. Dressing in the icy cold, she could barely feel her fingers or toes as she scraped out the ashes. It was a job that had to be done at dawn so that her father could light it before he left for work.

As winter increased its grip, seldom a day passed when the funeral cart wasn't making its solemn way to the cemetery. Everyone blamed the incessant freezing fog for those taken by consumption, influenza and whooping cough. Old George Jenkins the grocer succumbed in his stockroom, leaving his wife to run the shop alone. The Hope remained closed for several days while landlord and wife battled unsuccessfully to save their youngest, and disputes between the Larkins and the Grants were set aside when Jessie's little brother Arthur was tragically lost to pneumonia. His mother had sat with him for five days and nights, constantly filling a steam kettle and renewing hot linseed poultices wrapped inside his flannel vest, but his body was just too weak. Sam helped the grieving father and grandfather carry the coffin through the churchyard as Flossie held her best friend's hand tightly.

'My ma's glad she took out a penny policy on our Arthur,' whispered Jess. 'There would have been no money for that coffin otherwise.'

Paying for life insurance to avoid the stigma of being unable to afford a proper funeral was commonplace for many working-class people. Families would go without food and coal just to put by a penny a week for each child, two for the mother and three for the father. By the end of winter, Reverend Southgate had buried an alarmingly large number of babies and young children, and it had become a contentious issue at Northfleet Council meetings. There was a suspicion that some poor people were insuring new born children, and then allowing them to die in order to collect the death money – which outraged bereaved families like the Larkins. When, after a domestic argument, the dead body of an infant was thrown out of a bedroom window in Samaritan Road, no one was arrested, yet the powers that be proposed a law preventing children under a certain age from being insured.

'They are tarring us all with the same brush,' George Larkin declared angrily in The Huggens. 'Criminals get away with murder, while a poor man's child isn't worth a penny. So much for the law!'

The bitter winds, hail and snow that heralded the start of 1879 continued right through until the spring. Flossie opened her curtains on Easter Sunday to see a blanket of snow which looked deep enough to cover her boots. Watching her warm breath melt the ice on the inside of the window, she doubted that the planned reopening of the Rosherville Gardens could possibly go ahead that day. The gates had closed abruptly the previous

September, after the sinking of the *Princess Alice*, and much had been written in the local paper about what should be done to bring back the crowds.

'You won't have seen the notice, then, since you weren't at school?' Maisy Turner said, stopping by the Grants' yard as she walked through the alley. It was a Monday, washday, and pleasantly warm. Flossie wiped the soap suds off her hands. She'd heard other children talking eagerly as they went by and now curiosity got the better of her.

'It's stuck on the pier gates,' Maisy continued at a speed of knots. 'Says it'll be half price to get into the gardens this weekend. Only thruppence for a grown-up, and children go free. Ma says they're trying to drum up business because the bank holiday weekend was a washout and the gala night fireworks were ruined. We're all going. I'm desperate to try the skating rink, it's free too but you'll have to pay sixpence to hire skates. Can't stop, need to spread the news.' And with that she was gone.

Flossie had never actually been inside the Rosherville Gardens, a magical place built in a disused chalk pit, yet she felt she could describe every inch of it. Annie Devonshire had been there right from the start and watched the seventeen acres of uneven wasteland being turned into a 'Zoological and Botanical Gardens'. Disappointed to find out that tickets for the official opening were seven shillings each, Annie had stood with her neighbours on top of the cliffs to see what kind of people were able to afford such a price.

'As the band of the Royal Marines played a merry tune,' she said, 'the Duchess of Kent arrived in all her finery.'

Flossie thought it sounded so majestic, especially the description of the two Bengal tigers that arrived on the *Roxburgh Castle* and were unloaded on the slipway.

Within a few years it was clear that the gardens needed to appeal to a wider public if they were going to succeed. By the time Annie first went inside, in addition to the Italian gardens, statues and the clifftop walks, there was a Gothic hall, bijou theatre and an open-air dancing platform where she twirled to the *Rosherville Polka*, performed by a quadrille band. Not only that, she got to see the fabulous Lupino family ballet troupe, and marvelled at a hot air balloon ascent. Flossie never tired of hearing about such wonders, though she shivered when told of the Peruvian mummy being kept in a watchtower.

'Church pews must be empty,' Kate whispered as they joined the long queue on that Sunday morning.

It seemed as if most of Northfleet had taken advantage of the half-price entry offer, and everyone was in high spirits. Flossie and Lottie's excitement had prevented them from sleeping the night before, and they were up with the lark, arguing about what to wear from the limited choice in their dresser – the older sister, not surprisingly, settling for something comfortable, whilst younger went for the brightly coloured and impractical. It was clear where Lottie got her fashion sense from when, a few minutes later, Mary, wearing her fancy hat with netting and feathers, came into their room to complain about the fuss. Flossie smiled to herself as she watched their mother putting the discarded clothing back into the drawers, holding on to her hat each time as she bent forward. It was nice to see her sober for once. She looked so much younger when her ice-blue eyes were sparkling, despite being so heavily hooded.

Joining Kate and her children waiting by the Calleybank – a column of chalk some eighty feet in height left by the early chalk diggers – both families made their way to the new London Road entrance of the gardens. Thankfully the crowd were constantly shuffling forward, so it wasn't going to be too long a wait.

'Oi, Kate!' a voice shouted from the back. It was Bessie Turner. 'Keep an eye out for the Prince of Wales. I have it on good account he likes it here.'

'Doubt he'd be so bothered about getting in for thruppence,' Kate yelled back, laughing.

Many a pub regular gossiped about how the Prince, on arriving by train, had been spotted by some girls of ill repute. Declining their mischievous offer of some shrimps, tea and a bed for the night, he went on to have some fun incognito in the gardens.

Eventually, their turn to pass through the turnstile arrived. Mary held Kate's basket as she wrestled with the barrier, her ample girth causing a hindrance. Once inside *The Place to Spend a Happy Day*, as it was described in the advertisements, they set off determined to make the most of every minute.

Before they could be stopped, the children rushed headlong into a large conservatory full of palms and ferns. The heat hit Flossie like a wall, the humidity taking her breath away. Never before had she experienced anything like it. With pent-up energy erupting, the gang ran the full length of the building, barely stopping to look at anything, and then hurtled out, eager to explore elsewhere.

'Shut the door,' yelled an old gardener waving his stick. A balding cockatoo, which looked as old as he did, screeched deafeningly, setting off the caged monkeys next door.

Grabbing hold of each other's hands, the party descended the steps inside a cliff tunnel. Kate took her time, which gave everyone the chance to admire the circular temple with its domed roof, columns and statues halfway down. As they reached the bottom they were greeted by a troupe of jugglers and sword swallowers, which proved too much for Lottie, who screamed and hid behind her mother's skirts when a grotesquely painted clown leered at her.

Promenading through the Italian gardens, they marvelled at the fountains and statues and then strolled around the lake, admiring the black swans. They climbed mossy banks to see Gothic ruins clad in mantling ivy and walked the winding paths to locate the chained eagle. After picnicking in a romantic dell listening to the dance bands, they poked at rare birds in an aviary and gawped at Bruin the bear prowling slowly round his deep, empty pit. When he saw that they had biscuits, the thick-furred grizzly stood on his hind legs and held out his great paws. An audience soon gathered, including some sailors. Bruin responded by ascending his pole, to the delight of the crowd. It was then that one of sailors dropped a lighted fusee down into the pit. Flossie watched in horror as the poor beast scurried down to get it, burning his nose in the process and causing him to roll about on the floor of his den, rubbing his nostrils with his great paws before plunging his head into his water trough. The look on his great face was pitiful.

Heading towards the maze, Lottie let out another scream when a tall, dark woman with an orange headscarf and black ringlets stepped out of the shadows.

'Shall Peggy tell your fortune, ladies?' she said. 'Will tell you true, ladies. Peggy always tells true.'

While Mary and Kate crossed Peggy's palm with silver, the children disappeared inside the maze. A young boy sat on a tall ladder to guide those who were lost, but with so many children running around finding the dead ends, the group located the exit with little trouble. Just as well, too, as weariness was setting in and it was time for a rest and something to eat.

Finding a patch of grass to sit on, Mary and Kate leaned against a sycamore tree and kicked off their boots. The girls stayed with their mothers, letting their picnic settle in their stomachs whilst Kate's lads, their energy restored, rushed off to play Aunt Sally. Flossie failed to understand the fascination for knocking things off wooden sticks, and found their brotherly bickering irritating.

It was a great relief when, near to three o'clock, the time came to see the African Blondin, Prince of the Air, a rope-walker of great fame, walk across the chasm from cliff to cliff.

Deciding that outside the Baronial Hall was the best place to sit; the group watched with fascination as men secured ropes and fastened sacks of sand at regular intervals to weigh down the edges of the huge safety net.

At half past three the band struck up with *See the Conquering Hero Comes* and all eyes turned upwards to witness the rope-walker, eighty feet above them, beginning his perilous journey, balanced only by a long pole. Dressed in tight-fitting white garments, with a short, dark blue skirt decorated with dazzling tinsel, he somehow managed to perform somersaults, even hanging on to the rope by his chin. Everyone cheered and clapped furiously, thinking that this was the high point of his act. But then he returned laden with heavy chains, which confined both hands and feet. Having accomplished this, he returned once again, this time blindfolded and enveloped in a sack. Just when the audience thought he could do no more, the African Blondin reappeared carrying a cooking stove on his back. At the centre of the rope, he kindled a fire and cooked an omelette. The ovation continued for many minutes, the children beside themselves, desperate to understand how he could achieve such feats.

With the light fading, an army of groundsmen painstakingly lit thousands of candles in coloured glass jars hanging from the branches of trees and dotted around the flower beds. Chinese lanterns were hung across the terraces and two bonfires ignited in readiness for the evening finale: fireworks. Flossie had often stood by the pier looking back at the star shells and rockets exploding in the distant sky, but being here, watching the display close up, was spellbinding.

Overwhelmed, the weary group wended their way slowly home. With memories to last a lifetime, it had most certainly been the place to spend a happy day.

5

It was almost midsummer before the weather finally improved. Eugene O'Sullivan, a local mush-faker from Samaritan Grove, had raked in more than a few bob selling umbrellas as the wind and rain battered the estuary, and was now enjoying the proceeds in The Little Wonder pub at the top of Hive Lane. For months he'd been wandering from street to street, knocking on doors with a bundle of old umbrellas and a few essential tools under his arm.

The day Mary responded to his knock, Flossie could barely conceal her amusement as she watched him lift his battered bowler and tug on his long, curly beard before extolling the virtues of his trade. Declaring the Grants' umbrella beyond repair, Mary gratefully accepted a few farthings for it. Her pleasure soon evaporated, however, when O'Sullivan was seen sitting on a scullery stool outside number 19 using Mary's 'ribs' to restore Bessie Turner's umbrella to its former glory.

'Get your best bonnets on, girls, we're going on an outing,' Sam yelled from the bottom of the stairs whilst trying to attach his rarely-used collar to his shirt.

'Where are we going, Dadda?' Lottie shrieked, flinging

herself at her father, who caught her in his strong arms and spun her around.

'The river's like a millpond today and the sun's shining. Perfect day for a boat trip.'

As he still wasn't giving anything away, Flossie thought she might have better luck. 'But where to, Pa? Please tell us.'

With a twinkle in his eye, Sam unveiled his plan. 'Thought we'd go on a steamer to the Embankment. That Cleopatra's Needle's up now. See what all the fuss is about. What do you think?'

Lottie squealed with excitement. Flossie could barely hide her own, and hurried off to get their things together. This was one experience she certainly wasn't going to miss. The previous January, the whole school had been given the afternoon off to watch a huge granite obelisk that had come all the way from Egypt being towed up the Thames by the *Anglia*, a local paddle tug. Not that you could see the obelisk, hidden inside a watertight, ninety-three-foot-long, cigar-shaped cylinder. It seemed a miracle it could float. The children had learned all about its turbulent journey across the Bay of Biscay, where six men had lost their lives. Conjuring up images of pharaohs and pyramids, Flossie was eager to see it standing upright in its new home.

The last to leave the house, she stopped to catch a shawl her mother tossed her at the last minute. 'You'll need this, it'll be chilly on the way back,' Mary said, having declined to accompany them, feeling sure she'd suffer seasickness. She'd packed some bread and cheese, for which Sam had given her a tanner, knowing all too well how she was destined to spend the day.

Having caught up with Sam and Lottie, the three of them linked hands and set off along The Creek just as the water cart came round the corner. Within days of the rain stopping and the mush-faker moving on, it was well and truly needed.

Rising dust was intolerable at the best of times, so water carts sprinkled the roads to lay the dust for a while. With The Creek in such a bad state of repair, Sam shouted at the driver to take care. William Bailey had had an accident with his horse recently and the owner of the road had supposedly paid someone to undertake a repair.

'Bodge-up, that's what I call it,' Sam growled as he watched the water cart lurch to one side going over the hole.

Being Sunday, the factories were silent so for once they could chat whilst walking through the alleyway leading through Bevan's yard.

'I'll show you *The Rocket* if you like,' said Sam. 'Just mind your boots on the tracks.'

Picking their way across tramways heading in all directions, Lottie pointed when she saw a small locomotive engine, appropriately named after Stephenson's first engine, at the entrance to a long tunnel.

'Its wagons are empty now,' explained Sam, 'but come tomorrow they'll be full of chalk chipped away from the cliffs above the quarry at the end of this tunnel.'

'It's just like snow,' laughed Lottie, attempting to brush off the soft, powdery chalk layer settling on her clothes.

Sam looked around. Usually the scene was one of general confusion, with men and horses everywhere. The lack of noise unnerved him. He was used to the steady stroke of the steam engines above the rattle of the coopers' hammers, and the squeal of the steam saws.

'It's the quarrymen I admire the most,' he said to Flossie, as they made their way out. 'They stand on the narrowest of ledges, sixty feet up, breaking away the chalk with long crowbars. Pitchers, they're called. Work in all weathers, no matter what.'

Carrying on along the Undershore, it wasn't long before Lottie was complaining of tiredness, so they stopped for a brief rest at the lighthouse on the India Arms Wharf. Fearing the day was going to be a test of her patience, Flossie secretly wished they had left her sister behind. She wondered if they were going to make it to Rosherville Pier on time, and jumped when the ear-piercing screech of the paddle steamer's horn announced its arrival.

Right on cue, half a dozen women carrying steaming baskets appeared from nearby Teapot Row.

'Shrimps! Shrimps! Buy me lovely hot, brown shrimps,' they shouted. 'Penny a pint unpeeled, tuppence if you want 'em done for you.' Jostling for position close to the gangplank, they bombarded the passengers making their way to the tunnel leading to the gardens. But trade wasn't as brisk as it used to be. People were still reluctant to trust the paddle steamers after the *Princess Alice* disaster, so numbers were down and there were few takers for the local delicacy.

It seemed that the 'better off' were choosing to continue their journey by the new railways to the seaside resorts of Margate and Ramsgate. The posh Rosherville Hotel, at the bottom of Burch Road, rarely had hansom cabs outside it these days and the older Bailey boys had long since given up their shoe-blacking business there. Having to pay five shillings a year for a licence to join the Boot-Black Brigade just wasn't worth it any more.

There were even fewer people heading back to London, and the Grants had the boat almost to themselves. Sam noticed how many empty ale glasses were lying around. Considering it wasn't yet midday, he felt sorry for the workers and entertainers in the gardens. There had been many reports of drunkenness and disorderly conduct of late, even some arrests. Priscilla Lee, who told fortunes while people were queuing to find a space round the bear pit, enjoyed regaling her audience with the tale of an overzealous Irish labourer who, having pushed his arm through the bars of the cage to offer the bear a biscuit, got a nasty surprise. Bruin, mindful of his status among the carnivora, proceeded to avail himself of the arm rather than the biscuit. Sadly, Bruin had to be beaten off with an iron bar before the man could be extricated and rushed to the Middlesex hospital.

From the top deck of the *Elfin*, the girls' excitement grew as the steamer moved gently away from its mooring. The ebb tide revealed encrusted barnacles below the waterline of the gleaming white pier posts and, as the paddles churned up the mud, ropes of black seaweed could be seen flailing around the great wheels. The smell of the sea was overpowering.

Flossie watched the captain as he sought out a channel to navigate the busy river and noticed him motioning to a boy standing below at the engine-room hatch. Thinking she recognised him, she looked again. It was Stanley Bull, Albert's older brother who, at thirteen, already seemed proficient in his job as the call boy. With no bell or telegraph from the bridge to the engineer, the call boy had to fix his eyes on the skipper, who, by hand motions, signalled what he wanted done.

'Stop her easy! Half a turn astern,' Stanley yelled down the hatch. Flossie was impressed. She was quite taken by how grown-up he looked in his smart navy-blue trousers and shiny boots. Such an important job, she thought, blushing slightly at her unexpected interest in a boy.

'Full speed ahead,' Stanley confirmed, before heading back to the bridge. Flossie watched him duck beneath a sign that read *Do not speak to the man at the wheel.* Then he was gone.

Sam got the girls lemonade from the *Elfin*'s refreshment bar and they made their way to the dingy forecabin – the aft being for the sole use of first-class passengers. It was a lovely day and the girls so ached to be in the sunshine that they downed their drinks quickly and returned to the deck, where the breeze past Purfleet was now quite strong. Sam took off his cap and, folding it carefully, pushed it into his trouser pocket. The girls tightened their bonnet ribbons. Nearing Greenwich and the magnificent Naval College, the *Elfin* jostled with three other paddle steamers for a turn to come alongside a floating pier. Flossie smiled when she saw that they were called *Sea Swallow*, *Gannet* and *Petrel*, imagining what the other boats belonging to the Diamond Funnel Company might be called.

As they moved closer there was a commotion on a sloping beach exposed at low tide, which caused Stanley Bull to bellow more instructions down the hatch. The small chunk of seaside was full to bursting with Londoners enjoying themselves, their children wading, bathing and sailing model boats. Lottie, deciding that this was where she was going to get off, made for the gangplank and had to be restrained by Sam. Embarrassed at how much noise a near-seven-year-old could make, Flossie offered her sister a handkerchief, which was refused. With tears streaming down her pink face, Lottie was left to her own devices.

The crew cast off again and the paddle steamer headed upriver through the increasingly polluted waters of the Thames. The further they travelled, the more the view deteriorated. Elegant church spires could be seen in the distance, but only above ugly wharves and the sooty backs of warehouses lining the banks on both sides. The bleakness was only broken by the occasional lively alehouse reached by a flight of lightermen steps ascending out of the water. The vista was not entirely without excitement, though; barges were everywhere, weaving expertly in and out, delivering and collecting cargo from the jetties. At Pickle Herring Wharf there was a slight collision, but not severe enough to deter the watermen from their business. Along the Rotherhithe and Bermondsey waterfront, barges were tying up right alongside the wharves, their bags of flour and grain unloaded by overhead hoists. The walls of the warehouses were powdered white by the stuff.

'Poo,' squealed a recovered Lottie, holding her nose and pointing to thick smoke coming from a tall, thin chimney.

'That's horrible,' agreed Flossie. 'Whatever's causing it, Pa?'

'Ah, that'll be the Queens Pipe,' Sam replied. 'At Tobacco

Dock. There's an oven burning bad tobacco day and night. Come on, come over here. Look at all the sailing ships.'

Sam's attempt at distraction proved successful. Flossie and Lottie gasped at the size of the vessels unloading in the docks, their tall masts too numerous to count. The thought of the vast distances they had travelled, combined with the rich aromas issuing from them, simply overwhelmed their senses. The delightful scent of fresh fruit quickly gave way to the musky aroma of hides, skins and vast mounds of wool. As they neared St. Katherine's Dock, sweet molasses, rum and wine mixed unpleasantly with rubber tapped from the impenetrable Amazon basin. Meanwhile, Sam fuelled the girls' imaginations with stories of Chinese silks, Russian furs, coffee from Brazil, ostrich feathers from South Africa, oils and spices from India and perfumes from the Orient.

'Ivory tusks from Africa have their own warehouse,' he continued. 'I've seen it. Lost count how many hundreds of whole elephant tusks there were, and tons more sawn into pieces and stacked like drainpipes. Even had giant hippopotamus teeth for sale.'

'And every bit of it has passed by our Creek to get here,' marvelled Flossie.

Sam did his best to explain that the Port of London was the centre of a world trade, and the River Thames the artery along which the great ships came and went, carrying the goods and produce that made the British Empire the envy of the world.

'The trouble is, not everyone benefits from all the riches. Compare the wealth locked up in the docks to the meagre rewards the workers get for handling it. James and Tom Luck say they don't get any wage at all when unfavourable winds stop the sailing ships from coming up the estuary. It just ain't right.'

Flossie asked why Henry Luck bragged so much when his father had no guaranteed daily work.

'Sometimes people brag to hide what their lives are really

like,' Sam suggested. 'Maybe you shouldn't be too hard on him, young Floss.'

Flossie nodded, filled with remorse.

As they entered the Pool of London, there were so many ships in dock that they found themselves delayed alongside Billingsgate's pungent fish market. Gangs of market porters were landing huge crates of fish, almost treading on each other's heels as they made their way across a narrow bridge of shore planks that vibrated under their weight.

'If they get out of step they'll be jerked into the water,' Sam said, 'load and all.' Then, pointing out the ice ship with its flag flying, he added respectfully, 'No harder work on the river.'

Flossie couldn't see why, until her father pointed to two men hoisting a yard-square block of ice – a huge mass – onto the back of a third.

'He has to carry that over the narrow plank, up a steep hill and gangway, through the market and out into Thames Street. A porter told me he once watched a man slip with a load like that. It fell on him, staving every rib, just like they were bacca-pipes.'

Lottie buried her face in her sister's shawl and covered her ears.

Relieved to be on the move again, they watched gangs of men, naked to the waist, their bodies, faces and hair frosted black with glistening coal grit, hauling huge baskets of coal out of the holds of colliers and swinging them over the side to be emptied into barges waiting in the pool.

'Some of them will end up back at Northfleet.' Sam shrugged. It certainly looked like back-breaking work, Flossie thought, slightly embarrassed to find herself staring for longer than seemed proper.

It wasn't long before they were stepping onto firm ground at the Old Swan pier. Weaving their way through a maze of bales and barrels to Thames Street, they followed the river along the Victoria Embankment in search of the mysterious obelisk.

'There it is!' shouted Sam, quickening his step and almost pulling Lottie off her feet. The sixty-eight-foot-high, 180-ton red granite obelisk was impossible to miss, with its two imposing bronze sphinxes protecting it on either side. They wandered around it in awe, Sam stopping to read the plaques mounted round the base, which told the history of the 3,500-year-old 'needle' and its journey to London at a cost of ten thousand pounds. The girls chattered about the contents of a 'time capsule' said to be buried at the front of the pedestal. Flossie could see why someone from the future might be interested in maps, coins, a *Bradshaw's Railway Guide*, copies of the Bible in different languages and an explanation of how the obelisk was erected, but not a box of hairpins, a shilling razor and a baby's bottle, let alone photographs of a dozen beautiful Englishwomen.

After they had eaten their bread and cheese, Lottie was beginning to yawn. It had been an exhausting day so Sam carried her back to London Bridge on his broad shoulders. On reaching Thames Street, dozens of other adventurers like themselves were milling about, searching for the sign saying *This way to the steamboats*. Luckily for the Grants, they had their return tickets, as there was an unholy crush at the payment kiosk.

Being one of the first parties to board, Sam ushered his girls into the forecabin and wrapped Flossie's shawl around them both, knowing that when the departure bell rang the chances were that a cloud of dirt and dust would descend. This often happened with the larger steamers when the funnel had to be lowered to allow passage under the bridge at high tide. Lottie stopped complaining about not being able to go on deck when she saw the women's frocks dotted with black smuts.

'Lucky you're in here,' laughed a man, poking his head through the door. 'Look at these blacks,' he said, pointing to his mottled collar and cuffs. 'Can you squeeze up and let me and the wife sit down? Ain't too comfortable on deck. No seats left. What's more, there'll be loads more getting on at Cherry Gardens, mark my words. Slums they may be, but they'll be finding a shilling for a jolly evening at Rosherville, that's for sure.' With that he tapped his pipe on the arm of the bench and folded his arms.

As the steamer swept through the centre arch of London Bridge, a band of instrumentalists with harp, fiddle and cornopean emerged from the drinking saloon. The jig they played wasn't too bad, but the ballad was horribly out of tune, causing great hilarity amongst the passengers. Thankfully the musicians moved on to the sixteen-penny end of the boat as the steamer pulled alongside the Cherry Garden floating pier, where dozens more brash people, carrying their own food and drink, flooded onto the decks.

By early evening they were well on their way home. The stretch of green countryside opened out and the river became brighter and the smell less unpleasant. Two hours passed quickly and the girls, now rested, wandered happily around the steamer for the remainder of the trip. At one point Flossie couldn't help but notice an old couple sitting close together, beaming with happiness. His hand was in hers as it rested on his knee and all around them were family – a thickset son with his attentive wife and their half-dozen children. It was a touching scene, something she wasn't familiar with.

Flossie hadn't met any of her relations. Mary occasionally spoke of her own mother, Fanny, in Essex, and Sam had said that his father went in and out of the workhouse depending on how much work he could get in the fields, but that was all. Flossie knew that everyone regarded going into the workhouse as the absolute last resort, so her grandfather's life sounded very sad and lonely. She couldn't ever imagine not being close to Lottie and looking out for her. Glancing over at her father, she caught him looking wistfully at the happy scene too.

'Look, look, there's the windmill,' someone shouted, 'on the top of the hill.' Necks craned in the general direction of the old mill in Gravesend.

Determined to join others who were waving at a bargeman lifting his brown tarpaulin hat in friendly greeting, Lottie had to be held tightly to stop her from leaning too far over the barrier. Slowly people started getting up and making ready to disembark.

At Rosherville Pier there were a few drunks, as was common at most landing places, but with such a surge of revellers determined to alight they did not cause a problem. Sam held on to the girls tightly, mulling over the best way to get home as the crowd pushed and shoved impatiently through the tunnel. Remembering that the gas lamps along the Undershore were constantly being smashed, he made the decision to go via the main road, where there would be more people.

Unfortunately, it turned out to be a rash decision. With gangs of men leaving the gardens much the worse for drink, the road from St. James' in Gravesend to Rosherville had become the haunt of prostitutes. Holding Lottie on his hip and telling Flossie not to stare, they rushed along the main road. Outside The Leather Bottle a group of dishevelled old women, using the foulest of language, were accosting every man or boy passing them. It was a disgraceful scene, and Sam was relieved when he finally put some distance between them and his girls. As they reached the High Street it began to rain. Three young women, somewhat unsteady on their feet, passed them. Cackling like witches and without an ounce of shame, they lifted their skirts over their heads to protect their hairstyles and disappeared up Station Road.

Times were certainly changing, Sam thought.

6

Flossie seemed to be waiting much longer than usual outside The Huggens. It was a hot day and there was a fragrant aroma of strawberries wafting on the breeze.

She watched enviously as a coster pushed his cart past her, yelling, 'Fine strawberries, all ripe, all ripe!' Not having any coppers, she hung her head dejectedly. He lingered a few moments, then reached forward and threw her a single juicy strawberry, before heading off up College Road towards the alms houses.

Hearing a commotion nearby, she turned to see a gang of local boys chasing up and down The Creek pretending to be Zulus and redcoats in pitched battle. The Zulus were taunting the soldiers with driftwood spears, the soldiers crouching behind the jetty wall pointing sticks and finger-rifles back at them. Suddenly a loud cheer went up from the warriors as, from around the corner, the Zulu chief, Henry Luck, appeared. With a headband fashioned from pigeon and seagull feathers, his face daubed with mud, and a straw skirt rolled up over his trousers, he looked every bit the warrior king. Waving his shield made from barrel staves, he leapt onto the jetty in full cry. Soon chaos ensued. Warriors lay dead in the gutters. Soldiers hung limply over the wall.

Flossie approached the Zulu chief, who was standing with arms raised on top of the jetty wall. 'This looks fun,' she said smiling, trying to be friendly.

'It's serious stuff, silly. We're fighting the Battle of Rorke's Drift,' he stated triumphantly. 'It's not for girls.'

'Well, you don't look much like a Zulu chief to me,' she snapped back, turning on her heels and marching off. Not being hard on Henry was going to be a challenge.

As the long-suffering landlord, Robert Scott, finally succeeded in getting rid of his regulars, a dishevelled Mary emerged along with other residents of The Creek, all of whom were deep in discussion about something. Unrolling a crumpled newspaper from under his arm, Jacob Turner silenced everyone with a wave of his hand.

'Right, I can read it proper, now I'm out in the daylight. Says: *On this 15th day of June 1880, the two Judges of the High Court of Justice assigned to the Election Petition trial against Thomas Bevan, determined that the said Thomas Bevan was not duly returned nor elected and that the said Election was void.* Then it goes on to list the ten men found guilty of bribing or being bribed.'

Silence descended, even Mary managing to contain herself. Reading on, Jacob Turner pushed his cap back and cleared his throat.

'Listen to this last bit, then. It says: *No corrupt practice was proved to have been committed by, or with, the knowledge or consent of any Candidate at such Election.*'

'So, Bevan himself's not guilty, then,' came a voice from the back.

'Seems not,' confirmed Jacob. 'But there'll have to be a by-election next month.' With that, he strode off and the crowd gradually dispersed.

Thomas Bevan had been elected Liberal MP for Gravesend

in April 1880 – the year that William Gladstone took office for a second time as Prime Minister. Voting irregularities were commonplace. Only five per cent of Britain's thirty million citizens had the vote and they had to be male householders, tenants, or lodgers paying at least ten pounds a year in rent. Bevan was an employer of a thousand in the town, of whom 180 were voters. On election day, the employees clocked in as usual. Each received a rosette in Bevan's colours and then those eligible were given the afternoon off with pay to vote. It was this that was seen as constituting bribery and cost Bevan the election.

Jacob Turner shook his head at the sight of Flossie holding Mary upright as they tottered past his front door. Bessie would have killed him if he'd ever returned from the alehouse in that state. It had been a bad week for him. He'd already lost a week's pay on account of an accident in Bevan's cooper's yard and, with six children to feed and clothe, he felt up against it.

Every works had its own cooperage, as cement for exportation was better kept dry in barrels. Bevan's churned out over two thousand casks a day. Jacob was on a production line, manhandling flaming casks before a cooper hammered metal hoops onto them to form barrels. It was when the burning staves were being doused with water and compressed that a momentary loss of concentration resulted in him burning his hand.

'I'm only surprised it hasn't happened before,' he said as his wife coated the wound in flour and wrapped cotton wadding around the hand.

Bessie Turner saw things differently, not that she'd ever say a bad word about her husband. But he was a sickly sort, always ill or having accidents. The bread on the table and the coal in the grate were, in the main, down to her hard labour. With a baby strapped to her back and a toddler at her ankles, she did other folks' washing and cleaning by day, then cut out and sewed workmen's flannel shirts at night, sometimes straining her eyes until two in the morning to finish three at a stretch. For this she'd receive a meagre tuppence ha'penny each. Watching Mary Grant squander hard-earned money on drink made her so angry that she found it impossible to be civil, and no one could blame her.

It always came as a relief to Bessie and many other mothers when the stave ships would arrive from Scandinavia, the treacherous journey only possible during the summer. Several vessels would arrive at once, packed to the gunnels with timber. There was a great need to unload as quickly as possible, so vast numbers of local boys were employed to carry as many staves as they could manage down the gangplanks. You had to be over ten years old to avoid compulsory education, and for a small, nimble lad like Robert Turner, being able to clamber between the tangled masts and rigging was a perfect way to earn ten pence a day working for Lawrence & Wimble's Crown Cement Works. The only problem was the splinters. His hands and arms were already embedded with them.

'Me ma pulls out the worst ones and dabs the sores with iodine,' the eleven-year-old informed Henry and Albert when they enquired why his arms were yellow. 'But it's just one of them things. Your turn will come.'

Some late afternoons, Flossie and Jessie would keep Maisy company outside The Ship Inn, looking out for her brother amongst the other boys on L&W's own wharf. When all three berths were in use at once, Robert could sometimes be spotted as part of a human chain, conveying staves from vessels to shore and packing them onto wagons.

'If I'm lucky,' he said to Flossie one day, 'come winter I might be strong enough to load the barrels onto the barges. That way I'll still have a job.'

The Crown Works owned four sailing barges – the *Lady Edith*, *Victoria*, *Jessie* and *Alfred* – all of which were well-known sights on the river. Flossie knew that when the barrels were full of four hundred pounds of cement they'd be far too heavy for Robert, but she couldn't bring herself to say anything in case she hurt his feelings.

Edwin, Robert's younger brother, also earned a few farthings at the butchers on the village green. With its own slaughterhouse at the back and meat hanging on display rails at the front, there was always blood for him to wash away and sawdust to replenish when he wasn't at his lessons. The boys knew their mother needed every penny they could muster to buy decent shoes for all of them. It was a matter of pride that they should have them, and Bessie often wondered when she passed a fancy-ware barrow how so many women could be out buying ear drops or combs for themselves when their clinging youngsters went barefoot. Survival in The Creek was only possible if whole families pulled together.

Discovering there was nothing for their evening meal, and with Mary too drunk to care, Flossie climbed onto the kitchen stool and reached for the money tin on top of the dresser. It was Wednesday, three days until payday, so what few pennies were left had to last. It was hot work dashing uphill to the fishmongers on the High Street, but being near to closing time she knew there was a good chance of picking up a bargain. Herrings at a penny each were usually five a penny by the end of the day. With pairings of tripe, leftover bread and cocoa, there would be a reasonable meal for everyone. Heading back, her basket full, she had to be quick.

Taking a shortcut through the maze of back alleys leading down to the river she soon realised her mistake. Blowflies quickly engulfed her as they swarmed all over the fishy contents of her basket.

'Oh no, the bluebottle boats!' she said out loud, swishing her hand through the cloud of marauding insects. Barges moored in Onward Creek were laden with London rubbish. After being dumped on the banks to rot, the residue was then used to make breeze for the brickworks. During the summer months the boats would be covered in flies, hence their 'bluebottle' nickname. 'Disgusting,' Flossie murmured as she fled the area, flies still lingering on her parcels.

With just one last errand to run before going home, she struck out along the shore to find Sylvester Lee and purchase a pennyworth of Arabian Family Ointment. Mary, having lost her job at Hive House due to a disagreement with Agnes Avery, was now a scullery maid at the Manor House on the hill. Through constant immersion in tepid water, her hands had become chapped and raw, causing the hard skin on her fingers to crack. Arabian Family Ointment eased the pain and took the edge off her complaining.

No sooner had Flossie entered her front door than Mary snatched the balm from her and flew into a rage.

'Where have you been?' she spat. 'They'll all be wanting their tea.'

Flossie was well aware of this. She'd heard the klaxon announcing the end of the working day as she shut Sylvester's caravan door, and had barely made it back ahead of the mob. The pain in Mary's fingers was probably what saved Flossie from a smack on the leg.

'This liniment's all I have to relieve my suffering,' Mary wailed, the numbing effect of gin clearly wearing off.

The lodgers, tired from their day's toil and hungry for their seared herrings, sat patiently as their temperamental landlady threw the fish into a pan and reeled around dangerously in front of the range.

'Do you remember the story about that old reverend doing indecent things to a servant girl on a train and then disappearing before his court case?' she shouted over her shoulder.

The men all looked at each other, before shaking their heads in unison.

'You must do. It was only a year or so ago. In the local papers, it was. His son wrote a letter saying his father was innocent, but he'd gone abroad 'cause no one would believe him.'

Swinging the pan off the range, Mary wobbled precariously towards the group. Joe flashed a look of desperation at his two compatriots as they expected the fried fish to land in their laps. Flossie wished her father were there to restrain her mother, but these days he rarely made an appearance until well after teatime.

'Turns out it's them I work for. The son took over the Manor House Asylum when his father absconded – you know, the one that used to be the workhouse. It's properly licensed now, but three years ago the rev was prosecuted for running it illegally and keeping a lady against her will. He was fined fifty quid...'

Flossie grabbed the pan out of her mother's hands and started to serve the grateful lodgers. Within minutes they had wolfed down the meagre portions, bones and all, and soaked the juices up with crusts of bread.

'Anyway,' Mary continued, oblivious to what was going on around her, 'it's now a home for dipsomaniacs with money. Captain Dalrymple is one of them. He came in the scullery today and couldn't wait to tell me the whole story. There's only him and that mad Susannah Lydon as inmates now.'

Exhausted, Mary signalled to Lottie to get her the last of the herrings. 'Put some bread on the plate with 'em, then,' she snapped as the lodgers made their escape to the front room. 'How the mighty have fallen, eh?' Mary shouted after them.

It was decided. Upon leaving church the following Sunday, the children of The Creek and beyond were going to walk to Springhead. Flossie was so excited she found it impossible to listen to the sermon. Instead she let her eyes wander over the wood carvings decorating the chancel arch. Then, as the congregation sang the last hymn, sunlight burst through the stained glass of the east window, refracting with the cement dust to create a glistening array of colours. It was a glorious day, for which they all heartily gave thanks.

The gang assembled outside St. Botolph's National School, which most of them attended regularly, apart from Flossie. The south side of the churchyard adjoined one of the many chalk pits and had a steep drop which, whether by divine intervention or not, no child had yet fallen down.

'Right, all here?' yelled Henry Luck over the crackle of gunfire coming up from the bottom of the cliff where the 20th Kent Volunteer Rifle Brigade were training. 'Albert, you bring up the rear and keep a check on stray little ones.'

Albert Bull did as he was told and the group headed off through some cornfields and over a narrow railway bridge leading to the Marsh – a rich piece of pasture fed by a number of streams.

Henry walked over a plank which was fixed across the first stream. 'It's stable,' he yelled. 'Single file and no jumping.' Everyone obeyed his instruction and all crossed safely. Unlike the surrounding muddy marsh, the fast-running water was clear, and Henry picked his way cautiously, avoiding the places that looked dangerous. After a while, though, some of the children found the need to explore too tempting and broke free from the line. Shrugging his shoulders, Henry continued on regardless, following a well-trodden path.

Flossie stopped to admire some overhanging willow branches while Lottie gave chase to a kaleidoscope of blue butterflies hovering and fluttering amongst the reeds. Suddenly the peace and tranquillity were shattered by a piercing scream. Flossie instinctively turned to see her sister beginning to sink into a pool of black, slimy water which oozed up through the rank grass, enveloping her shoes. The more she struggled, the worse it got. Quick as a flash, Albert Bull threw a nearby plank across the mire. Henry shinned along it, grabbed Lottie around the waist and hauled her to safety. Lifting her up onto his shoulders, he carried the sobbing, bedraggled bundle back to her much-relieved sister. It took a whole bag of dolly mixtures before the crying finally stopped, allowing Flossie to clean her up as best she could.

The drama over, they stopped to rest awhile beside a broad stream covered in cultivated watercress stretching as far as the eye could see. Men in punts were collecting handfuls of the lush green plants, pushing themselves about with the aid of long poles. In some parts where the vegetation was dense, the pickers were wading waist-deep. Watercress sandwiches for breakfast, and shrimp, watercress and bread for dinner were staple meals for most in Northfleet. There were even times, like on the night before payday, when watercress was eaten on its own, earning it the nickname 'poor man's bread'.

'This was the first watercress farm ever to be opened in Britain,' Henry announced proudly as the gang of young faces crowded around him. 'Here, at Springhead. Worth a fortune now.'

And he was quite right, it had indeed become a lucrative business. The key to growing quality cress is the quality of the water and, as the name Springhead suggests, the pure water rising from the eight springs in the chalk landscape ensured that. The Roman town of Vagniacae had been sited there for that very reason. Springhead had been privately owned by one James Sylvester, who expanded the site to include a tea garden with access to the watercress beds. People came from far and wide to enjoy the gardens and sample newly introduced types of cress. However, things started to go wrong when the South Eastern Railway Company built a new and improved line, but failed to provide a bridge allowing access to the gardens. Sylvester eventually won a case in court against them, but by then it was too late to save his business.

'Do you know what happened?' Henry Luck said to his by now captivated audience. 'Blew his brains out, he did.'

A chorus of 'ergghh's greeted this revelation. But it was true: James Sylvester committed suicide by discharging a brace of pistols simultaneously, one on either side of his head. The resulting verdict was temporary insanity.

With the expansion of the railway, tons of cress plants packed in wicker 'flats' were now being regularly transported up to Covent Garden market. Flossie had heard Sam tell of street sellers – including tiny children – flocking out of the great watercress market at dawn with verdant basketfuls of the stuff, heading straight for the water pump where they jostled for a chance to freshen their wares so as to tempt passers-by. They had to work swiftly, splitting the cress into little bundles, to be first amongst the coster cries heard in time for breakfast. How any of them survived in such a squalid, smoky, fog-bound city of four million was a mystery to Flossie. What's more, she thought, none of the costers would ever see the beautiful place their bundles of cress had come from.

The hot sun had finally dried Lottie's mud-splattered summer dress as the children wandered back through Springhead's rustic archway into the gardens. Pretty flower beds, dotted with vivid scarlet geraniums, surrounded a velvet lawn. Some of the group sat under a walnut tree, relieved to be in the shade. A monkey fastened to a neighbouring tree trunk was straining against its chain.

'It's called Jenny,' said Henry, returning from a fruit stall with some nuts. On seeing the brown-paper bag, Jenny immediately started screeching and leaping up and down. Henry thought it far more entertaining to place some nuts just out of the creature's reach and then watch it pull on its chain, for which the girls chastised him, but this just egged Henry on. Beckoning all the boys to watch, he lay on the ground at a calculated distance and, flashing Flossie a look of defiance, tempted the now-agitated monkey by placing a nut between his teeth. That was a mistake. Extending her claws, she seized the nut in one fell swoop, leaving Henry with his pride and his cheek in tatters.

Camphor oil would relieve the latter, but not the former, Flossie thought. *He was such a contradiction: one minute, the hero saving Lottie; next, the silly show-off.*

Albert got short shrift for offering Henry his handkerchief and they all walked home in silence, following their leader's bloody trail.

7

Flossie took one pace forward out of the line and shouted across to Jessie, 'Can you see Lottie? Is she still crying?'

Jessie turned to scour the infants following on behind, but couldn't see her in the procession. Unfortunately, their schoolmistress, who was marching at the front, had eyes in the back of her head and on noticing the disruption, lowered the school banner she'd been holding aloft and prodded Flossie in the stomach. 'What are you doing, girl? Get back in step. The whole village can see you.'

Flossie felt her face reddening. Miss Boulter hadn't finished.

'Hang your head in shame, Florence Grant. You are fortunate to be in this parade at all, considering your poor attendance. I'd be speaking to your mother if I thought it would do any good.'

Flossie wanted the ground to swallow her up. Thankfully the crowd was so noisy that only a few witnessed her embarrassment. She'd just have to hope her sister was all right after being dragged from her side when their marching orders were given – boys in front, then girls, lastly infants.

Preparations for the annual church school treat had started early that morning. Tents were erected in the meadow and swings set up. Carts arrived from the vicarage laden with food. After that, the parade had commenced. Flossie's mood greatly improved as they reached the High Street just in time to see the train from Greenhithe arrive at the station and the band from the *Arethusa* alight from it. The boys in their smart blue jackets headed the procession playing *Nancy Lee*, and soon everyone was singing along to the music.

Of all the wives as e'er you know, yeo-ho! Lads, no! Yes-ho!
There's none like Nancy Lee, I trow, yeo-ho! Yeo-ho!
See there she stand and waves her hands,
Upon the quay and every day,
When I'm away, she'll watch for me
And whisper low when tempests blow,
For Jack at sea, yeo-ho! Lads, ho!

Everyone came out to watch the spirited band of rescued boys, some as young as eleven. Several of the mothers lifted the corners of their aprons to their eyes to wipe away a tear, knowing the deprivation and misery these 250 homeless lads had experienced. It was a joy to see them so well fed and clothed now they were part of the 'Boys' Navy' – each one being taught the skills to become a qualified sailor.

The Bailey boys were always talking about the fifty-gun frigate, the *Chichester*, loaned by the Admiralty and anchored at Greenhithe. But when the *Arethusa*, the last British ship to go into battle under sail, took her place alongside it, they harried poor old Tom Handley to take them out in his rowboat for a closer look.

'Not sure I'd like to be one of the boys, though,' Matthew Bailey told his mother. 'I've heard life on board is hard and the boys are only known by a number.'

The band ceased playing as the bells of the church rang out, calling all the village children to join in the day's celebrations.

They came trooping along from every quarter to join the procession, some from as far as Springhead Lane, carrying their bright tin mugs. Flossie was amazed to see so many unfamiliar faces walking alongside her waving banners and flags. The sudden roll of a big drum, followed by a clashing of cymbals, announced their arrival at the great gates of the Rosher estate. The well-to-do family had granted access across their land and, without further ado, the bluejackets marched under the great archway followed by the army of children. Flossie had often wondered what Crete Hall and The Mount looked like up close, and couldn't help staring as they filed past. The homes of Miss Rosher and Mr Sturge looked huge compared to her own home, yet just as unwelcoming, she thought.

Winding their way down the slopes to the meadow, a great cheer went up as the procession reached its destination. Flags and banners were planted at intervals along the terrace and a general rush ensued for the swings and donkey rides. Football and cricket with the *Arethusa* boys provided welcome entertainment, especially for the girls, who were not usually to be found at the side of a pitch. Henry Luck, realising he was no match for such fit and able boys, played the fool in the races instead. He dragged poor Albert Bull all over the track in the three-legged race without gaining the winner's penny. There was even less chance in the sack race, where you were required to run twenty yards in a straight line inside a meal bag tied round the neck. Each entrant had an attendant to pick him up if he fell, which required as much effort as the competitors. Stumbling and shuffling towards the distant winning post, few made it more than a few yards before toppling over. Ten utterly failed to reach their goal, and when the remaining two fell flat on their faces before it, they were declared winners and presented with a tanner to share between them.

Flossie and Jessie had meanwhile made their way over to the ponies that were being tended by some of the boys in blue.

Assisted onto their mounts, they were supported in their seats by one lad, while another made the ponies trot.

'Oh, we *are* having such a lovely gallop,' Jessie squealed coquettishly, tossing her abundant hair back and fluttering her eyelashes at her groom. 'Can we go faster?'

Flossie shot her a look of dismay. She already felt she was on a fairground dobby ride and certainly had no desire to increase her speed. Jessie dug her heels into the pony's sides and went off at a canter over the brow of the hill. As the boys ran to catch up, Flossie realised that something was wrong when she heard one of them shout. Jessie's pony had stopped short of some trees. Within seconds they reached the spot to find her lying on a patch of soft turf. Her white face had a little trickle of blood coming from her nose, but she seemed otherwise unhurt. 'The silly pony threw me,' she simpered as a boy with dark hair and green eyes lifted her gently up and held on to her hand. 'I think I need to sit here awhile.'

Flossie watched in amazement at the ease with which her friend chatted to the young man. It was obvious she liked him, and he clearly liked her.

'The other training ship, downriver, is the *Worcester*,' he told her, 'for boys whose parents can pay. They end up being officers on the great merchant vessels. But our lives are a bit different.'

Jessie nodded, wide-eyed, as he continued.

'We can get the birch now we're fourteen. There are strict rules, though, and only the captain can do it. You get ten cuts for stealing and twelve for absconding.'

'Oh my goodness, how shocking,' said Jessie, sounding quite different to the girl Flossie knew.

'Worst crime is immoral behaviour, that's twenty-four cuts and dismissal with disgrace. None of us would take the risk of getting thrown out of the old *Arethusa*, though.'

His name was Silas, not that Jessie was aware of it as she stared into his green eyes. Nor was she taking in the additional facts he imparted about the *Arethusa* being a warship with fifty-three guns, having bombarded Odessa during the Crimean War six-and-twenty years ago. But Flossie did, and breathed a sigh of relief when the church bells indicated it was time for tea.

As they made their way back up the slope with the ponies, Jessie bid a lingering goodbye to Silas and re-joined her friend, who was already scouring the lines of infants opposite the catering tent to see what had happened to Lottie. Luckily she found her smiling and laughing, which brought her great relief. Before the band struck up again they all sat patiently waiting while Reverend Southgate said grace, then with a loud 'amen' made a beeline for the cakes and buns.

With the light fading, the meadow dimmed to a dark green and the final part of the special day got underway. The verger busied himself setting up a magic lantern show while some choirboys shinned up two adjoining trees and hung a large white sheet between them. With the younger children having gone home, all the rest grouped together on the grass in eager anticipation. *Alone in London* and *Overland to India* weren't much fun, but *The Pied Piper of Hamelin* was suitably gruesome and thoroughly entertaining.

Much revelry followed as Pied Piper Henry and his assistant Albert chased the girls from The Creek along the Undershore before bolting off somewhere. Stopping to get their breath back, Flossie and Jess gazed in awe at the bright lights appearing on the Essex bank and the blue lamps of the numerous ships lying at anchor on the shimmering steel-grey belt of the river.

It had been a lovely day, but the end of the school treat meant the end of the school year and Jessie's last days of freedom. Nell Larkin had wasted no time in securing her daughter a position the moment she turned twelve. Jess, who was almost a year older than Flossie, was soon to start as a scullery maid at number 16 Burch Road, the home of Mr Dunlop, master of

Rosherville Pier. The girls had already walked past the house a few times and stared in at the finery.

'I wonder how many fires there are?' Jess groaned as they stood at the bottom of the flight of white marble steps leading up to the glass-panelled front door. 'I've been told I'll have to get up at five to light them all.'

Too sad for idle conversation, they took each other's hands and walked home, listening to the lapping of the water and the swishing sails of the tall ships leaving on the evening tide. Flossie wondered where Mary would find her a scullery-maid's job, and hoped that her one afternoon off would coincide with Jess'.

Having finished her chores at home, Flossie was only too pleased to accompany old Annie Devonshire on an afternoon walk to Gravesend. Annie's stiff legs made the going slow, so there needed to be frequent rests to look at the scenery and chat. Once past the noisiest of the cement works, they stopped at Ben Woods Old Wharf where Humber coal was being unloaded from a picturesque Yorkshire Billy-Boy schooner. It was a clear day and they could see that the construction of the new docks at Tilbury was moving along fast.

On passing two impressive properties that had the London Portland Cement Works sandwiched in between them, Annie sighed. 'It looked very pleasant here until the factories came,' she said wistfully. 'Look at that monstrosity stuck between Cliff House and Howard House! Just like Orme House in The Creek. That was beautiful too until they knocked it down, just before you moved here.'

Continuing on, Flossie felt like they were walking in a wild garden, through flowering brambles that spread up the steep chalk escarpment. So many years had passed since the chalk had been dug out that the huge, desolate pits now resembled a prehistoric valley.

'Everyone around here suffered from the whiteness at the time. Some of the older women wore thick veils to protect them from the reflection in the sunlight,' remembered Annie.

As they continued through the overgrown wasteland, the noise of the factories began to recede and they found themselves at Pitcher's deserted dockyard. Entering though a castellated gateway, discoloured by weather and years, both stopped to observe the forlorn remains of the castle, once the residence of the shipyard owner.

'Supposed to have been built using stone from the old London Bridge,' Annie said, resting against a tree stump. 'Pitcher's was respected the world over. Even the imperial Russian fleet was refitted here. In fact, they were here so long that midshipman Rimsky-Korsakov had time to compose his first symphony.'

Flossie's eyes widened in amazement.

'I can remember when the East India Company had *their* ships built here, the place was so busy. The noise of a thousand workmen pounding hammers all day long was tremendous, my father being one of them. People round here used to love the sound of the hammers. Meant that food was going to be on their tables. But after they had built gunboats for the Crimea, the yard closed and all the men were thrown out of work. That's until the cement factories came, of course, then the jobs returned.'

Annie signalled to Flossie to help her up. She straightened her neat bonnet, linked arms with her young companion and the pair shuffled off down Dock Row, built by Pitcher for his workers, to the edge of the river. Looking out towards the estuary, Annie became very quiet. Sensing she was deep in thought, Flossie moved away slightly and, picking up a few stones, threw some into the water, watching the circular ripples as they skimmed the surface. Eventually Annie called Flossie over.

'My Joseph's been gone seven years now. Just been working it out. Did I ever tell you what happened to him?'

Flossie shook her head. She knew from Mary that Annie's husband had drowned, but not how.

'He was on the *Northfleet* when it sank. Two hundred and ninety-one were drowned. He'd only been on board nine days, heading for Tasmania.' Annie wiped her eyes with her handkerchief and took a deep breath. 'My father helped build that ship twenty years ago and Joe had been all over the place – Australia, India, China, you name it. Then he goes and drowns in the English Channel. What makes matters worse, the steamer that rammed her reversed engines and left without doing anything to help. Didn't even signal to others. Terrible shock, it all was.'

The *Northfleet* was a full rigged ship, chartered for three months to carry 376 assisted emigrants, mostly navvies and their families; forty crew members and a cargo of 450 tons of iron rails and equipment to build a railway line in Tasmania. After leaving Gravesend, bad weather forced the ship to drop anchor two miles offshore from Dungeness. During the night, a large, outward-bound steamer travelling at full speed struck the *Northfleet* amidships, making a clean breach in her timbers beneath the waterline. The ship went down in three quarters of an hour. Eighty-five people were saved, but of all the rest, only six bodies were ever found, four of them never identified. The Spanish iron-hulled steamer *Murillo* was named as the vessel responsible. When the undamaged ship docked at Cadiz, the watch crew were arrested, but they were never tried, there being no extradition treaty between the two countries.

'The only thing I have to console me is a letter sent from the pilot in charge, who had taken to the mizzen topmast and was rescued. He wrote that he last saw my Joe manning the pumps below, sticking at it till the bitter end, even though it was pointless. Did me good knowing that because the newspapers said the crew were out to save themselves first. The captain had to draw his revolver and shoot one of them in the leg when they defied his orders to put the women and children in the lifeboats first. Even then, only one woman and two children were rescued. The *City of London* picked up one little girl about your age. Nobody knew who she was, or what to do with her, as both her parents had perished. It was hard to live that down, I can tell you.'

It was all too shocking. Flossie held on to Annie's hand tightly as they continued silently in the shade of the cliffs on an ever-widening path that eventually joined the smart Clifton Marine Parade. Deciding that she could go no further without a cooling drink, Annie went into The Hit and Miss for two glasses of ginger beer, while Flossie gazed in awe at the multitude of pure-white sails circling around the Royal Thames Yacht Club and the shimmering domes and minarets of the exotic Clifton Baths.

'Joe always said how they made it look like the buildings he'd seen in India,' Annie said as she handed Flossie her drink on her return. 'Inside there's one pool for men and another for women, and hot, cold and vapour baths for the languid. Never fancied it meself, but I've made use of the old bathing machines on the foreshore to take a dip in the river.'

Reaching the town pier, they paid the penny entrance and descended the steps at the end to the landing stage. If the ships and steamers looked large passing Northfleet, they appeared gigantic here, riding at anchor. Flossie gasped as one of the great steamships of the Orient line swept by on her way to the docks. It was as close as she'd ever been to one of these leviathans, and it took her breath away.

'There was as many as three thousand tall-masted ships in the river on any one day,' Annie continued with a sweep of the hand. 'That's why they tried building a tunnel from Rotherhithe to Wapping to get cargo across without having to stop the ships. Brunel came up with a way to dig it out and used our Roman cement, but it was the worst job in the world. Six men drowned and Brunel himself barely escaped with his life.'

Flossie vaguely remembered Sam trying to tell her about the tunnel debacle, but she had been too young to take it in.

'Took a while to finish and in the end, it was only used by pedestrians. The money ran out before they could build the ramps for the cargo. Mind you, on the first day, fifty thousand people paid a penny to walk through it and by the end of three months, a million had done it. They called it the Eighth Wonder of the World.'

'Did you go?' Flossie was now utterly engrossed in the story.

'Certainly I did. Couldn't go down all those marble steps today, but I was younger then and, besides, the walls were full of pictures and statues to take your mind off being underwater. What's more, when we stopped to rest on the first platform, someone was playing a huge organ. At the bottom there were some fifty arches lit with gas burners that made them as bright as the sun. I've never seen shops like it – polished marble counters and gilded shelves full of fancy wares and curiosities. And there were all sorts of contrivances to make you spend your money, from Egyptian necromancers to dancing monkeys.'

'Gracious!' Flossie exclaimed. 'I wish I could have seen it.'

'Very different now, my girl. About ten years ago steam trains started to run through the tunnel. Some say it's terrible down there now for the drivers and firemen – no ventilation shafts under the river.'

As the sun started to weaken, Annie declared she was too tired to walk all the way home. So, after buying a pint of brown shrimps for her supper, they made their way back up Bath Street, to St. James' Church. Mr Jennings, of The Wheatsheaf Tavern opposite, had recently started a horse-drawn omnibus service between the church and Huggens College.

'If we make out we are ladies of reduced means from the alms houses, we might get on for half price,' Annie joked.

Riding back in comfort, the old lady slept with her latest penny dreadful unopened on her lap. Flossie mused over all the things she had seen and heard on their long walk. Annie had experienced so much during her long life – some wonderful things, some very cruel – yet she had managed to rise above it all and survive. Flossie had great admiration for her.

8

'Can you hear the voices? Must be more than half a dozen of them, poor souls.'

Sam was perched right on the end of the slipway, desperately trying to peer through the dense fog. Everyone was quiet, listening for the faint cries of help coming from the freezing water. Unfortunately, surrounding vessels were sounding their foghorns, which only made the situation worse. It was hopeless.

'Get the children back indoors. Nothing good's going to come of this,' Sam shouted.

Flossie couldn't make out where her father was in the murk, despite him being only a few feet away. The cold, wet, cement-ridden air was hurting her lungs and her clothes were soaked through.

From somewhere Mary emerged, ghostlike, her sodden hair falling limply about her shoulders. 'Go find Tom Handley,' she rasped, grabbing hold of her daughter's arm, 'and fetch him here. Go on, girl...'

Sam had seen Tom tie his fishing boat up earlier, so with it being Christmas Day, he was likely to be at home. Pushing her eldest daughter off into the greyness, Mary located Kate Bailey's boys and, forming a human chain, they made their way slowly back to the safety of their house.

It was a terrible end to what had been a wonderful day in The Creek. The Grants and their lodgers had been welcomed into the Baileys' warm, bright parlour while nine sailors from a ship moored in the estuary had rowed over to enjoy the hospitality provided by The Hope Inn. Come the evening, the men finally dragged themselves away from the warmth of the bar to make their return. Several minutes later, as Patrick Delaney opened The Hope's privy door, he heard a commotion which he immediately recognised as the sound of their boat overturning. Raising the alarm, Creek residents arrived en masse with as many lamps as they could muster and lined the shore to create a beacon of light. But there was nothing to be seen through the impenetrable fog, and it soon became clear that the men were lost.

As Flossie ran along Grove Road on her mission, she became aware of footsteps close on her heels.

'I'm not chasing you, just think I can get there faster than you,' a voice rang out from behind her. It was a young man running at breakneck speed in the direction of Park Place. As it was obvious he was going to get to Tom's house before her, she decided to turn back.

By the time Tom and his messenger arrived at the slipway, there was just one eerie cry sounding far out from the shore, and soon, it too was no more.

Sam's voice eventually broke the silence. 'Thanks for coming, Tom, but there's nothing you can do,' he said forlornly. 'They are all lost. Best get back here as soon as the fog lifts, I expect it'll be five bob a body, like usual.'

As the crowds started to disperse, Flossie felt a tap on her shoulder.

'I'm sorry if I startled you earlier.'

Swivelling round, she found herself staring into the eyes of the young man who had raced past her.

'I hoped we might get to the men in time. I wonder if anyone is left aboard their ship?'

Taken aback, it took a few seconds before she realised she'd seen him before, standing by the large gun, a Crimean War trophy, in front of Grove House. He had looked important in his blue steel spectacles with papers under his arm and, close up, he was very different from the other boys she knew. For one thing, his cap and coat looked sturdy and warm and obviously not second-hand. His fingernails had no trace of dirt under them and his fair skin wasn't rough. He was of slight build with no sign of ugly muscles, and every inch of him looked well-scrubbed. Florence Grant was intrigued, if not a little smitten.

'I'm Sydney, Sydney Gibbons,' he said, removing his cap.

Suddenly aware of her cement-coated teeth, she didn't dare smile. Hearing Mary calling for her, she turned briefly, then turned back to say goodbye, but Sydney had already been swallowed up by the fog.

'I can't stop long, Floss. I have to see my mam,' Jessie said, looking flustered and red in the face, having run all the way up Burch Road.

It had been three weeks since the drownings and they'd hardly seen each other, which made Jessie even keener to find out about Sydney Gibbons. Clutching each other's hands in expectation, the girls ran quickly to a seat outside The Elephant's Head where they knew they wouldn't be disturbed. Flossie composed herself as her friend got her breath back.

'He knows such a lot of interesting things, Jess. I can't begin to tell you all of what he's told me.'

'Wonder why he chose *you* as his confidante?' Jessie responded.

'It seems he finds it hard to make friends of his own kind,' Flossie continued, ignoring her friend's condescending tone.

'He's got a sister, Esther, who's a year older but looks much younger. He brought her to the slipway when we watched the ship finally go.'

'What ship?'

'You know, the one the drowned men came from. It took Tom and the others days to find the bodies.'

'I can't believe I missed all that, what with having to work on Christmas Day. Would you like a toffee apple?'

Jessie had spotted a young boy pushing a cart full of tempting treats. Flossie nodded and soon the two of them were tucking into sweet, sticky, golden delicacies.

'Well I never, fancy you meeting a gentleman in the making,' Jess teased as she prised lumps of hardened toffee from her teeth. 'The upper-crusts living in my house rarely give me a second glance, let alone talk to me. I have to "know my place", the cook says. Even the lady's maid is stuck-up. Anyway, tell me more.'

'He seems pleasant enough, and is devoted to his sister,' Flossie said, blushing slightly. 'He's studying to be a land surveyor, the teacher comes to the house especially. They have a governess, a cook, a housemaid and a nursemaid to look after Thomas, the baby.'

'Very grand,' Jessie said with a note of sarcasm in her voice. 'My pa's often talked about Mr Gibbons at the factory. Not sure he likes him much. Says he might be the manager of Robins, but he's full of his own importance. Still, perhaps his son is different. Look, I'd better be going now. Same time next week?'

Flossie nodded and smiled as she watched her friend throwing her rotten apple into the gutter. Food purchased from street sellers often held hidden surprises. What she hadn't mentioned was that Sydney and Esther were going to meet her on this very seat later that afternoon.

'He's very good,' Sydney said as the trio sat in the sunshine watching a strange little man performing a clog dance on the pub's cellar flaps beside them. 'Who is he?'

'That's Harry Relph,' Flossie replied. 'He's often here on a Saturday when the crowds are queuing for the gardens.'

'He looks very queer. How old is he?' Esther asked. 'Maybe we should put a penny in his pot.'

'A bit older than us, I think, but it's hard to tell.' Flossie was fascinated with Harry Relph, having often watched him perform. On one occasion Henry Luck had pushed Albert Bull forward to ask why he always wore white gloves. The boy said it was because he had five fingers and a thumb on each hand and six toes on each foot. That, along with being only four foot six inches tall, made him something of a spectacle, but it was his exceptional dance routines that stopped the passing crowds in their tracks.

When the ale keeper of The Elephant's Head left a glass of ginger ale by the pub door, 'The Young Tichborne', as the audiences had nicknamed the portly thirteen-year-old, took a grateful break. Slipping out of his heavy footwear, he reached for his much-needed drink and slumped against the wall. The name 'Tichborne' had become synonymous with being overweight thanks to an infamous twenty-five-stone fraudster, Arthur Orton – otherwise known as the Tichborne Claimant. Playing on the hopes of Lady Tichborne, who could not accept that her son had drowned as a child, he materialised in Wagga Wagga, Australia, pretending to be the said son and heir. In truth, he was nothing more than a Wapping butcher's son. Thankfully the family was not taken in and Orton was sentenced to fourteen years' penal servitude.

Keen to impress her new friends, Flossie plucked up courage and went over to talk to Harry. It was perfect timing as he was only too happy to share some good news.

'It's paid off. I've been spotted by the manager,' he said,

nodding in the direction of the Rosherville Gardens. 'I'm joining a troupe of blacked-up minstrels. All the fashion now. You do it with burnt cork. I'm to dance and play a penny whistle and if it goes well, I'll get a regular booking. With any luck I won't have to go back to lathering for a livin'.'

The sixteenth and final child of seventy-seven-year-old publican Richard Relph, Harry had moved to Gravesend at the age of eight. His schoolmaster had recommended him for a watchmaking apprenticeship, but his father ignored the advice and had him taken on as a lather boy in a Gravesend barber's shop. Taking advantage of his celebrity status as a local freak, he found he could earn extra income busking to day trippers, theatre queues and outside public houses, where he devised his eccentric dances.

'This is just the start. Got my eye on Barnard's Music Hall in Chatham,' he continued. 'Top-of-the-bill acts earn thirty-five shillings a week there.' Wiping his mouth with the back of his glove, he winked at Flossie, ambled over to his spot and, with a cherubic smile, burst into song.

Waving goodbye, Flossie, Sydney and Esther left the crowds behind and made their way home past Thomas Bevan's posh house with his initials in the railings. Convincing her friends to take a short cut down Hive Lane, they were forced to hold their noses on account of the stench. The lane was used as a public convenience by many a man on his way to work, and Flossie began to regret her hasty decision, especially when halfway down she sensed that they were being followed. As they started to walk faster, out of the shadows two oafs emerged and within seconds one of them had pinned Sydney to the wall, knocking his glasses into the scrub, while the other loomed over Esther menacingly and pointed to some pretty trinkets she was wearing.

'I'll have some of them fine things o' yourn,' he laughed roughly. 'Make 'em over sharp.'

Esther was so terrified she started to shake.

'You see this?' he spat, waving a stick in front of their faces. 'It'll be best for all of you if you do what I say.'

Flossie watched in horror as Esther handed over her bracelet and fumbled with the clasp of her brooch while the boy grabbed the gold chain attached to a watch hanging from her waist. Stuffing the jewellery into his pockets, he then made off. His accomplice deftly punched Sydney in the ribs, rendering him incapable of giving chase, and then strolled off as if nothing had happened.

The girls rushed to Sydney's aid. Though winded, he soon recovered and took charge of the situation.

'We need to find a policeman. There's no time to lose,' he said, brushing the cement dust off his cap.

As they made for the London Road, Sydney stopped under a street light and turned to Flossie.

'You should go straight home,' he said, freeing his sister's hand from hers. 'I think it will be for the best if you don't come with us. The police may well think you were in on it. You could have lured us down that unpleasant lane and given the robbers a sign to follow. It is likely that the authorities will be suspicious of you.'

Taken aback at being thought an accomplice to the attack, she flashed him a disdainful look and, lifting her skirt away from her knees, ran off down the lanes, not slowing down until she caught sight of the flaming kilns of The Creek.

John O'Connell let her in. 'Your mam's been looking for you,' he said reproachfully. 'She's gone along the Undershore to get our meal, not best pleased that you weren't here to go. So be warned.'

Flossie shrugged her shoulders. Glancing around the kitchen, it was obvious that her father wasn't home. Without him to give the orders, the lodgers hadn't washed, and powder from their caps and clothes was falling off them like snow. The three of them were sitting with their feet up on the table. Things had become very lackadaisical of late.

This was payday, but without her husband's earnings Mary had to shop with no more than a tanner and a few farthings. Pluck would be the best she'd get, and sheep's lungs needed a long time cooking. Better hope for some broken fish if she didn't stop off at The Staff of Life on the way. Lottie had done her best with what was left in the pantry and the lodgers were picking at some dry bread and wilted watercress while they waited.

As it turned out, Mary didn't make it to the shops, nor did she get home until after the girls had gone to bed. When she eventually rolled in, well after closing time, she crashed around the kitchen for another hour. Luckily Lottie didn't wake.

Flossie, on the other hand, couldn't sleep. The events of that afternoon were weighing heavily on her mind and she felt responsible for putting Sydney and Esther in danger. There were always pickpockets outside the gardens and gangs of local youths often obstructed the footpaths. If arrested by the police, they usually got fined a shilling and were named in the local paper. She should have known better than to leave the main road, and sighed on remembering what Sydney had said to her. Though his motive for sending her away may have been to protect her, perhaps he really did believe she was in on it? Whichever way it was, she doubted she'd ever see him again. Maybe Jessie was right: the upper-crusts keep themselves to themselves.

A few weeks later the Grant girls were at a fancy bazaar when Flossie caught sight of the *Reporter*'s headline: *Two boys commit wilful murder stealing pocket watch*. A chill ran down her spine. Moving closer to read the story while Lottie was choosing a penny pipe for Sam, it stated that the victim was Thomas Eves, proprietor of the Pavilion Theatre. Named simply as Clarke and Henderson, both aged ten and Eves' employees, the killers had apparently *beaten him with sticks until he died*. According to the police, Clarke *had treated the situation with great indifference.*

When they admitted to further violent crimes, including one involving the son and daughter of Mr Robert Gibbons, cement manufacturer, the judge had no hesitation in meting out a sentence of penal servitude.

The lodgers were full of the story come the evening. Flossie kept quiet, only too aware that she'd had a lucky escape.

'Wake up, girls, and get dressed.'

It seemed like the middle of the night and Flossie tried desperately to stay asleep despite being shaken by her mother. Lottie inevitably started crying.

'Hush, girl,' Mary whispered. 'We're going on a trip. Now hurry up, the pair of you.'

Confused, Flossie rubbed her eyes, braved putting her bare feet on the cold floor and went over to the window. It was pitch-black outside. Fumbling around, she eventually found and lit her bedside candle and started to do as her mother said.

'Where are we going?' Lottie whined.

'Don't know yet,' Flossie replied, trying her best to calm her younger sister. 'Best do as she says. Happen it'll be a pleasing day.' It was too dark for Lottie to see the worried look on her sister's face.

There was something different about Mary that spring morning. It was only five o'clock, yet she was dressed, with tidy, straightened hair. There was no evidence of a hangover and she wasn't slurring her words. Barely ten minutes had passed before she returned and placed a carpet bag, not seen since the day they first arrived in The Creek, on Flossie's bed.

'We'll be gone for a while, so pack all your clothes,' she instructed. 'I've made you both a drink of warm cocoa before we leave. Now be quick, we have a train to catch.'

Suddenly excited at the prospect of an adventure, Lottie started dancing round the room. 'Maybe it's to celebrate your birthday,' she squealed, trying to make her sister join in. Flossie resisted, continuing to pack. Birthdays usually came and went without any fuss, she thought.

Peeking into the other bedroom while her mother was downstairs, Flossie saw that her father was not there. An early start, even for him, she thought. Yet the room seemed strangely empty with Mary's bag, coat and best bonnet neatly laid out on top of the tidy bed. Flossie couldn't remember the last time she'd seen it that way.

Dawn was breaking as they walked down the London Road to the Town Pier and the ferry to Tilbury. Mary walked with purpose, one bag balancing in each hand. She looked taller, somehow. Lottie was jabbering happily, which thankfully made up for Flossie's silence. There was a light mist on the river as the small steamer *Cato* came alongside. The girls buttoned up their coats for the short, but damp, ferry ride to the opposite side in Essex. The vessel filled up quickly with construction labourers heading for the new docks. Everyone jostled for position on the cramped deck and there was much pushing and shoving. A man who looked like he hadn't washed in a week of Sundays leered at Mary, and got so close that Flossie could feel his hot breath on her face. Thankfully someone else elbowed him out of the way to give the girls some space. Flossie tried to concentrate on the shimmering lights reflecting on the water.

It was a relief to disembark, but the distasteful experience proved to be just the start of a tortuous journey. Sitting in an icy train carriage, standing on a smelly omnibus and a noisy walk through crowded streets left the girls bewildered and tired. They soon gave up asking where they were going. At one point, with stomachs rumbling, the sound of a nearby street market offered hope of some sustenance. As it grew louder, the hubbub and din of bellowing voices alarmed Lottie.

'Walnuts, apples, onions, turnips, penny a lot. Herrings, whelks, any of it for a copper…'

Allowing her exhausted girls to rest on a small green, Mary

toured the stalls for a cheap meal. Eyes darting everywhere, Flossie realised they were in Barkingside, a place evidently far, far busier than Northfleet. Horses and carts were everywhere and large groups of men jammed the footpaths, talking and smoking pipes, while their women rushed from stall to stall with purchases spilling from their apron pockets. It was not long before the girls were tucking into eel pies so hot that they burnt their mouths, followed by penny licks to cool them down. Try as hard as she might, Flossie couldn't quell her suspicions over her mother's sudden generosity. Ice cream was an unheard-of treat.

'We're almost there, girls,' Mary said as they turned a corner. Flossie noted that they were in Tanners Lane, and remembering that her father had given her a silver tanner as a keepsake, she now fondled it in her pocket.

Mary suddenly stopped. They were outside a pair of large metal gates.

'This is it,' she said, ringing the bell. 'Now let me have a look at you both. Got to make sure you look smart.' Pushing some stray ringlets back under Lottie's bonnet, Mary proceeded to spit on her handkerchief and wiped some spots of grime off both their faces.

A tall, serious-looking woman opened the gates and ushered them in. Lottie looked up at Mary.

'What is this place? Tell us now, Mama,' she pleaded. 'Are we going to stay in one of those houses?'

Mary remained silent as they crossed a manicured lawn and stopped outside one of a row of thirteen identical cottages all named after plants or flowers. Flossie gasped on reading the plaque on the wall: *Dr Barnardo's Village Home for Destitute Girls.*

9

Disputing it didn't make any difference. The governess was adamant.

'Your name is Oxer, Florence and Charlotte Oxer. It says it here in clear English.'

Flossie's head was spinning. She'd been left in a room for more than an hour 'to calm herself' before being allowed to see the handing-over papers. Permission to do so had only been granted on the express condition that this must bring an end to her obsession with her surname. Now the proof was in front of her. In faint spidery writing, it read:

I, Mary Ann Oxer, of no fixed abode, do hereby hand over my rightful daughters, Florence and Charlotte Oxer. Cause: destitution due to husband Henry Oxer's imprisonment in Ipswich, Suffolk, for drunkenness and thievery.

Flossie fell silent. It was no wonder that the governess had grown tired of hearing her yelling that her father, Samuel Grant of The Creek, Northfleet, needed to know where they were so he could come and take them home.

Slamming shut the admissions register, the governess looked stern. Running a bony finger down the perfect creases of her apron, she made it clear: 'Dr Barnardo forbids his children to speak about their pasts, so that is how it will be from now on. Do you understand?'

Exhausted, Flossie nodded. Drained of emotion, she fixed her gaze on a mass of girls in white pinafores streaming silently past the window.

'We create an environment here that leads to a pure, purposeful and happy life, and soon you will be taught how to achieve it.' Seeing that she was losing Flossie's attention, she rapped her knuckles on the desk. 'In essence,' she declared, staring deep into the girl's eyes, 'the well-ordered and gentle life of our Village Home casts no backward shadows.'

The rest of the evening was spent in a whirlwind of unfamiliar and disagreeable tasks. Every stage of their initiation caused Lottie to burst into floods of uncontrollable tears. She had to be dragged to have her photograph taken, fearing that it might hurt. Next she was unceremoniously dropped into a steaming bath, where she was convinced she would drown in such deep water. It was a far cry from the second-hand, six inches of tepid water that she was used to. The final straw came when her hair was roughly searched for nits. Too distraught for supper, she was put to bed by Miss Adams, their new housemother.

Left on her own for a while, Flossie stared at the pictures on display. The pitiful images of ragged, sad-eyed scraps of humanity were more reminiscent of the scavenging mudlarks wading in the Thames after the *Princess Alice* went down than of herself and Lottie.

'Dr Barnardo is a great believer in documenting the plight of poor children,' Miss Adams said on her return. 'Many are orphans rescued from the East End gutters; "street Arabs", he calls them.' Peering over the top of her spectacles, she looked

Flossie up and down and sniffed. 'But the Doctor also removes children from neglectful parents to save them from corrupt influences.'

So that's how they see us, thought Flossie. It had all happened so fast. Struck dumb with fear, the girls had been whisked away even whilst Mary was pleading her case for abandoning them. By the time they were brought back to the reception house, their mother had been shown out, leaving only the carpet bag behind with a scribbled note on top. *Be good*, it said.

Inside Primrose Cottage, Lottie lay shivering, unable to sleep. Her sister crept in beside her and they huddled together for comfort. In turmoil, Flossie tried to make some sense of what had happened. Their world had been turned upside down. They were in some kind of a workhouse and been told that family contact wasn't encouraged. Were they never going to see their mother again? Was that what Mary wanted? Was that why she had abandoned them? Did she feel nothing for them? It didn't make sense. And why had she used a false name? Their name was Grant, not Oxer. How could Sam, whom they loved dearly, find them if their names had been changed? And how did Mary come to hear about this Dr Barnardo, so far away from everything and everyone they knew? Why would *he* care enough about destitute children to build such a home?

The London into which medical student Thomas Barnardo had arrived from Dublin fifteen years earlier was, by now, a city struggling to cope with the effects of the Industrial Revolution. The population had more than doubled over the previous fifty years, much of the increase being concentrated in the East End. New railway lines cut through former residential areas, pitching thousands of families from their homes at a time when the dispossessed from rural areas, and Irish immigrants fleeing from starvation, were flooding in. Overcrowding in bad housing, unemployment, poverty and disease were rife, with one in five children dying before their fifth birthday. London had a higher illegitimacy birth rate than anywhere else in the world. Rather than face the humiliation of being branded 'paupers', many families did anything to survive outside the workhouse. Thousands of children slept on the streets and many were forced to beg after being maimed in factories.

So disturbed by the plight of these destitute children was the philanthropic Barnardo that he opened an all-night shelter at 10 Stepney Causeway. Initially concerning himself with the welfare of boys, he soon realised that though fewer girls were evident on the streets, their plight was greater than that of the boys. With the age of consent being thirteen, girls were in grave moral peril, being bought for five pounds for local brothels. In an extraordinary act of charity, when he and his new wife Syrie were given Mossford Lodge in Barkingside as a wedding present, the Barnardos converted the rear of their home to accommodate sixty girls. With the help of her Christian lady friends, Mrs Barnardo set about turning these starving, half-naked girls with street cunning into industrious, respectable, God-fearing servants. Whatever their background, she believed Christian influence, stern love and industry would mould the children.

After only a short while, however, Thomas Barnardo declared that they were failing, having discovered that the barrack system of large dormitories was 'propagating evil' through older street girls corrupting younger ones with their appalling tales of degradation and inhuman behaviour. He therefore embarked on creating a Girls' Village Home in the sixty acres of grounds adjoining Mossford Lodge. A series of doll's-house cottages were built clustering around a village green, each offering a home for fifteen to twenty girls of mixed ages. Placing a 'mother' in charge, he wanted each home to function as near as possible to a normal family. A perfect world in miniature.

The upper classes viewed poverty as shameful and a result of laziness or vice. They lived in terror that the 'dangerous classes' would cause the breakdown of law and order, with mobs of juveniles threatening their peace and security. Orphaned children were summarily placed in institutions where they were clothed in pauper uniforms, ticketed, drilled and herded into vast workhouses filled with thieves, beggars and other examples of human failure. This offended Barnardo. He refused to discriminate between the deserving and undeserving poor and accepted all children, including disabled and illegitimate ones, stressing that every child deserved the best possible start in life whatever their background. Soon, news of his innovative Home for Destitute Girls, where no one was turned away, had spread far and wide.

As dawn broke, the sound of birds chirping in the trees came as a surprise to Flossie. Uncovering her face, the air felt cold, but not damp. There was no howling gale rattling the window frames, and no piercing foghorns or factory sirens either. Peering round the bright yellow room, she counted three other beds besides her own and Lottie's, all occupied by sleeping girls. A fireplace, its mantelpiece heavily laden with ornaments, was on one wall and a washstand complete with jug and bowl against another. Over the door was an intricate embroidered sampler, bearing the message *Barnardo will be your true family*.

Seconds later, Miss Adams appeared at the door. Drawing a watch from her breast pocket and pulling it towards her face as far as the chain would allow, she flicked open its case with a fingernail and, pointing at the two new girls, whispered, 'It's six o'clock. Collect your new dresses and pinafores from the laundry room and be ready for breakfast in one hour.'

Flossie and Lottie hurriedly dressed in their own clothes for the last time while the other girls continued to sleep soundly. Closing the door quietly, they followed Miss Adams across the green. In the daylight, the grounds looked immense. Flossie counted twenty-four ivy-clad cottages in all, surrounding a large green with pretty flowerbeds and almond trees. Lottie nodded towards the wrought-iron gates that Mary had led them through the evening before. They clanged in the wind as if to remind the girls of their loss of freedom.

Issued with fresh clothes, Miss Adams told them to memorise their number as every item of clothing had that number chain-stitched on it. Braiding their newly-washed, unruly hair took some doing, but finally they were ready to join the other hundred or so girls performing physical exercises on the green before breakfast.

'Your Sunday bonnets will be waiting for you later,' said Miss Adams as she forced Lottie to let go of her sister's hand. 'All the girls have ribbons to match the flower their cottage is named after.'

After breakfast, with unlimited bread, the girls had time to take stock of their new bedroom. Flossie admired her snowy-white quilt, proper cotton sheets and rag rug. Further investigation revealed a straw paillasse covering a rust-free green iron bedstead.

'Bedding gets changed every week,' an enthusiastic girl, who turned out to be called Betsy, told them. 'We gets meat twice a week too. I ain't ever 'ad so much meat.'

Delving under her bed, Lottie pulled out a round chamber pot with her name freshly painted on the enamel underside, followed by a wicker basket filled with neat clothes.

'They come from well-wishers,' Betsy added gleefully. 'It's like Paradise 'ere.'

Cleanliness of person and property was an early, and important, lesson for the girls to learn. During their medical check-up later that day, they were given a toothbrush which Miss Adams had to teach them how to use. Fresh water was plentiful,

Barnardo having sunk a three hundred-foot-deep artesian well to serve all of their needs.

'At home,' said Lottie to an unimpressed Betsy, 'we only get water for two hours a day, and that includes Sundays too.'

As the days and weeks turned into months, Flossie slowly began to appreciate her new surroundings. It seemed impossible that there could be such a peaceful place, graced with an abundance of fresh, clean air. To be able to walk far from a foul, poisonous river without the relentless din of factories was bliss, and she woke every morning with a huge sense of relief that her chest wasn't clogged with damp cement dust.

Living in a totally feminine world was hard to get used to, but she found the reliability of the routines and schedules preferable to her haphazard life in The Creek. Her cottage seemed like a palace, with a kitchen, a large dining room, a playroom with pigeonholes for toys, four bedrooms and a bathroom. You could see your reflection on the polished floors and there were pictures on the walls, albeit all of religious scenes. Miss Adams had her own room, which, when the opportunity arose to peek inside, was seen to be small but cosy, with fresh flowers on the table and a patterned carpet on the floor.

Primrose Cottage's spinster 'mother' was a strict total abstainer, according to Betsy. Such self-control impressed Flossie. A Christian lady of private means, she had apparently answered an advertisement for volunteers in the early days and the work had become her vocation in life. She seemed content to spend all her free time alone in her room.

Miss Adams ensured that the girls' physical welfare was always attended to, with a guaranteed one-course hot dinner every day and clean, dry clothes, which Flossie received gratefully. Nevertheless, she found the emphasis on moral welfare somewhat tedious. No organised games were allowed on Sunday, only Bible studies at half past ten and half past six, followed by choir practice. The extra devotional service at half past seven on Wednesdays was bad enough, but on rainy days, when the girls were unable to exercise, they were made to sit silently and memorise psalms.

As far as their emotional well-being was concerned, sympathy was in short supply. Two new girls who cried constantly over the loss of their parents, having been abandoned on the grounds of extreme poverty, tried the patience of their new 'mother'. It was well known that some parents decided to separate *in order* for their children to be taken in – desertion by at least one parent being the qualification for entry.

Flossie understood their grief, having by now given up hope that her father was coming to claim them. She missed Jessie, Kate Bailey and old Annie Devonshire, even silly Henry Luck, yet she didn't miss her old life in The Creek. Lottie, being younger, was finding it much harder.

The whole tone of the children's upbringing in all the cottages depended on the disposition of the housemothers. There were general rules, but the way an individual mother interpreted her duties varied greatly. From what Betsy was saying, some were clearly kinder than others.

Every hour of the children's day was organised, starting with the older girls getting up at half past five to light the fires. Once breakfast was over and all the chores done, elementary lessons took up the rest of the morning, leaving the afternoon free for domestic training. Barnardo had started his village at a time when employing servants was increasingly a mark of social status. Well-turned-out and properly instructed plain cooks and maids were difficult to obtain, so the girls were taught from a young age to make beds, lay and light fires, clean grates, scrub floors, sweep and greet visitors.

Suspecting that Mary had sung her daughter's praises over the weekly washing in The Creek, Flossie found herself working in the vast new steam laundry that undertook all the washing for the houses. It was a soul-destroying environment. The girls washed over six hundred sheets and garments on a Monday and ironed them all on a Tuesday. The washing was tedious enough, but ironing was worse. Eight girls were positioned around a huge ironing board, four on each side, pressing sheet after monotonous sheet using a heavy box iron. Flossie counted ten such boards side by side and several other tables where linen was being folded.

Fainting from exhaustion was common. When one young girl collapsed alongside Flossie one day, the intolerant laundress shouted, 'Take her outside for some air, and make haste!'

As she helped the fragile, exhausted girl up from the floor, Flossie saw that her legs were encased in heavy metal braces.

'Don't feel sorry for her, she's a hopeless cripple,' the laundress snapped. 'You'll find yourself helping all sorts here – blind, deaf and dumb, deformed and diseased. No one gets turned away here.' The sarcasm in her voice was biting.

Ethel, as Flossie discovered, was fourteen, though she looked no more than twelve, such was her tiny frame. 'I'm a factory cripple,' she whispered as she began to recover. 'Started in the rag factory before me tenth birthday, but me bones were too young, couldn't stand up to the job.'

As the girl continued, Flossie was appalled by the awful conditions in Bethnal Green.

'I reckon there were over two dozen lodging in our 'ouse and most of 'em 'ad been in clink one time or another. Rotten 'ouses like ours was all us poorest could afford; last stop before the work'ouse. That's where me ma is now, as it 'appens. We used to call it Sweaters Hell, down the old Nichol.'

The Nichol, a notorious area where Ethel had lived in one room with her mother and father and seven brothers and sisters, had been described in *The Illustrated London News* as *a monotonous round of vice, filth and poverty, where people huddled in dark cellars and bare and blackened rooms reeking with disease and death and without the means for the most ordinary observations of decency or cleanliness.* The houses, if they could be called that, were constantly damp, having been built with ash bricks and billysweet, a rough mortar made from street dirt mixed with the by-products of soap-making from local factories, which led to sagging and unstable walls that never dried out.

During Ethel's short lifetime every back yard and open space had been built upon. Homes doubled as workshops producing anything and everything, from clothes pegs to couches. Carts and barrows constantly plied their way through the maze of yards and alleyways. Fetid cowsheds and donkey stalls were everywhere. Tailors, hawkers, pawnbrokers, pie shops, fish curers and drunkards lived side by side.

'Every blighter earns just 'bout enough to ward off starvation,' Ethel added matter-of-factly. 'Me pa was an ivory turner and could turn 'is 'and to French polishin' given a chance, but he got taken with consumption and we 'ad to move to Boundary Street. Fings went from bad to worse then. In the end, there was only the workhouse left. I'm the lucky one. Dr Barnardo took pity on me.'

Relishing having escaped the steamy atmosphere of the laundry for a while, the girls carried on talking, warming to each other as they did so.

'So you don't know yer real father then?' Ethel asked after hearing a little of Flossie's story. 'He wasn't the geezer who brought you up, then?'

Flossie shook her head, long past shedding tears over it. 'So I'm told,' she said ruefully. 'They say my ma left me here to go back to him. In Ipswich. That's why I've got the name Oxer. Never, ever heard it before.'

'You'll find out the truth one day, don't worry,' Ethel said, touching her new friend's arm. 'She's got some nerve, yer ma 'as, I'll say that fer 'er.'

At that point the door opened and the laundress shouted for them to return to work, lest they fancied going up before the governess.

When two of the older girls in Flossie's room secured employment, Ethel moved in, along with another waif from the East End, Rose Roberts. They were only too glad to get away from their old housemother as she had a way of punishing her girls by locking them in the bathroom or making them lie under their beds all night.

Flossie found her new friends refreshing. They were down to earth and irreverent, though Lottie was less impressed.

'I can't see why you find them so entertaining,' she said grumpily. 'You'd never make friends with their sort if we were back in The Crick.'

Though Flossie couldn't disagree with that, over a year had passed and her attitude towards others had changed. Lottie still declined to mix with those she considered below her.

'If I remember rightly, we didn't mix with the matchgirls when we were off hopping. Now you chat to that common Rose Roberts all the time.'

Dismayed at her sister's snobbish tone, Flossie saw no point in arguing. There was little difference between any of them as far as she was concerned. They were all destitute.

Rose was fifteen and an orphan. She'd first been employed as a matchgirl at Bryant & May, aged ten.

'Told 'em I was twelve, of course. Worked fourteen hours a day fer five bob a week. Mind you, never got that much, 'cause we was always gettin' fined,' she told Flossie. 'Lost 'alf a day's pay if we was a few minutes late, thruppence if we was caught talkin' and even more if we dropped any of the lucifers. White slavery, they called it.'

Prolonged exposure to white phosphorous produced a condition called 'phossy jaw'. Many suffered, and even died, making the 'strike anywhere' matches. Rose was one of the lucky ones. She escaped necrosis of the jawbone, but three years carrying boxes of matches on her head, as the younger girls were made to do, had taken its toll. Her hair had been rubbed off, causing baldness.

'Think it looks bad now?' she said, when she saw Lottie staring at her one morning. 'Take a look at this.' Fumbling in her pillowcase, Rose pulled out an album of picture postcards which she opened and held up to the sisters. Before them were two 'before and after' images. 'This is me when I first come 'ere. This one's after six months.'

Flossie was stunned. She could hardly believe Rose was the same person in the pictures. The left-hand photograph was of a pale, bald and undersized urchin standing in rags. The one on the right was of a slightly healthier-looking girl dressed in a smart pinafore and bonnet, holding some embroidery. Lottie snatched the album from Rose's hand and stared at the cover. Titled *Once a Little Vagrant, Now a Little Workman*, it was a collection of pictures, each one showing the transformation from orphan in a state of neglect to child scrubbed clean and full of promise.

'Where did you get this from?' Flossie asked a little too sharply, conscious of the fact that she and her sister had had their photographs taken the first night they'd arrived.

'I nicked it. Old Barnardo flogs 'em to 'is rich friends to raise funds, by all accounts. Five bob for a pack of twenty or sixpence for a single.'

Retrieving her one and only possession from Lottie, Rose added, 'I won't 'ear a word said against 'im, though. Saved my bacon, I can tell ya. I'd been sleepin' in shop doorways on the Roman Road since me ma died of phossy. Me only 'ope was that Fanny Allbright would take me in 'er lodgin' 'ouse, but she said I 'ad to save up fer a wig wiv some ringlets first or I'd scare off 'er clients. That was when the beadle found me, thank the Lord. I'm not allowed to grow me fringe back, though, Miss Adams says it's "a most immoral hairstyle".'

Rose lifted her head and flicked her nose as she impersonated their housemother. The girls muffled their giggles, fearing that the woman herself might overhear.

'It seems we factory girls are the 'ardest to transform into respectable domestic servants 'cause we lack womanly graces – Gawd knows what they are.'

As time went by Flossie felt increasingly isolated from the world and wondered what effect leading such a cocooned life was going have on her future. There had been the occasional tastes of freedom on day trips by horse tram to Epping Forest, but it was an age since she'd walked through a busy street, visited a shop or talked to a man. So many subjects were taboo, and there were too many Christian endeavour meetings for her liking. She wondered how those incarcerated as babies would ever learn to cope with the outside world when their time came to leave. Watching the little girls playing Mothers and Fathers on the green was heart breaking. They were recreating family life they had no experience of.

One fine May morning, there was great excitement everywhere.

'Ain't been this much fuss since Princess Mary come to open Hyacinth Cottage,' Ethel said, tightening the straps on her leg braces. They were all lined up on the green wearing their best clothes, the housemothers fussing around rearranging hair and straightening smocks. There'd been days of preparation and Flossie was looking forward to it all being over and done with. Houses had been scrubbed and best quilts put on the beds. Enamel mugs had been temporarily removed and dainty cups and saucers stacked in the kitchen cupboards.

Forced to practise their musical drill yet again, arms outstretched to maintain formation, out of the corner of her eye

Flossie noticed Dr Barnardo emerging from Mossford Lodge. He looked exceedingly dapper in a straw boater and freshly polished shoes, his military moustache smartly trimmed and tweaked, curled upwards even more than usual. Mrs Barnardo followed behind, her eyes barely visible under a huge, elaborate hat. Together they stood waiting by the porter's lodge with the rest of the senior staff, everyone towering above the exceedingly short doctor. Every now and then one or other would check a pocket watch or straighten a tie or ribbon. Some of the girls were excited, others less so, knowing that they were on show to upper-class visitors on a tour of their Village Home. Soon they'd be poking around in the girls' bedrooms and, later, having dinner in their cottages. Flossie wasn't sure how she felt about being treated as some kind of spectacle, but when the gates opened and the visitors arrived, she waved her Union Jack and curtseyed with the rest.

After some exhaustive handshaking, the ladies and gentlemen, in all their finery, were guided towards the waiting girls. They strolled past at a safe distance, pointing and whispering behind gloved hands. Flossie wondered why it was that people with money imagined poor people lacked feelings. A select group of girls then danced around the maypole before joining together to sing the *Song for our Little Servants*, to which the assembled audience responded with nods of affirmation and gentle applause at such a display of Christian piety.

When I go to service
I must watch and pray
That my Heavenly Father
Will direct my way.

May the love of Jesus
Fill my heart and mind
And his Holy Spirit
Make me good and kind.

Keep me strictly honest
Steady and upright
Thoughtful of my mistress
In and out of sight.

If her things are broken
By my carelessness,
Let me mind 'tis better
Always to confess.

10

During her fifteenth year, the stable and contented life that Flossie had slowly begun to take for granted at Dr Barnardo's was turned upside down. Many of her friends had moved on – Rose, unhappily, back to the match factory and poor, fragile Ethel into service as a lady's maid. But losing her friends was nothing compared to losing the only person she could truly call family.

'I'm going to live in Canada,' was how Lottie broke the news. 'I wasn't allowed to speak of it until our mother agreed, but it is definite now.'

Flossie couldn't believe her ears. Her sister, going to live in Canada? Their mother, whom *she* hadn't heard from in three years, being in contact with Lottie and giving permission for this to happen? Surely that couldn't be right. She felt old wounds opening up again.

'I'm the pick of the crop,' Lottie sighed. 'I feel faint with joy.'

Flossie raised her eyebrows at the sight of her sister swooning and fanning herself with a handkerchief.

'Only the brightest girls get to go on the Great Canadian Adventure – that's what Dr Barnardo calls it. Miss Adams put me forward for the interview with the governess and said I'll gain a healthy independence and a comfortable home far from the bad influences of my early life. I'm leaving next month for a place called Toronto, where I'll be found a respectable position. I can't wait to get away from this stifling place.'

Flossie was dumbstruck and her head was spinning. Apart from her amazement that all this had been hidden from her, she was shocked to see that Lottie, not yet thirteen, so obviously relished leaving everything and everyone she knew behind. How different could two sisters be? Seemingly unaware of the pain she was causing, Lottie rushed off to find out who else had been chosen to go with her.

With tears welling up in her eyes, Flossie started walking in the direction of the governess' office. She wasn't going to have her sister taken away from her without a fight, and there were many questions that needed answering.

'I can only spare you two minutes,' the governess said curtly, pushing a few stray strands of iron-grey hair into the tight bun on the back of her head. 'It's quite simple. I contacted your mother in Ipswich and asked for her permission for both of you to emigrate. She eventually replied, declaring that only Charlotte could go, not you.'

Flossie gripped the desk, her legs turning to jelly.

'Mrs Oxer is of the opinion that her youngest daughter has the countenance and disposition to find a rich husband, but that *you* will be more likely to obtain responsible employment here and be able to aid her financially in the future. I imagine she found someone to write the statement, but the signature is clearly hers.'

With that the governess stood up, walked round her leather-topped desk and guided a stunned, silent Flossie towards the door, adding as she did so, 'Don't go listening to the rubbish that some people will tell you. Our children's welfare is of paramount importance. Most of the reports of ill treatment stem from the Catholics. It's just part of their propaganda. They think

Dr Barnardo is spiriting children away to Canada in order to convert them. Stuff and nonsense.'

Gently pushing the unwanted visitor across the threshold, she closed the door firmly behind her. Rooted to the spot, Flossie sobbed as the governess' words echoed in her ears. How could her mother still have some say in her future after abandoning her daughters in such a callous manner?

As for Catholic propaganda and ill treatment, it seemed that Boards of Guardians had been permitted to send workhouse children to Canada for thirty years. Now that economic depression was causing mass unemployment, homelessness and destitution, Christian philanthropist Barnardo saw it as his responsibility to try to relieve 'population pressure' in congested cities. *Overcrowding is a primary, if often unrecognised, cause of the moral cesspools I and others are continually engaged in deodorising*, he wrote at the time. *Every boy rescued from the gutter is one dangerous man the less; each girl saved from a criminal course is a present to the next generation of a virtuous woman and a valuable servant.*

His zeal had convinced governments, like that of Canada, of the advantages to be gained from child migration as a way of populating the colonies with British stock. Less scrupulous operators, however, saw it as a means of providing a source of cheap labour dressed up as child welfare. Private agencies were soon capitalising on the advantages of sending children overseas. While caring for a child in an institution in Britain cost around twelve pounds a year, sending one overseas involved a one-off payment of fifteen pounds. It wasn't difficult to see how money could be made out of destitute children.

The first party of fifty Barnardo boys left England in 1882. A year later, when girls were included, rumours began to circulate about abuse, neglect and even slave labour amongst thirteen-year-old girls sent from Barkingside to live with farming families in Winnipeg. As a result, a vetting and inspection system was hastily installed. By this time the numbers of children being sent to Canada had risen into the hundreds.

The scheme wasn't without its critics, though. Canadians feared that their country would be contaminated by the dumping of slum children on their soil. To counter this, Dr Barnardo promised to send only the 'flower of the flock'; children who were morally, physically and mentally sound. If any should become 'definitely immoral or criminal', he guaranteed that they would be shipped back.

My poor sister, Flossie thought. *Too young to understand.*

The following weeks were unbearable. Flossie watched her little sister move into a cottage where girls destined for Canada were being housed and given special lessons to prepare them for their new lives. Increasingly despairing, she felt unable to show her emotions for fear of being criticised. Instead she put all her energies into embroidering a sampler with the words *Home is Where Your Heart Is*, praying that, tucked into her luggage, it would remind Lottie of where she belonged.

When the fateful day came, the governess encouraged the remaining girls to give three cheers as they watched the pioneering group march out of the gates. Flossie stayed silent as they turned the corner of Tanner Lane, heading for Liverpool and the *SS Sardinia*. Lottie was indistinguishable from the rest in their Ulster overcoats and red hoods, each child bearing a large tag with their name and a Barnardo's number on it.

Realising that something needed to be done to take Flossie's mind off her loss; Miss Adams decided to give her a 'project'. Six new girls, rescued in dire circumstances, had been hastily placed in Primrose Cottage. The sudden death of a Smithfield brothel-keeper had thrown them onto the streets. Every one of them was younger than Flossie and she found it hard to hold back her tears as they undressed for their initial bath, exposing their fragile, bruised bodies.

Kitty was the first to speak of her experiences. 'He courted me for quite some weeks and made me believe he was going to marry me. Then one day he said he'd take me to London and show me the sights. I'd never been, so it sounded exciting, and it was at first. Took me here and there, gave me plenty to eat and drink, even treated me to the theatre. That's when I missed the last train home. I was a bit drunk, so when he offered me nice lodgings for the night, I agreed.

'Course his client was waiting in the next room. I screamed and yelled all the way through it, but no one came. I didn't dare go home after I'd lost my character, so I became a "mark". The brothel-keeper got twenty quid commission that first night with me being a virgin; after that he called me "newly seduced" and got a tenner. The madam checks I'm on the streets every night as my keeper's off most of the time looking for fresh girls to replenish his stock.'

One by one the girls opened up and talked of their misery. None could offer any serious resistance. There was no escape, no matter how brutal the men could be. Two had even been seduced with the consent of their mothers, who were paid handsomely for it. Matilda, at barely thirteen, was in obvious pain and much distressed. Listening to her sobbing during the night, Flossie cradled the tiny slip of a girl in her arms. Her story was all too familiar. She'd been given a 'drowse', probably laudanum, or 'black draught' as it was known.

'It makes you lie like you're dead and you don't know what's happened till morning,' she whispered. 'Then the pain hit me, I could hardly move. He was charged fifteen pounds for the first of me, less after that. The brothel-keeper said it was no use crying as what was done couldn't be undone. Besides, no one else would take me in now so I should be grateful to be one of the attractions of his house. After a week I gave up all hope, until now.'

Hearing how the girls had been recruited as 'marks' to

join the eighty thousand prostitutes already on the streets of London was alarming enough, but to discover that three of them had been bred for the task was beyond belief. Worse still, the practice of keeping the female babies born to women within the brothels, so that there would always be a supply of 'merchantable maidens', was an undisguised secret in the dark recesses of that world.

There were many sleepless nights ahead for Flossie worrying about what might be happening to Lottie, so young and so far away. It was a great relief when news finally came.

10th September 1884
Winnipeg, Canada

Dear sister,

I have arrived safely and am living on a farm. I'm sorry that I haven't written sooner, I simply haven't had time until now as the last weeks have flown past in a whirl of excitement.

We girls felt so very important as our ship pulled out from the port of Liverpool. A band played and people were waving banners. We all sang hymns until they were out of sight. It turned out to be rough crossing the Atlantic and I was seasick many times. Luckily there was a wooden trunk, made in Stepney, waiting for each of us in our cabin which was packed with new clothes. I had to smile when I found a Bible, a Sankey hymn book and a copy of The Pilgrim's Progress *on the bottom.*

Within a few days of landing on Canadian soil, we were sent off aboard a 'Barnardo special' train with all our belongings and a packed lunch. Oh, Floss, it was such a long and dusty journey across vast plains called prairies. There was nothing to see for miles. When the train eventually stopped there were lots of strangers waiting in horse-buggies.

Do not worry about me, Flossie, I am very happy. Mr and Mrs Rourke are kind to me and say I am the daughter they never had. Besides, there will be an annual visit from a Barnardo inspector to check up on me.
I think of you often.
With love,
Lottie

Flossie pressed the letter to her chest. *Oh Lottie,* she thought, *I pray that Mrs Rourke is the mother that you never had. Canada sounds like such a strange land – when will I ever get to see you again?*

Six months later, Flossie was summoned to see the governess. She had just celebrated her sixteenth birthday and her time at Dr Barnardo's was almost over.

Miss Adams, who, along with the matron, was also present, spoke first. 'I believe Florence Oxer has an excellent chance of securing a superior position. In addition to the basics, she is proficient at baking, dressmaking, knitting, embroidery, needlework, crochet and lacemaking.'

The governess fixed the girl applying for her dismissal papers with a matriarchal stare. It seemed an age before she addressed Matron.

'And what of Miss Oxer's time in the infirmary?'

Matron shuffled to her feet. 'The girl has learnt some basic nursing skills and coped well when we lost a few weak babies during the recent scarlet fever outbreak. Furthermore, she displayed both a practical and compassionate nature towards the Shoreditch brothel girls.'

'Very well, Florence Oxer, come back tomorrow at two o'clock for my deliberations.'

Crossing Babies Green on her way back to Primrose Cottage, she smiled at the army of pram pushers, promenading as they did every afternoon, come rain or shine. Nineteen large Elizabethan-style cottages had just been built around the new green, each occupied by twenty-five girls, with one specifically equipped for tiny babies. In fact, there were so many girls at Barkingside now that there was talk of a school, hospital and children's church on the agenda.

The smell of fresh creosote wafted on the breeze and, in the distance, old Jack, the gardener, could be seen painting fences. Beyond him the goats and ponies were waiting to be fed. Flossie surveyed the idyllic scene with a heavy heart, and although keen to get the formalities over, the thought of eventually leaving the security of Barkingside was daunting. For better or worse, it had become her home, one she trusted and relied upon. What she would find outside the gates was unknown.

The governess sat pondering the imminent loss of such an adept, diligent, though somewhat headstrong ward and pupil for quite some minutes before calling her into her office at two o'clock.

'Congratulations, Florence,' she said, handing over a money order. 'You are a credit to Dr Barnardo's and all that we stand for. I have great faith that you will shine and have pleasure in judging you first class.'

Flossie flushed and thanked the stern woman who, for so long, had epitomised nothing but authority and discipline. The monetary award system was often talked about amongst the girls, but it had never dawned on Flossie that she might be considered one of the best. To enter the world of employment, first-class girls received an outfit to the value of five pounds, which they could keep, provided they did not change their job for a year. Second-class girls, found guilty of ill temper, disobedience, insolence or laziness, were given an outfit worth three pounds and ten shillings. Third-class girls – those deemed to have grave faults – were issued with an outfit costing three pounds, but had to pay the money back out of their wages. Dishonest, violent or vicious girls, and those uncontrolled in temper, were declared fourth class and sent from the village in disgrace.

As Flossie stood up to leave, the governess stood up too. Her countenance softened slightly as she fumbled in her desk drawer.

'I have something else for you,' she said, handing her a grubby envelope. Flossie immediately recognised the postmark: *Ipswich*. 'From your mother,' the older woman said quietly. 'I am already aware of its contents. Take it out into the garden and read it in peace. And take this as well…'

Flossie looked stunned as a second, much larger envelope was placed in her hands.

'You will have much to think about. You may come and talk to me again when you have had a chance to digest this information.'

Finding a quiet spot beneath a heavily-laden apple tree, Flossie found herself trembling in anticipation of what she was about to learn. Slowly opening the letter, she saw a sheet of cheap, flimsy paper inside which she unfolded and began to read:

Dearest daughter,

I am truly bereft at what you must think of me and I will try my utmost to explain my reasons for leaving you and Lottie on that fateful day. I feel sure that once you understand, you will forgive me.

I have charged those in power to find you a respectable position here in Ipswich so that I can make amends and I truly look forward to seeing you soon.
Your loving mother,
Mary Oxer

For a moment, she found herself unable to breathe. So many thoughts whirred around inside her head that she felt quite faint. Looking again, she checked to see if the sprawling signature was really that of her mother. If it *was* from her mother, why the sudden change of heart towards her abandoned offspring? Dismissing the cloying sentiment present in those few lines as a ploy, Flossie quickly resolved to confront her mother face-to-face over her past actions. As for seeking employment in Ipswich, that was not on Flossie's agenda. She had no intention of watching her earnings disappear behind the bar of the local alehouse.

Turning to the larger envelope, she wondered what else she was about to discover. Lifting out a mass of newspaper cuttings tied together with string, the name *OXER* was written in capital letters on the front sheet. The reports seemed to be in date order. Scanning the lines of the first, she realised that she was reading an account of Henry Oxer's arrest and appearance at the Magistrates' Court for being drunk and disorderly. It transpired that, at only twenty-two years of age, this was the first of many such appearances leading to periods of incarceration in gaol.

Not far down the pile, Mary Oxer's name appeared. There were details of her arrest for stealing a shirt from a neighbour. The sordid story was difficult to take in. '*I took it for want of bread*,' Mary had pleaded, but the magistrates showed little sympathy given the fact that she had neither sold, nor pawned the shirt until a full five days later. Her 'need' was in doubt and she was subsequently gaoled for fourteen days.

The more Flossie read, the more unbearable the truth became. With tears trickling down her cheeks, she learned that due to debt and unpaid rent the destitute pair were sent for a spell in the workhouse, and there Mary had given birth to a girl. Scouring the scrap of paper for a date, Flossie faced the uncomfortable truth as to the place of Lottie's birth. On release, and forced to live in lodgings in Bond's Court, a mean corner above Rope Lane, Henry continued to be arraigned before the magistrates for drunk and disorderly behaviour. Then, after he was shopped by his own mother for stealing a family Ulster coat, he gave her a black eye, for which he received a month in custody.

The final part of the wretched story concerned the welfare of Mary Oxer and her two daughters. They appeared destined for the workhouse again after Henry had deserted them following his release from gaol. When the workhouse guardians sought to get Henry's father, Fred, to appear before them over the matter of contributing to the cost, he failed to do so.

Flossie certainly did have more questions. She doubted that many of them could be answered by the governess, though. When did Samuel Grant get involved with Mary? Was she her knight in shining armour? Did Flossie and Lottie have the same father? Putting the paperwork back in the envelope, Flossie started walking back to the office; there was one question that could be answered now.

Thankfully the governess was one step ahead and assured Flossie that she had no intention of carrying out Mary's request to find the girl a 'respectable position' in Ipswich. She had been collecting the newspaper reports on the Oxers' visits to their local Magistrates' Courts for many a year and was under no illusions as to their motives. Barnardo's policy was such that Mary could have taken her children back whenever she wished, despite signing to hand them over. Obviously, she had chosen not to do so. Now that Flossie was of age it was up to her where her future lay and the contents of the buff envelope would help her make an informed decision.

Two weeks later, Florence Oxer passed through the wrought-iron gates that had insulated her from the world and all its influences for almost four years. Wearing a smart dress, coat and hat, she popped the Bible and pledge card given to her by

Miss Adams into her carpet bag and turned into Cranbrook Road. The clatter of iron-shod hooves and the yells from street vendors were deafening as she turned her back on what she had come to know as *The Largest Family in the World*. Whatever revelations lay in store for her on her arrival in Ipswich, she was resolved to discover the truth about her parentage.

11

Flossie surprised herself by how easily she coped with the hustle and bustle of London. After making her way by tram to Liverpool Street station, she waited in an unruly queue to buy a train ticket to Ipswich. Having saved money from her five-pound voucher by settling for robust, practical clothing, she now had enough for travel, food and lodgings for quite a few days. Miss Adams had found her an old map of Ipswich, so during the journey she plotted a route to Mary's address.

Leaning back and staring out of the window, she considered her past life. Try as hard as she might, there were no fragments of memory that threw light on anything before Northfleet. It was hopeless; she was going to have to rely on others telling her the truth. Whatever happened over the next few days, she was determined to find out about her own and Lottie's origins.

Passing a row of malt houses as the train pulled onto the platform, the sweet caramel aroma made Flossie feel quite nauseous. It was a relief to be out of the enclosed station and in a busy thoroughfare, full of imposing shops and coffee houses. A fancy window display bearing a sign reading *New Goods from China* caught her eye and, unable to resist the temptation, she went inside. Laid out before her in this veritable Aladdin's cave was an array of feminine items only previously seen on the pages of magazines. Combs encrusted with precious stones, ornate belt buckles, sleeve links, earrings and delicate ivory fans. Purchasing a tortoiseshell hairpin for herself and a dainty marcasite brooch which she thought might suit her mother if she felt inclined to give it to her, she watched excitedly as they were wrapped in decorative paper. Elated with her new-found sense of freedom, she continued on her journey, disappointed that the department stores came to an end as she turned into Eagle Street.

With the pavements becoming dirtier and more crowded, she found herself being jostled by rough-looking people, some appearing the worse for drink. *Hardly surprising*, she thought, given the large number of alehouses she had already passed. She couldn't fail to notice the numerous pawnbrokers with their golden spheres suspended above their doors, or the many shops in the vicinity with signs offering *left-behind clothes*.

From Upper Orwell Court towards her destination, the streets narrowed alarmingly. Rowdy groups of street children disappeared down passages and alleyways as quickly as they appeared. She stopped momentarily to push her delicate parcel to the bottom of her old carpet bag for safekeeping and checked her street map to see where she was. Looking around, she spotted a jagged piece of wood hanging over an archway with the misspelt name *Bond Cort* roughly painted on it. With some trepidation, she entered what initially looked like a dark tunnel. Within a few feet a foul stench engulfed her, then, emerging into the light, she found herself in a small yard surrounded by a cluster of one-up, one-down, blind-backed cottages. All forms of life seemed to coexist there. A quick glance revealed mangy dogs, chickens and even a pig or two. There was clearly no proper sanitation. Finding Mary Oxer in this filthy rabbit warren of a place was going to be a solemn challenge.

'She be barred from The Mitre Tavern and even The Cow

and Pail, except on Saturdays when they put up with trouble,' a grimy, dishevelled woman told her as she emptied a bucket of human dung into a storage tank in the corner of the yard. 'Might find 'er in The John Barleycorn on Pottery Street, or even The Safe Harbour. Chequers be worth a try. That be a rough house. All else fails, she'll be in The Angel. They ain't at all fussy.'

Seeing the smartly-dressed young girl's dismay at the overflowing slop-tank, the woman cackled. 'What you pulling a face at? There's over an 'undred of us living in these eighteen cottages. We're never short of this mess, and we gets a good price fer it. Farmer buys it to manure 'is fields.'

At that point a swarm of flies, disturbed by the latest delivery, descended on both of them. Flossie waved her arms about to get rid of them when, as if on cue, a flypaper man appeared in the yard. Wearing a cone-shaped wizard's hat, he demonstrated the value of his headdress as marauding flies were magically drawn to the sheets of sticky paper wrapped round it. Within seconds his teeth were visibly vibrating with the desperate buzzing of his trapped prey while a few lucky ones that had missed the target emerged from his grey, unkempt beard.

Keen to escape into the fresh, early evening air, Flossie left the fly-man and the dishevelled woman arguing over his fee and headed off along Rope Walk. Living conditions couldn't get much worse, Flossie thought. It was always the same in areas catering for the lowest strata of inhabitants – numerous shops and dwellings crammed together, plagued by open, stinking cesspits and disease. Unscrupulous landowners building poor-quality housing were never short of tenants, so desperate was the need to put a roof over their family's heads that they often moved into unfinished premises.

Children were out in the streets, skipping or playing hopscotch, their houses too hot for early bedtime. Flossie watched one lucky little boy playing with a whip and top as a water cart clattered into view, its contents slopping over the cobbles. Those with shoes stopped to remove them before joining the others running barefoot behind the cart, all splashing excitedly in the cascade. For a moment she felt ten years old herself, with uneven pigtails and smutty pinafore, innocently playing whilst waiting for her mother to leave The Huggens. It seemed like history was close to being repeated.

Rounding the corner, a massive crenellated building overshadowed the street. Realising it was the town gaol – the place where Henry Oxer spent much of his time – Flossie felt a shiver run down her spine. The sight of disembodied arms hanging out of iron-barred windows may have served as a reminder to those below of the gravity of the law, but it shocked her to the marrow.

In Pottery Street, the scene just got worse. In order to get to The John Barleycorn, she encountered a scene of horror before her. Several butchers were outside their shops hanging freshly slaughtered carcasses. Gutted rabbits with distorted faces dangled by their ears. A rag-and-bone man waiting nearby was offering purchasers tuppence for their skins. Flossie found the shrill animal noises issuing from the abattoirs simply terrifying, and she was forced to lift her skirts to avoid the river of blood running down the cobblestones. A dozen or more children were in a yard watching the poor creatures being dispatched, laughing as the beasts writhed and twitched. The sight and sounds of pigs feasting on the discarded offal and clotting blood made her retch. It was a great relief not to find Mary drunk at the bar at the down-at-heel alehouse here; the smell was as bad inside as out.

On entering Woodhouse Street an assemblage of street entertainers – barrel-organ grinders, accordion-players, tin whistle and fiddle-players – helped Flossie regain her composure. It was obviously a popular meeting place and the crowds were reluctant to move on. A sad-looking bear was being made to stand on its hind legs and twirl around. But there was one act so intriguing that it prompted Flossie to open her purse and drop a penny in the collection pot. A man with ebony skin held a pair of animal rib-bones, about six inches in length, between the fingers of each hand. By moving his wrists in a certain way, they knocked against each other, creating a *clickety-clack* sound reminiscent of Harry Relph's clogs on the cellar flaps of The Elephant's Head in Rosherville. It made Flossie smile and brought more memories flooding back.

The clock on the outside of the Baptist chapel served as a reminder of her mission. The Safe Harbour alehouse had a welcoming name, at least. She forged on, passing densely populated terraced houses with front doors opening directly onto the pavement. Hawkers working out of lodging houses were everywhere selling small quantities of coal, wood, fish and poultry. Despite passing at least two milk shops, a crowd of small children were crowding around a barrow to buy a farthing's worth to drink on the spot. Behind them, a sign outside Cant's the Baker advertised its bake office, where you could get your meat or pudding cooked for a penny. For many women without the means to slow-cook meat, this was where you came to cook your piece of clod for Sunday dinner.

It was getting late. Mary wasn't in The Safe Harbour, but someone had just seen her holding forth in The Chequers Inn. It was just as well because a trawl around any more of the fifty or so inns and beer houses of Ipswich was unthinkable. Cheap drink was available literally a step or two away from every labourer's workplace or front door. It was no wonder that drunkenness and domestic violence were such a problem.

Flossie braced herself for the reception she might receive as she pushed open the heavy, glazed door of The Chequers. Mounds of sawdust heavy with spilt beer and spit made it slippery underfoot as she fought her way through the crush. Trying not to catch anyone's eye for fear of confrontation, she was on the verge of retreating when a familiar voice stopped her in her tracks.

'Well, you're a sight for sore eyes, that be sure. All grown-up and fancy-looking.'

Plonking her glass down on the bar, a tall, intoxicated woman with dirty clothes and unruly auburn hair held out her arms. 'Come closer and give your ma a kiss.'

Flossie had imagined this moment a thousand times. Raw emotion took hold. Sorrow, anger, disapproval and embarrassment surged through her as she stood rooted to the spot. If this was a demonstration of motherly affection, it had failed. It felt more like an attempt to impress the gang of cronies at the bar.

'Well now,' Mary spat, with hands on hips, 'I see you're as stubborn as ever. Maybe you'll be buying me a drink instead.'

The bar fell silent as Flossie approached the landlord and purchased a large gin. Mary snatched at the glass, but Flossie pulled it away and, fixing her mother with a cold stare, proceeded to pour it very deliberately onto the floor in front of her.

'That'll be your last drink tonight. When you're ready, *I'll* be waiting for *you* outside.'

The slow walk home to Bond Court was excruciating. Mary stumbled and cursed, shouting abuse at her daughter for having shown her up in front of her friends. Flossie ignored it all, intent only on getting the inebriated woman off the streets. On entering the house, she was horrified to see the filthy conditions her mother was living in alongside her husband Henry's parents, Mary Ann and Fred Oxer. Henry's latest incarceration had left the family in dire straits.

It was then that Flossie discovered she had a brother, Henry George. At two years old, he still wasn't walking and appeared weak and emaciated. It occurred to Flossie that had his grandmother not been there to look after him, it was unlikely the boy would have survived this long. They all shared two tiny rooms without a window and Flossie realised she now faced having to bed down in the scullery with her mother, listening to the cockroaches running between the cracks in the poorly-constructed walls. It was a far cry from the spotlessly scrubbed Primrose Cottage she'd just come from, but at least she had the comfort of knowing that she wouldn't be there long. Just long enough to get some much-needed answers.

Mary had wasted no time in touting her daughter's superior domestic-service training and fully intended to reap the rewards. Ipswich girls generally worked on the premises of tradesmen, shopkeepers and publicans, while country girls became servants to the middle-class households in Church Street. But Mary was aiming for something grander than this. She had her eyes on Holywells at the top of Bishops Hill. This large residence and park belonged to the Cobbold family, owners of the Cliff Brewery and its many public houses. Having frequented them all, she had obtained some useful contacts. There was talk of a new chambermaid being sought soon.

Flossie waited the whole of the next day for her mother to sober up. During this time she sat with her grandparents who, although disinterested in her, were inoffensive. They seemed happy enough to sit on a couple of rickety wooden chairs, each holding a pint of porter, with Mary Ann balancing the listless Henry Junior on her knees. By afternoon both were dozing off, so Flossie offered to watch the infant whilst they took a nap on an old iron bed without sheets or pillowcases, and just overcoats to keep them warm.

Once Mary was clear-headed enough to pay some attention to her son, Flossie busied herself collecting rubbish stored in the privy to heat up the range. Knowing full well there was no food to be had, she visited the nearest grocers, purchased a few meagre ingredients and provided the family with a rare hot meal. Using an old newspaper as a tablecloth, the family tucked into a feast of whelks and batter pudding, bread and pork dripping.

With food in her belly, Mary seemed ready to impart her side of the story. Indeed, once she'd started, she couldn't stop. So much information gushed out of her that Flossie's head began to reel.

In a nutshell, it emerged that she was powerless to resist the charms of handsome young Henry Oxer. However, after marriage, he rarely worked, was violent and had introduced her to the demon drink, causing the lurch from workhouse to prison. Sam had come along and rescued her, not just once but twice. She'd tried hard to make it work with him, but he finally betrayed her, forcing her to abandon her girls to Dr Barnardo's and return to Henry in a state of destitution.

Knowing her mother's penchant for lying, Flossie found this tale of woe hard to swallow. How had Sam betrayed her? And why *would* he have done? He had saved her and put up with her drinking and slovenly behaviour for years, so surely if anyone was to blame, it was her.

Seeing that her daughter doubted her word, Mary's tone changed.

'You always took his side – always blaming me, never him. I slaved to earn the extra pennies to put food on the table when he didn't come home nights.'

'You can't possibly remember half of what happened in The Crick, you were too drunk!' Flossie lashed back, her eyes flashing. 'You spent our money in The Huggens. We often had no tea. Then you decided to come back here and abandon us without as much as a hint of guilt. Four years, Mother. Four years not knowing what happened. How could you?'

Mary shifted uneasily in her chair.

'Then we find out our name's Oxer, not Grant. How is *that*?'

'I think you should see this,' Mary said, pulling a crumpled piece of parchment from a nearby drawer and handing it to her daughter.

Flossie unfolded it and started to read. A quizzical look crossed her face. It was a birth certificate.

Florence Gant, born 2nd March 1869 at 10 Duke of York Court, Milton. Father: Samuel Gant. Mother: Mary Gant, formerly Allen.

'So, Sam *is* my father, not Henry Oxer. But Florence *Gant*? Is that a spelling mistake?'

'No, it's Sam's *real* name,' Mary said quietly.

'What do you mean?'

'It's as I say. Sam's family name is Gant, although it was never legally my name, of course. We changed it to Grant later so as people couldn't find us.'

Flossie's eyes rolled in confusion. 'What are you saying? You are not making any sense. First you have me called Florence Oxer these four long years, now you tell me my name is Gant!'

Mary turned to face her daughter. 'I cannot be certain that Sam *is* your real father. You could be Henry's, as Lottie most definitely is.'

Flossie's jaw dropped open. 'But you've just shown me my birth certificate.'

'That is the absolute truth,' Mary continued, casting her eyes to the floor. 'Of course I told Sam I was positive he was the father, but I had been with both of them.'

Sensing her daughter's dismay, Mary tried to justify her actions. 'With a husband in and out of gaol, I was lonely and in need of a man's company. Sam was kind and gentle, so different to Henry. I was pretty in them days, but when Henry had been using his fists on my face, it would send Sam into a rage, the like of which I hadn't seen before. He'd have killed Henry if I hadn't begged him not to. "He ain't worth going to the gallows for," I used to say. Anyway, I felt safe with Sam; I knew he'd protect me.'

They sat in silence for a while, Flossie utterly mystified.

'So why on earth did you return to Henry? And then have Lottie?'

'You're too young to understand, girl. But you will one day. Things happen between people that you don't expect. You make mistakes and then you pay for them. That's why I wanted better for you and your sister.'

Flossie was still finding it hard to believe her mother, but decided to let her continue to reminisce about the past, absorbing information along the way.

It seemed that when Sam first arrived in Ipswich he found work at Ransome's Works, which dominated the dockside with its foundries, workshops, warehouses and timber yards. Nearly half of the workforce were migrants who, according to the Oxers, had changed the character of the community beyond recognition. Down Bishop's Hill, ancient timber-framed merchants' houses were now accommodating dozens of families, with shacks erected in their back gardens to house yet more.

Mary first met Sam in Dalby's lively Ales Store. She had noticed him looking at her, and when he finally plucked up courage to ask her where she worked, she'd replied, 'At Pretty's, in the boning', which hadn't meant anything to him. 'Don't you know a Pretty girl when you see one?' she'd added coquettishly, running her hands over her pulled-in waist. The confused look on Sam's face made her smile. 'William Pretty the Drapers, on Westgate Street, making boned stays and corsets'…

When Sam saw the joke, he laughed out loud. That was how it all started.

Mary's expression changed as she described what followed. Once convinced that she was with child and in fear of Henry's wrath should he doubt her fidelity, she and Sam left Ipswich in the dead of night. They found lodgings in Milton near Northfleet, and Mary's mother Fanny Allen came from Essex to help with her confinement. But finding a job that paid enough to keep them all proved hard for Sam and the money soon ran out. With Flossie just a few months old, Mary decided to return to Henry.

'I couldn't keep up the pretence and be the "wife" Sam wanted. I was young, I missed Henry. Oh, he's a wrong 'un, that's for sure, but he had a twinkle in his eye I couldn't resist. He wanted me back, so I decided to give him another chance. Course, I realised in time, a leopard can't change its spots. He didn't pay no bills, got into trouble again, so they sent us all to the Union Workhouse. I gave birth to Lottie there. You were barely three years old. They let us out after three months when Henry was sober enough to get a job, and his parents agreed to let us live with them here in Bond Court. All of us in just one room. It was hard, but with both Henry and Fred pinching stuff we got by. Not long after I was pregnant again, and we was all delighted when it was a boy... John, we called him, after my brother.'

After draining the dregs of porter in Fred Oxer's tankard, Mary took a deep breath. 'He was only a month old when he died. Overlaying, it was. Could have been me or Henry that did it. We were both near unconscious, been in The Angel, you see.'

Overlaying, or suffocation when a sleeping parent or sibling rolled on top of the baby, was common when entire families slept in the same bed. In fact, a quarter of all babies died this way before their first birthday in one-room homes, and more often on Friday, Saturday and Sunday nights.

Mary slumped into a chair, tears rolling down her cheeks. Flossie was quite taken aback by this show of seemingly true emotion. *The first of her lost boys*, she thought. She left it a few minutes before asking her next question.

'So what happened after that tragedy?'

'Henry just carried on with his old ways. Got so drunk once, he was arrested for throwing the first punch outside The Kings Head, then failed to turn up for his court appearance and got fined ten shillings and sixpence, with twelve shillings costs. Of course we couldn't pay, so he went to gaol for a month. They put him on the treadmill every day in St. Helens. No point to it, just slow, back-breaking punishment. He abandoned us good and proper after that and went missing. His mother blamed me, so I had to find somewhere else for us to live. I knew Sam had come back to Ipswich; I'd seen him around so I waited outside Ransome's and talked him into giving us another try. That's when we changed our name to Grant and came to The Crick to throw the debt collectors off the scent.'

'So you were just using him,' Flossie said, unable to hide her disgust.

Mary shot her a look of indignation, her piercing eyes creating a chill in the air.

'I gave him best part of ten years, didn't I? But you don't know the half of it. There's more to tell, but it'll have to wait. I need to get something nourishing for my boy; he's started a dreadful cough.'

Flossie knew only too well what that really meant. There was no drink left in the house, so wrapping her shawl round her shoulders, Mary tucked an empty gin bottle out of sight under her arm and headed for the door.

'Wait,' Flossie shouted, 'I'm coming with you.' She knew it was the only way of ensuring that Henry George wouldn't go to bed hungry.

It was icy as the pair turned the corner.

'Henry will be out of clink soon,' Mary said, the moisture in her breath forming a tiny cloud before her. 'Happen things will get back to normal for a while.' In the dark, she couldn't see her daughter shaking her head.

Chapman's on the corner of Waterworks Street denied Mary's

plea for groceries on tick, so Flossie reached into her purse and bought a quarter of corned beef for tuppence, a pennyworth of pickles and another pennyworth of milk. Against her better judgement, a few more of her pennies disappeared over the counter at The Cow and Pail getting her mother's gin bottle refilled.

As they passed a fishmonger's drying house, several children were enjoying the warmth of a crackling fire, ducking and darting between the smoking herrings and sprats. They all looked so innocent, Flossie mused. Just like her and Lottie all those years ago. Now there'd been so many revelations, nothing would ever be quite the same again. They'd never know for sure if they shared the same father.

'I thought you were going to make Ipswich your home now,' Mary stammered unconvincingly when Flossie announced she was leaving. 'I was just getting used to having my daughter back. What will I do without you?'

Casting her eyes around the insanitary court with its overflowing tank emitting a choking stench, Flossie could find no words. Mary dabbed her eyes with the corner of her apron. *Crocodile tears, that's what those are*, Flossie thought. *Money's in short supply, and will be even more so when Henry gets back with an unquenchable thirst.*

Seeing her daughter was clearly not going to change her mind, Mary's simpering tone quickly changed to sarcasm. 'I dare say you'll be heading for Northfleet, then. Do as you will, but I'll let you find out for yourself what really happened there. That will be plain to see.' Grabbing the old carpet bag, she thrust it at Flossie. 'I wasn't the one at fault and, as I told you before, I had no choice but to leave you and Lottie at Barkingside. I did it for your own good.'

Flossie stared silently at the shabby woman standing before her, then picking up her carpet bag, walked slowly down the rotting staircase. As she waited for two women carrying steaming, stinking buckets to pass in front of her, Mary shouted down her final words.

'You lived a life of luxury at Dr Barnardo's compared to what it would have been like if I'd brought you back here. So be grateful for small mercies.'

Flossie passed through the tunnel without looking back.

Mary had reason to be pleased the next day, despite the rent being due. It was Monday, pawn day. She joined the brigade of women making their way down Fore Street pushing their possessions in prams, or carrying them underarm, towards Sneezums pawn shop. There was always a long queue on rent day. In the slightly better-off streets, a runner with a handcart would call for freshly washed sheets wrapped in brown-paper parcels so no one could see what their neighbours were pawning.

Mary had no need to pawn her chenille hat with its tattered feathers this week; she had a brand-new marcasite brooch, still in its pretty wrapping, which Flossie had left on the table. Mr Sneezums would be surprised she'd been given such a gift of quality, and once he'd looked at it through his magnifying glass, would give her enough money to buy a quarter of gin. Then Mary would be off to the bottle department at the back of The Fruiterers Home Inn, which opened early on a Monday.

12

20th January 1886

My darling sister,

It was so good to hear from you and I am relieved that you have left Barkingside and found employment, even if you look upon it as only temporary. I was never greatly happy at Dr Barnardo's, but I accept that it suited you more. Hearing of your harrowing experiences in Ipswich made me despair, and I am desperately sorry that our mother is in dire circumstances and so sadly unchanged in person. Though I find it hard to come to terms with the possibility that we have different fathers, rest assured, dearest Flossie, that I will always consider you to be my true sister. It was you that I looked up to for support and guidance and you who never let me down. I concur that the bond between us should not, and will not, be broken by this. Please write to me again when you have found Sam and discovered what caused the 'unbearable state of affairs' that led our mother to abandon us so heartlessly.

Well, as you surely can tell, I have grown up these

past eighteen months. No longer the complaining child. My time on the farm was hard and I suffered hugely from loneliness, despite the kindness of my guardians. I am now living in Winnipeg, which is so much better, and have secured a position as a general maid in the household of local businessman J. Y. Griffin. He has a pork-packing business which dresses 250 hogs a day! His cook told me that the city was little more than a collection of shacks ten years ago, but now, with the opening of the Canadian Pacific Railway, we are experiencing a period of great prosperity. Already hundreds of Chinese immigrants are arriving every day to work on the railroads and settle here in the Prairies. Once there was only Charley Yam and Fung Quong who sold Chinese medicines in town, but now they are everywhere. They will surely find the bitterly cold winters and the Red River springtime flooding hard to get used to.

Some things here, Floss, remind me of home. Winnipeg Lake has paddlewheel excursion boats, and there are freighters and steamboats transporting fish on the busy Red. Other things are completely different, Main Street is extremely wide and all the buildings well spread out. There are long planks stretching across the mud for you to walk from side to side. It seems a new shop opens every day now on Portage Avenue, and we also have an opera house. I'm afraid to say our frontier town also has more than its fair share of saloons, variety theatres and places of disrepute as we have been flooded with young men seeking employment. You would be amused to hear of the vaudeville show I attended quite recently. The acts rivalled any we saw at Rosherville Gardens all those years ago. A particular highlight was Oscar, who made the sweetest music imaginable with the aid of forty wine glasses! However, most of the theatres are being forced to close now as the newspapers are calling them 'shops of harlotry'.

Anyway, I must *tell you about the biggest event Winnipeg has ever seen – the return of our own Little Black Devils, back from the North-West Rebellion. I doubt you will have heard about it, sister, but the Canadian Government have won the last in a series of battles fought to protect the British Empire from another native uprising. I will now endeavour to explain the cause of my own excitement.*

We spent three days in the heat of summer welcoming several thousand volunteer soldiers returning from the front – our city's own 90th Winnipeg Rifles (named the Little Black Devils by the enemy) amongst them. A hastily erected Victory Arch, spanning Main Street, was decorated with electric lights, bunting, flags and banners, and all the shops had spruce trees with lanterns. I had just managed to find a space on the platform when the troop train arrived, and I was shocked by the sight of our ragged, sunburnt soldiers who have been gone these four months. Most now had beards and some marched in trousers fashioned from oat sacks, while others had hats made from supply bags dyed with coffee. Still, none of that mattered or lessened the cheering. It seemed as if every Winnipegger was there to cheer the two and a half thousand volunteers marching down Main Street and under the arch. It was an age before the official business was over, but finally they were released to celebrate. You can imagine what it was like! The taverns remained open all night and the police were instructed not to interfere.

We girls, being greatly outnumbered, had the time of our lives and it will come as no surprise to you, my clever sister, that I met the man of my dreams. Private Daniel O'Keefe, B Company of the Queen's Own Rifles – so tall, so handsome, with such ice-blue eyes. We danced in the streets, hardly noticing the rain which began running like rivers between our feet. Looking like a pair of drowned rats, we eventually sought refuge in a shop doorway and spent the rest of the night engrossed in one another's company, oblivious to the damage being done all around us.

We were so shocked the next morning to see that the storm had ripped the decorations to shreds. Evergreens littered the sidewalks and the streets resembled a quagmire.

Thankfully, the bright sun quickly dried everything and by evening the city was ablaze with Chinese lanterns. From every quarter, rockets were firing. The parades continued, and without fear of further rain we young ladies were able to dress up for the occasion. We don't always wear bonnets these days, so I let my hair fall in rag curls. I wore a white cotton dress adorned with lace collar and pockets. I had seen it in a shop window and managed to save enough to buy it – even though it took three months. I am so glad I did, as I had, without doubt, the best night of my life. Daniel said our pretty faces brought gladness to the hearts of the returning soldiers.

Some boisterous fools put an end to the fun by firing Roman candles at people and setting fire to the arch, but Daniel told me this was just the soldiers painting the town red. One soldier did exactly that: he painted a horse that colour and rode it about the town!

Oh, how my heart ached when, all too quickly, the eastern regiments were boarding trains for home. The Queen's Own are based in Toronto, and that is where Daniel has returned to. I open each of his letters with excitement hoping for a proposal, which I am positive will come once he is settled.

How things have changed for us,
With all my love,
Lottie x

Flossie's joy on receiving word from her sister was tempered by the thought of her expecting such a proposal long before her fifteenth birthday. How different Lottie's new life seemed compared to her own. She sounded so confident, so self-assured and yet so vulnerable.

A creaking of the floorboards above Flossie's head jolted her back to reality. Cook was stirring and would be expecting her first cup of tea. As the housemaid, this was Florence Gant's second task of the day. The first had been to clean and relight the range to ensure there was hot water for the household. Folding her precious letter, she slipped it into her apron pocket. There wasn't time to ponder her sister's situation any further. It would have to wait until later.

After leaving Ipswich, Flossie had travelled to London to enter service in the household of a wealthy stockbroker and his family, secured on the basis of her excellent references from Dr Barnardo's. Situated on a wide thoroughfare in Portland Place, close to Regent's Park, the impressive mansion was home to five members of the Galbraith family and a staff of fifteen. According to the chambermaid, there were twenty-two rooms upstairs, not that Flossie had much chance of seeing them given her lowly rank below stairs. She had found it hard to make friends as the other maids were all older than she was. The parlourmaid, with whom she shared a room, was twenty-four. Also, with hardly any time off, there had been few opportunities to explore, so she'd been saving the best part of her six shillings a week pay to finance her long-awaited return to Northfleet.

When the day came, almost a year later, Flossie stepped out of the carriage at the new Rosherville Halt station, gripping the same old carpet bag that held everything she possessed. She felt excited, if not a little apprehensive, whilst climbing the impressive staircase rising from the island platform. It was likely that this was not the only change she was about to encounter.

Sheltering from the hot sun under the canopied footbridge, she rested a while as the train disappeared into the cutting where she'd played as a child. The sails of Boorman's flour mill caught her eye as they glinted in the sun. *At least that's still here*, she thought.

'You'll be heading for the gardens then, lass?' a man's voice said from behind her.

Flossie turned to see a porter picking up her bag. 'Oh, thank you. No, not today, things to attend to first.'

'Quite a success already, this new railway. Only been open since May.' He continued to talk as they made their way through the gleaming ticket office to the carriage park outside. 'This Whit Sunday was a bumper day for the gardens. Fourteen thousand, by all accounts, went through the turnstiles. Loads of them came by train, despite the steamers trying to undercut our prices.'

Smiling at the porter's enthusiasm for his new railway, she handed him a coin from her purse and set off on foot along the well-trodden walk towards 'home', with no idea what she would find. Having been gone for nearly five years, she was only too aware that Sam might no longer be living in The Creek. Many times she'd picked up a pen and started to write to him, but each time something had stopped her. After all, it wouldn't have been impossible for *him* to have found *her* if he'd had a mind to. He must surely have thought Mary had gone back to Henry, taking both girls with her? So now she should be prepared for the possibility that he didn't care enough and could be lost forever.

Turning into Lawn Road, the sound of children laughing took her by surprise. It was the end of the day for the five hundred pupils at the new Northfleet Board School, and parents were gathered outside the infants' gate. *Something else new*, she thought as she picked her way through the crowds.

Stepping on and off the kerb to avoid prams and running children, she could have so easily missed him were it not for a dog barking as it chased after a ball. She watched as the excited mongrel returned his prize to a young boy with grubby knees and socks round his ankles. Thrusting the gnarled ball into his pocket, the child ran back to his waiting father. It was Joe Ollerenshaw. Despite being older, there was no doubt that it was indeed their previous lodger. Gathering his clan, he set off down the road with a baby over his shoulder, dragging a toddler behind him.

Flossie, seemingly unrecognised, studied the group closely as minutes later, Joe stopped to chastise his scruffy son for kicking up cement dust into the toddler's face. The resulting hullaballoo forced some passers-by to cover their ears until Joe bundled his trio of children into an open front door, which slammed shut behind them. *He obviously isn't Sam's lodger any more*, Flossie thought, *and he hasn't wasted any time in bringing children into the world.*

As the hordes dispelled and the street emptied, the familiar grinding and pounding of Bevan's cement works caught Flossie unawares and brought a lump to her throat. Skipping along the alley into The Creek, she was comforted to see that all the houses looked just the same – damp, grey dust clogging the gutters and grime piling high on windowsills. Even the old lamp was still hanging outside The Huggens Arms, albeit without its glass. Clinker balls – no doubt the culprits – were lying all around.

There were net curtains in the windows of number 32, something that Mary would have considered a waste of money. Apart from that, her old home looked much the same. Taking a deep breath, she banged the rusty door knocker and nervously stood back.

'Well, I'll be blowed, if it isn't Flossie Grant,' a young girl exclaimed on witnessing the visitor standing before her. 'Ma, come see, it's Flossie Grant come back to us!'

'Didn't expect to ever see you in The Crick again,' Bessie Turner said, peering from behind her eager daughter Maisy. 'Looking quite the young lady too, in all your finery.'

It wasn't long before Flossie was receiving a doorstep account of what had gone on since the time of her departure. The shock rooted her to the spot.

'He's got a new family now. Got married straight after you left. Right confused, we were, believing he was already married to Mary. Thought he'd get arrested till we finds out you'd all been living 'ere in sin.'

Flossie sighed at the thought of her family saga being a source of local gossip and her return starting it all up again.

'That's why we're 'ere in your old place,' Maisy continued in her shrill voice, oblivious to the damage already done. 'It's bigger, so we grabbed the chance to take it on, then Ma's family came over from Dublin. Dare say Kate Bailey can tell you more. She's not changed.'

It was such a relief to find everything next door exactly the same. Kate enveloped a tearful Flossie in her welcoming arms and held her tight. In fact, they both cried and laughed in equal measures for several hours.

'Bless you, my darling girl, if only you'd knocked here first. I could have saved you from Bessie Turner's venomous tongue.'

'She only said what everyone now knows,' Flossie sobbed, well aware that there were more folk she would have to face up to soon.

'I'm so glad you came back, Floss. We all worried about what had happened to you. I'd hate you to think I knew what your mother was up to. I swear I had no inkling. You do believe me, don't you? I was broken-hearted when I found your house empty.'

Flossie could feel nothing but affection for this kind woman who was prepared to take her in on the spot, shield her from prying eyes and listen patiently to her recounting what had happened in Ipswich. But Kate knew it wasn't yet the right time to tell what she knew of Sam. Best let the girl make her own mind up; there was a lot to take in.

Flossie stood on the jetty, waiting for her best friend. Jessie had been given the afternoon off to go to the official opening of the Gordon Recreation Gardens and the two girls had a lot of catching up to do. Old Annie Devonshire was sitting on a rusty bollard peering across at the comings and goings in the recently completed Tilbury Dock opposite. In her hand was a new fern-decorated spectacle case that Flossie had given her.

'I like sitting 'ere in the afternoons,' the old lady said, pointing at one of the big vessels. 'There's so many different ships nowadays, carrying the likes of jute from India. There'll be Madeira wine on that West African Line. Look, can you see it? Got two dry docks over there now.'

Flossie trained her eyes on the new dock, which already looked congested.

'Fifty six acres of water, so they say. I sat here and watched the *Glenfruin* be the first to steam in.' Fumbling in her bag, Annie pulled out a tarnished silver medal. 'Only had it a couple of months and it's already gone black with the damp. It's what I got on the day all the officials came. Here, you read it.'

Flossie could just make out the inscription on the back: *In commemoration of the opening of the Tilbury Deep Water Docks by Harry H. Dobree, Esq., Chairman of the company April 17th 1886.*

'I'm sorry I missed it all,' Flossie sighed, handing the medal back. At that moment, she caught sight of Jessie making her way gingerly towards them up the slipway, taking care to avoid the seaweed and tar.

'Can't afford to get my boots in a mess,' she laughed, hugging her old pal. 'Sorry I'm late, took ages for the boat to come across. Didn't you see me waving?'

Flossie had to admit she hadn't.

'Well, blow me down,' Jessie teased. 'Thought you'd be keener to see me than that!'

'I am, silly,' Flossie giggled, holding on to her tightly. 'You don't know just how pleased I am to see you.' The girls started gabbling away, the years apart melting away.

'So, a new job for you, Jessie. What's it like working over there?' Annie enquired when she was able to get a word in.

'Oh, it's a very fine hotel, Annie. We mainly get first-class passengers on overnight stays. Makes it especially hard work for me though, it's my job to change the sheets.'

The stately, red-brick Tilbury Hotel was impossible to miss. Standing at the entrance to the dock on what had once been deserted marshland, it had been built to accommodate passengers travelling to and from America, South Africa, India and Australia.

'I've 'eard it's got *electric* light throughout,' Annie said in a mock-posh accent. 'Bit of an eyesore, if you ask me. Another of them things what's happened since you've been gone, Flossie. I still haven't gotten over the shock of our General being murdered by those savages in Khartoum, and now there's the Darnley boy marrying beneath him. Poor Lady Darnley. Right upset the applecart that has.'

Flossie turned to Jessie with a bemused expression.

'Now off you go. Don't waste any more time staying with me. My old legs won't carry me to Gravesend any more. You come back and tell me what they say about General Gordon. I'll say a little prayer for him on me own.'

Giving Annie a peck on either cheek, the girls set off along the shore. The sun was hot and the river shimmering. They walked arm in arm, catching up on the past. As Flossie began to tell her story, tears welled in her friend's eyes and they had to stop, the pair collapsing on a bench.

'So you haven't seen Sam yet?' Jessie eventually managed to ask. 'Should I say Sam? Or are you still going to call him "Father"?'

'I don't know. I've gone over it in my head so many times. From the very first day in Dr Barnardo's I prayed that he would come and find me and Lottie and even now – now that he must have heard that I am back in The Crick – I am hoping that *he* will make the first move.'

'You know he has another family now, don't you?' Jessie said quietly.

Flossie raised her eyebrows. 'Yes. Bessie Turner was quick to impart that news. I just need to know if he still thinks of us – his first family. I've seen what my mother is truly like and I've heard her version of events. I'll withhold judgement until I've heard Sam's story and then decide if I am able to call him my father.'

'You've become a strong woman, Florence Grant.' Jessie smiled.

Flossie smiled too, knowing that the only certainty in all this was that Grant was definitely not her name. She didn't bother to correct her friend, though.

'Come on, let's get going or we'll miss the event. On the way you can tell me all the Darnley gossip.'

Jess looked momentarily confused.

'Lady Darnley's son marrying beneath him, I mean.'

'Oh, that… *Your* life is far more dramatic.'

Their smiles turned to laughter as they gathered up their bonnets and purses and dragged themselves to their feet. In that moment, Flossie felt like she had never been away, so familiar their relationship seemed. Yet she knew that Annie was right. It wasn't the same. Change was everywhere.

'Didn't Lord and Lady Darnley's son have something to do with cricket?' Flossie asked as they stopped for a penny lick by the pier. 'I remember us walking out to Cobham Hall at Eastertime to help them pick their daffodils. We got a penny a bunch. We used to peer at the Darnley's Elizabethan pile, with its fountains, and imagine what it would be like to live there.'

'Yes… and we found the Swiss chalet Charles Dickens gave them, where he did much of his writing! Anyway, to get to the point, the son in question is the Honourable Ivo Bligh.

He took over as captain of England's cricket team after we lost to the Australians four years ago. There was such a fuss about Englishmen losing on home soil that *The Sporting Times* published a mock obituary to English cricket, saying it had died, been cremated and its ashes transported to Australia.'

'But what's all that got to do with him getting married?' Flossie said, trying hard to grasp the connection.

'Hold your horses; I'm coming on to that bit. You see, at a friendly local match in Melbourne, a certain Florence Morphy handed him a tiny urn with the ashes of a burnt bail in it, symbolising the ashes of English cricket.'

'What, in jest?'

'Yes, in a playful way. He took a fancy to her, and she rather liked the look of this tall, dashing Englishman. He won the cricket as well as her heart, but when he returned to England with the ashes in his luggage and Florence, a mere music teacher, on his arm, hoping to obtain his parents' approval to marry her, they refused. So he went back to Australia and married her anyway. They've just come back here to Cobham Hall, and have a son now. It's said the ashes sit on his desk beside him.'

'How romantic,' Flossie said wistfully. 'I wonder if we'll see them all this afternoon?' She found the idea of an upstairs/downstairs romance rather appealing.

As the girls entered the gates, the newly laid out recreation grounds were filled to capacity with people attired in their Saturday best awaiting the arrival of the dignitaries. The perimeter trees provided much-needed shade for the Gravesend Town Band, which performed a mixture of rousing patriotic and military tunes. Each piece ended with a crash of huge brass cymbals, to which the audience applauded enthusiastically.

Eventually Lady Harriet Bligh, Countess of Darnley, was invited onto the temporary bandstand where she composed herself before beginning a moving tribute to General Charles

Gordon, who had died so tragically the previous year at the siege of Khartoum.

'It was inevitable that Charles Gordon would join the Army,' she told the assembled audience. The son of a Royal Artillery officer, he was commissioned as a lieutenant in the Royal Engineers, and after brave service in the Crimean War, was ordered to China where his extraordinary achievements during the Second Opium War earned him the nickname "Chinese Gordon". On promotion to the rank of lieutenant colonel, he took command of our Thames forts with the mission to reconstruct and update their defences, and it was during his six happy years here in Gravesend that he began the active charity work for which he has become so loved and respected. His fame as a Christian evangelist parallels that of his military exploits.'

Loud clapping greeted this evocation. Flossie took a moment to study the dignitaries sitting in the front row. Spotting Ivo Bligh with his wife, she nudged Jessie.

'He's certainly dashing,' she whispered with a giggle. 'If all it takes to catch a lord is to give him a box of ashes, there's hope for me yet...'

Jessie stifled a laugh as Lady Darnley continued her speech. Flossie found her mind wandering as she tried to listen to the account of General Gordon's selfless work with the poor and destitute of Northfleet.

'He worked amongst the riverside boys and strove to improve the slave-like conditions of those working in the lime, chalk and cement works. General Charles Gordon was a saintly man...'

Images of her own childhood flashed before Flossie. Both her and Lottie sitting on Sam's knees, feeling the warmth of his arms around them. He had been a loving, caring father, so how had it all gone so wrong? What was this secret that seemed to be hanging over him?

'Thus, to commemorate the loss of Gravesend's greatest benefactor, the town has created this permanent memorial in his honour. I therefore take great pleasure in declaring the grounds officially open.'

Flossie's head jerked as rapturous applause greeted Lady Darnley's tribute. With no sign of it stopping, Jessie grabbed Flossie's hand and gestured towards the gates. She had to get back to Tilbury before dark, so they had already planned to catch a tram from Wellington Street back to Rosherville. Thankfully it wasn't long before they were well on their way.

As they were deciding what to tell Annie about her hero's memorial garden, the girls became aware of a commotion going on around them. They seemed to be slowing down. A large group of boys had decided to race the tram horse along the long stretch of the Overcliffe and were getting too close to the tram.

'Urchins!' the conductor yelled as the raucous tribe weaved from one side to the other. 'You'll be for it!'

'General Gordon's boys wouldn't have done that,' whispered Jess.

Both girls laughed guiltily as they descended from the tram and rushed off down Pier Road.

Kissing one another on the cheek, they barely had time to say goodbye before the horn sounded and the ferry headed off across the river. Flossie waved frantically until she could see her friend no more. It had been wonderful see each other again, and they had already made plans for another get-together. As she turned to walk back towards The Creek, it didn't take long before thoughts of Sam returned. Mulling things over, it was clear to her that she couldn't put it off any longer. She had to find him and face up to the inevitable revelations that were bound to come.

13

It was Joe Ollerenshaw who opened the door of number 17 Lawn Road. He didn't recognise Flossie at first, which was hardly surprising, being distracted as he was by a bunch of small children hanging on to his legs. Two more were pulling him backwards into the hall by his braces. Every time he attempted to swat them off, they came springing straight back.

'Oh my goodness, it's young Flossie, isn't it?' he said with a surprised look on his face. Flossie was amused that he obviously still saw her as a twelve-year-old girl in pigtails.

'Whoa, Neddy!' a child shrieked from behind, at which point Joe's braces were pulled so hard that he and his appendages all fell backwards onto the floor. Fearing that the smallest child would be crushed under Joe's legs, Flossie jumped to the rescue and, with help from all the others, hauled him upright again.

'Thanks.' He grinned, picking up a squealing girl and tucking her under his arm. 'You'd better come in.'

As she squeezed past him the whole group lurched into the chaotic kitchen. There was nowhere to sit. Clothes lay everywhere, some damp, some dirty. Tidying was evidently one task Joe couldn't manage. Seeing Flossie's eyes darting from child to child, he scratched his head, weighing up what he thought he should say.

'They're not all mine. Been laid off. Moved to Crown but they fell on hard times, just my luck. So I'm lumbered looking after the kids while me wife goes out charring.'

Flossie nodded, studying the faces of the assembled brood carefully. Realising he had to say something, Joe grabbed three of the children and thrust them forward.

'These here are Sam's. I'm minding them today as well, while Lizzie's washing pots in The Red Lion.'

One was just a baby, a few months at best; the next a boy who looked about two; and then an older girl.

'I'm Henrietta Gant and I'm four,' the rosy-cheeked child with long ringlets piped up. 'Do you know my pa?'

'Yes.' Flossie smiled, touching her chestnut hair. 'But I haven't seen him in a while.'

'He's on late shift, but Ma'll be back soon. Do you know her too?'

'No,' I haven't met your ma,' Flossie replied with an anxious look. 'But I'm sure she's very nice.' The thought of meeting Sam's wife like this alarmed her.

Moving towards the door, she fluttered her fingers at the gaggle of children. 'I must be going. I'll come back another time.'

The little girl followed her out, with Joe holding on to her ringlets.

'I kept my nose out of what was going on when Mary took you away,' he half-whispered as he opened the front door. 'So I can only speak as I find. Sam cares for these bairns just like he did you and Lottie, and he's got a good heart. He's let me and the wife live here for nothing, till I gets another job.'

Flossie had to lift her skirts up high as she picked her way through debris and muck to the top of Lawn Road. Like many other roads in the area, it had been taken up by the gas company whilst laying the main and left in poor repair. Grateful to reach the hill with its new concrete pavements with deep kerbs, she smiled on seeing that the same family were running the post and telegraph office. Purchasing a stamp for her next letter to Lottie, she made for a seat on the green outside the church. Somewhere in the distance, probably at the entrance to the gardens, she could hear the familiar strains of the Webb Family Band. Her mind was racing – if Henrietta was four, Mary must have found out that Sam had made another woman pregnant. That's why she left.

Early the next morning, there was a knock at the Baileys' front door.

'Do you want me to answer it?' Kate said, both of them suspecting who it might be.

Flossie nodded, bracing herself for the moment she had longed for, yet dreaded.

'Go into the parlour, I'll keep the young 'uns busy in the kitchen.'

'Is she here?' a man's voice echoed from outside. There was no mistaking that voice. It was Sam.

Kate let him into the parlour where Flossie stood nervously, tears stinging the backs of her eyes. He looked smaller somehow, cap in hand, running his fingers through his thick hair as he spoke.

'Oh, my darling daughter, I am so pleased to see you.' He moved towards her with his arms outstretched and, despite her reservations, she let him hug her. They clung to one another for a long minute, the familiar smells of tobacco and cement dust reminding her of her childhood. But it was she who broke free first, her eyes flashing and anger in her voice.

'You *dare* to call me your daughter? If you believe that to be true, why didn't you come looking for me?'

Sam blanched and lowered his head, allowing Flossie to vent her rage.

'Not once in all those years did that question ever leave me. You *must* have known my mother would go back to Henry again, so you could have followed. Why didn't you? Do you expect me to forgive you for this?'

At that point she broke down, unable to hold back the tears any more. Sam wanted to comfort her, but she turned away, wiping her eyes.

'I have no excuses, Flossie, and no answers that will satisfy you,' he said wearily. 'I was simply worn out by it all. Mary had told me so many times in her drunken rages that that profligate Henry Oxer had fathered you as well as Lottie; it was easiest to believe it in the end. Easiest to think it was better for you to be with your rightful parents, who she seemed to think were destined to be together. Not like she and I were, with no contentment from the very beginning. I thought about you often, but I told myself that your mother would drink less if she was happier, and that could only be better for you girls.'

Pulling a grey handkerchief out of his waistcoat pocket, Sam placed his hands on her arms and turned her around to face him, gently wiping her eyes.

'You have to believe me, Flossie. I loved you girls and, had things worked out different, we might still be together. Now look at you – you've turned out to be a real beauty, lass. I hoped and prayed I'd made the right decision to leave well alone. Reckon I did.'

Flossie looked at him carefully, suspicious that he had done nothing more than what was convenient for him, and decided this was not the time to enlighten him as to what really happened, nor to confront him about his other family. There would be opportunity enough to inform him that Mary had never intended to include her daughters in her reunion with her husband, no doubt to spare them witnessing the Oxers' life of drunkenness, thieving and violence in Ipswich. If fate had decreed that the girls were to be left in the hands of Dr Barnardo, maybe that *had* been for the best, though Lottie would need a lot of convincing about that.

Two weeks later, Henrietta, Samuel George and Alfred James Gant were all baptised together at St. Botolph's Church. Flossie thought it churlish not to attend, but asked Jessie to come along for moral support. It was a somewhat unruly affair with so many around the small font, but Sam and Lizzie laughed and smiled as they juggled their children. Flossie was embarrassed to feel a pang of jealousy as she watched their obvious mutual devotion. It wasn't hard to see what Sam saw in this comely young woman with fair hair and clear skin. Her sparkling eyes were so alive, so very different from Mary's.

Heading for The Dorset Arms afterwards, Lizzie took Flossie's arm and held her back slightly from the rest of the party. 'I can see you are ill at ease being here,' she said, now so close that Flossie could feel her large bosom pushing into her side. 'I understand why you think badly of him, but men are weak, leastways that's what my mam always says. You can't expect anything else after the way Mary treated him.'

Lizzie stopped walking and turned to face Flossie squarely. 'It has to be said, I know she's your mother, but she near broke him. He turned to me for comfort and then cried like a baby himself when he heard I was carrying his child.'

Flossie suddenly became aware of just how young Sam's wife was as she watched the tears pour down her rosy cheeks, Sunday best bonnet all askew.

'I was worried sick whether he'd do right by me and Henrietta, but just look at him.'

Flossie turned to see Sam and Joe Ollerenshaw on the other side of the road by the old chalk pit, balancing perilously on the edge, pretending to throw a screaming Jessie over. All the children were jumping up and down excitedly as the men clowned about, causing as much mayhem as possible.

'See what I mean?' Lizzie said to Flossie.

Flossie couldn't deny Sam looked the perfect father, but it did nothing to relieve her own feelings of abandonment by him.

By the time Jessie had finished straightening her skirts and ticking the men off for their foolishness, everyone was in much need of refreshment. Turning into Dorset Close, a safe cul-de-sac where the older children could be left in charge of the babies, Sam bought them some fruit pastilles and chocolate beans from a confectioner's cart before heading into the pub with the adults.

Through Lizzie, Flossie came to learn that when Sam and Mary first arrived in Milton, Sam got a job as a coal porter with Lizzie's father. The Davies family lived in Crooked Lane, and after Mary went back to Ipswich the first time they invited Sam into their home and did their best to console him. Lizzie was still young then, but by the time her father died, she was seventeen and working as a domestic servant. Sam returned the support given to him all those years before by helping Sarah Ann Davies and her four children when, almost penniless, they were forced to move into Brewhouse Yard. It was here that Sam started a relationship with Lizzie, and here that she gave birth to Henrietta in 1882, six months after Mary left Flossie and Lottie at Dr Barnardo's. Sam subsequently moved in and made Lizzie his real wife at Holy Trinity Church, Milton in February the following year.

As Sam raised his glass to his freshly baptised family, Flossie had to smile at the irony of the situation. Albeit with a new wife and different children, Samuel Gant was firmly back in Northfleet.

'I'll tell you what,' Lizzie said a bit later, 'it's too lovely a day to be stuck in here. Let's go up Windmill Hill.'

'Be full of Londoners off the steamers, seeing as it's a Sunday,' Sam replied uncertainly.

'Nothing like as many as used to come. Do let's, it'll make a lovely end to the day.' Lizzie had clearly made up her mind, and was already putting the baby back into his pram.

'You'll come too Floss, won't you? And you Jess? Sam added almost pleadingly. I promise we'll be back in time for your ferry.'

Jessie and Flossie looked at one another knowing they couldn't refuse.

Strolling up Windmill Street an hour or so later, it wasn't hard to see why it was one of the most prominent and frequented streets in Gravesend. Set back from the road, the cottages and villas had extensive frontages with lime and flowering laburnum trees bending gracefully in the breeze. Out of breath climbing the hill, the adults were overtaken by the children, who had spotted some donkeys. Sam and Joe chased after them, ferreting in their pockets for pennies. Flossie thought the windmill, which was well over a hundred years old, was looking a bit frail, but she joined Lizzie and Jess in the queue to climb the twenty feet to the viewing balcony. With its sails no longer turning, it was now being used as an observatory and camera obscura. Flossie lifted her skirts to mount the rickety steps, holding on tightly to the rail at the summit. There was no denying that the view was splendid. Wheat fields, orchards and arable lands stretched out as far as the eye could see.

'I told you it would be perfect,' sighed Lizzie. 'Hardly a cloud in the sky and no cement dust in your lungs. Wouldn't it be wonderful if you could hang your washing out up here?'

The girls roared with laughter as Lizzie pictured Sam's combinations and her bloomers circling on the sails of the windmill. Despite her initial misgivings, Flossie found herself warming to Sam's wife. She was a straightforward, down-to-earth woman who was doing her best to welcome Flossie into her family.

A passenger liner, the size of which Flossie had never seen before on the Thames, suddenly caught her attention. It was undertaking some deft manoeuvring into Tilbury Dock.

'That's the *RMS Ormuz*, destined for Australia,' Jessie said proudly. 'The Orient Pacific Line has just transferred its business here from Liverpool.'

Excited by what they had seen, the group descended the windmill, Sam and Joe heading for The Belle-View hostelry while the women enjoyed a welcome cup of tea at a kiosk. Refreshed, they took a short cut down Shrubbery Hill, a beautiful, natural wilderness that proved hard going, tangling their stockings in the wild brambles and catching the wheels of the pram in the undergrowth. Confronted by a stagnant pond, Sam and Joe rolled up their trousers and waded in, forming a human chain to allow the children to be carried across to Lizzie. Each delivery soaked her best skirt with foul water, but it didn't bother her in the least. Looking at all their beaming, happy faces Flossie realised what she had missed out on. Sam was a different person with Lizzie.

Further on, the terrain became crumbly and unstable. The children loved it. For them it was a great adventure – akin to Livingstone and Stanley in deepest Africa – which they re-enacted all the way to the pier.

Having bid farewell to Jess, they treated themselves to a much-needed tram ride home, despite it costing tuppence each. Exhausted, Flossie slumped into her makeshift bed at Kate's and had the best night's sleep she'd had in ages. She had no inkling then that within a very short time, she would find herself back in church, this time on a less joyful occasion.

Still holding the letter from Fred Oxer, she stepped off the train in Ipswich, heart in mouth, barely able to believe it had been just a few short weeks since she'd left.

With no time to spare, she took the horse-drawn tramway from the railway station to Cornhill, in the town centre. Counting the passengers to take her mind off her destination, it struck her how strong the single horse must be to pull twenty-three people and a heavy tram. Soon she would see another single horse leaving St. John's Home, the children's branch of the Great Whip Workhouse, this time bearing a far lighter load.

It had taken some time for Bessie Turner to pass on the scribbled note sent to Flossie at Sam's last known address. There was nothing much in it, just the barest details surrounding the death and impending funeral of little Henry George. It seemed that constant diarrhoea had left him too weak to survive in the workhouse where he'd been put shortly after Flossie had left.

There had been little time to make arrangements, but Flossie knew she had to attend. Now, standing around the grave in the freezing air, grief overcame her. The circumstances of his death were bad enough, but seeing that her mother was not amongst the mourners was too much to bear. Fortunately, Henry Senior had been released from gaol on compassionate grounds and so was able to place his son's tiny coffin into the ground – paid for by the Union. This was Flossie's first encounter with him. As they listened to the service, she fixed her gaze upon his fair, wavy hair, so similar to Lottie's and so unlike her own. He had dulled, sunken eyes, no doubt the result of the demon drink.

The sombre gathering headed for The Lion and Lamb, where, with a tot of rum warming her insides, she watched Henry slowly drown his sorrows before starting a rant against Mary and her family.

'Of course *you* wouldn't know this,' he spat at Flossie, spilling his beer as he swayed to and fro, 'but why would you? It all began when we lived in Dove Lane with her mother, Fanny Allen. It was she who looked after you and Lottie all day while my esteemed wife was in the alehouse. Trouble was, she kept arguing. Right nasty, she could be. Started hitting me one day, so I told her to sling her hook. Our Mary didn't like that, not that it stopped her drinking, and she still left you children on your own. So I gets cross and hits her for it, but she tells the coppers I'd hit *her* for complaining about not having any money for food!'

Flossie just stared at him, his indignation lost on her. Irresistible as he might be to her mother, all she could see was a feckless, weasel-faced, small-framed wastrel who bragged constantly about who he was going to fight next. Having taken an immediate dislike to the man, there was no way she was ever going to believe that he was her father.

'Then I gets charged with assault, bound over for the sum of twenty-five quid to keep the peace with my wife for six months.' He let out a caustic laugh, causing his ale to drop on the floor, separating the sawdust. 'Turned out not to be so hard, seeing as how she goes back to Northfleet with Sam Gant straight after leaving the court.'

Draining the last dregs, he studied his dejected reflection in the bottom of the glass and fell silent. Flossie wondered briefly what he might have been had the drink not taken its toll.

Then, turning to her with a pathetic look on his face, Henry added, 'Thought that was all in the past and things were going well. Shows you how much I know. Lord knows who she's with now. Been gone a while. Wisbech, the neighbour says. Up to her old tricks again. Asked my pa to take responsibility for his grandson, so when he says no, she leaves him at the workhouse on her way out of town.'

Turning out his pockets in search of a stray penny, he uttered his last word on the subject. 'She don't even know she's lost another of her boys.'

When Sam found out that Mary had abandoned her girls, the shock stopped him in his tracks. Flossie decided to tell him only after she'd received the letter about the death of little Henry George Oxer. Overcome with rage and remorse, he'd been all set to go to Ipswich himself until Lizzie begged him not to. Instead he spent every waking hour trying to reconcile himself to his infidelity being the cause of it all. Not that that could ever excuse Mary for despatching Lottie off to Canada, or the story she gave for doing it. Learning that yet another abandoned child had died alone was gut-wrenching. Thinking back to when his son James Samuel departed this earth, Sam remembered that Mary had been so bereft over losing their much-longed-for boy that he somehow excused the excessive drinking that followed. But what kind of creature could put a sick child in the workhouse, only for that child to die and be buried without its mother knowing? Chances were that she had gone to Wisbech pregnant again.

'God help *that* child,' he heard himself saying.

14

'So Lottie never got a proposal from her volunteer soldier, then?' Jess said, trying to get a comb through her friend's tangled mane.

'No, nothing came of it. She was far too young anyway,' Floss replied, flinching with the pain.

'Your hair is just like your mother's. Very pretty when it's tamed.'

The combing continued amid grimacing. Then Floss felt her friend hesitate, as if she had something on her mind.

'Is it hard not knowing who your real father is?'

Flossie smiled. Jess wasn't one to mince her words.

'I said when I came back from that poor child's funeral that I cannot accept Henry Oxer as my father. He has done nothing to earn that title.'

'And Sam?'

'Are you nearly ready?' Kate shouted up the stairs, stopping the conversation in its tracks. 'Time we were going.'

Getting ready for an evening at the Factory Club should have been a happy affair, but not on this occasion. Three children had lost their lives at the 'mud-hole' and a benefit concert was being given in support of their bereaved parents. The tragic event had cast quite a gloom over the neighbourhood, deepening the already melancholy mood Flossie had been trying hard to shake off all winter.

'The mud-hole's been unsafe for years,' William Bailey said, bracing himself against the biting wind. 'It's one thing to blame it on ice, but there's been eight deaths there that I know of. Bevan should fill it in.'

It was true; Flossie remembered going to the pond as a child. It had been dug out for its chalk and used as a playground, especially when you could slide on the ice.

Deaths due to accidents in the factories, or by drowning in the river, were common, but those involving children really touched the heart of the community, affecting everyone. Two years earlier the death of the blacksmith's son had been especially shocking. Bizarrely, it took place during the funeral of Reverend Frederick Southgate, vicar of St. Botolph's for nearly thirty years, who had died after a long and painful illness on 6th February 1885. Whilst workmen were busy preparing his vault in the churchyard, fourteen-year-old Edward Gray had just taken a bar of iron into the vault for use by the men and was returning up the steps when one of the bricklayers asked for his chisel. Not knowing that it was propping the stone up, the boy removed it, and no sooner had he done so than the massive slab fell on him, crushing his head and killing him instantly. Suddenly thrown into darkness, the men struggled to raise the stone, and with the greatest difficulty extricated the body, which they solemnly carried up to the belfry.

'Terrible, it was,' Kate had told Flossie. 'We were sad enough, what with it being our Reverend Southgate's funeral in the first place. He'd baptised every one of my bairns. We were in the same pew as the boy's parents when they were told of the tragic accident. I couldn't bear to look at them. Then William Honeycombe, one of the workmen, goes and dies. Never got over the lad's death. Held himself responsible. We all knew he suffered with his nerves and the accident was just too much for him.'

By spring, the weather thankfully improved, as did Flossie's mood. She had secured a position at Northfleet House, new home of Mrs Knight, now widow of the cement manufacturer. It had been a stroke of luck that the old gardener at the House got his tools sharpened by William Bailey on his horse and cart. Mrs Knight's need for a new housemaid had made itself known during a conversation over a pint or two in The Huggens and Flossie was quick to rush round with her references. Mundane as her tasks were, the job came in the nick of time as her money was running out.

One evening, the sight of a large ship coming up the estuary sparked some much needed excitement. *The State of Nebraska*, from the United States of America, looked like a regular sailing ship, yet, for some reason, every local craft from rowboat to barge was bobbing about on the tide, trying to get close. By the next day, rumours about its extraordinary human cargo had quickly spread. Cowboys and Indians anchored off Powder Magazine sounded like madness, yet here they were, the cast of Buffalo Bill's Wild West Show. Anchored at Tilbury briefly before transferring to London's Albert Dock, Flossie had asked for the time off she was owed and persuaded Tom Handley to row Kate and herself out to circle round the ship. In no time at all, a hundred or so foreign-looking individuals were staring down at the people staring up at them. Red Indian men, most of them upwards of six foot, stood in dignified silence, their faces painted and their powerful bodies swathed in blankets. Their squaws, leaning against the boiler house for warmth, were carrying their little ones on their backs.

'See the tallest redskin?' shouted Tom, struggling to keep from colliding with others. 'He's the chief, calls himself "Red Shirt".'

Flossie turned into the wind, her bonnet spiralling into the air, fortunately landing at her feet. She studied the striking man, about the same age as Sam, proudly walking up and down the deck smoking a cigarette. There was a single streak of vermilion down each side of his face extending from the eyebrow to the chin, and his forehead was girdled with a silk handkerchief. Occasionally leaning over the larboard rail, silently watching the activity below, nothing, it seemed, disturbed his placidity.

The next day Flossie found Jess more animated than usual. Colonel William F. Cody – Buffalo Bill himself – and some of his cowboys had been in the Tilbury Hotel, and she and the other maids had hidden behind the banisters to survey them.

'Oh, Floss, they are so dashing. I thought they'd be rough and ill-mannered, but not a bit of it. We all sighed when we saw Buck Taylor. He's very handsome and extremely muscular. I reckon he could pick me up with hardly any effort.' Jess fanned her face with her hand. 'His comrade, Dick Dolman, stands six foot three inches tall, and that's without his hat! They were talking about the ladies in the troupe. There's Miss Emma Lake, the champion female rider in all the United States, and Miss Annie Oakley, who is a better crack shot than any man. Oh, how I wish I could see the show at Earl's Court.'

Flossie nodded in agreement, knowing full well it was impossible at a guinea a ticket. But she had another idea. The *Nebraska* was due to set sail again after discharging its extraordinary cargo, so if they timed it right they could be on Tilbury dockside to watch all the performers disembark.

The trouble was, they weren't the only ones with the same idea and it took some very unladylike barging and shoving to get to where they wanted to be. People were everywhere, even leaning out of upstairs windows and hanging on chimney pots to see the Wild West cargo being unloaded. Special trains from Galleon's Station were being diverted onto tracks running alongside the wharf to transport the company directly to West

Brompton. Even hardened stevedores chuckled in amazement as out of the fore and aft holds swung horseboxes, immense bales and innumerable wooden crates holding unknown treasures.

Flossie and Jessie covered their ears as men shouted at the tops of their voices over the pounding of the steam winch. Then the unmistakable figure of Buffalo Bill strode down the gangplank to the cheers of the crowd, his wide-brimmed hat raised in appreciation. Flossie gasped on seeing his long hair tied back in a ponytail, which she imagined was as long as her own when let down. She marvelled at his brown leather outfit fringed with tassels that rippled in the breeze, somehow magnifying his presence.

'Here come the cowboys,' Jessie exclaimed excitedly, prodding her friend in the ribs as the spurs on the men's high boots scraped across the wooden slats. 'That one's Antonius Esquivel, chief of the Mexicans... and look that must be Annie Oakley!'

To everyone's surprise, Miss Sure Shot, as Annie was known, was tiny – barely five feet tall – with long, flowing hair and a skirt that, shockingly, ended just below her knees. She was carrying a pair of rifles.

'She can shoot dimes thrown in the air and riddle a playing card at thirty paces,' Jessie boasted, having gleaned the information from one of the performers back at the hotel. The idea of a woman being a crack shot made Flossie smile.

But the undoubted stars, as far as Flossie was concerned, were the 'Noble Savages' – Sioux, Cheyenne and Pawnee. She could hardly take her eyes off the horsemen, each carefully guiding his mount down the creaking wooden gangplank. They looked stunning in their wide trousers tacked all the way down, moccasins, feathers, beaver skins, beads and war paint. All in all, 160 horses were disembarked, each with a scarlet-and-blue blanket in place of a saddle, followed by buffalo, cattle, elk, deer and other animals never before seen in Europe. The overpowering smell as the last were unloaded finally persuaded the girls that it was time to wend their way home.

The press made much of the arrival at Earl's Court of the Wild West Show. Prime Minister Gladstone was reported to have asked Chief Red Shirt if he liked the English climate, while *The Referee* magazine welcomed the grand spectacle in verse:

We hear that the Cowboys are wonders,
And do what rough riders dare,
So wherever the 'pitch' is in London,
Its wild horses will drag us there,
O' fancy the scene of excitement!
O' fancy five acres of thrill,
The cowboys and Injuns and horses,
And the far-famed Buffalo Bill!

The weather continued to dominate everyone's lives during the first half of 1887. Over Whitsun a severe storm swept through the district, causing flooding in Northfleet. The strength of the wind and rain brought trams to a standstill. Drains were blocked and workmen had to clear inches of mud from the streets.

'Weather hasn't put off the Salvation Army march,' Lizzie confirmed, folding up her umbrella. 'Might stop the usual disputes, though.'

Sam looked at his pocket watch. 'They won't be arriving till about one o'clock so we don't need to worry yet.'

'I think we'd better be prepared, Sam,' Lizzie added, looking her husband squarely in the eyes. You know it's the sound of the brass band that brings out the Skeletal Army. Don't want anyone running down here throwing stuff, breaking windows.'

Taking the hint, Sam set off to check whether there was any trouble brewing. About 170 officers of the Life Guards column of the Salvation Army, dressed in white helmets, red jerseys and leggings, were assembling opposite Huggens College for an open-air meeting. It was a relief to see the police were out in force too. For most people, this annual training march was nothing more than a nuisance.

The Salvation Army regarded alcohol as a social evil, believing in total abstinence rather than moderation. Unsurprisingly, they were opposed by many members of the public. Small groups began organising themselves against the Salvationists. Calling themselves Skeleton Armies, they sang obscene versions of songs, threw rotten food and daubed meeting halls with tar. With actions designed to humiliate rather than cause physical injury, their attacks on Salvationists were treated leniently by police and magistrates.

Sure enough, it wasn't long before a contingent of Skeletons appeared carrying a flag with a crudely drawn coffin and skull and crossbones upon it. They did their best to disrupt the proceedings by beating drums, playing flutes, whirling rattles and shouting through trumpets. Sam had to smile as a man ringing a bell and attired in a coal-scuttle bonnet was carried shoulder-high past him, followed by several of the town's publicans waving their hats.

Despite all the commotion, the Salvation Army carried on regardless and Sam was able to report back to Lizzie that at least no dead rats had been thrown, as had been the case in previous years.

During Monday morning rain continued to fall heavily, but miraculously, just before noon the leaden skies cleared and the sun reappeared. Holidaymakers began arriving via all three railway lines, though not a single steam boat plied its way down the Thames from London bound for Rosherville. The pier was unnaturally quiet, and the ladies of Teapot Row had no customers for their afternoon tea of watercress and shrimps. Most train-travellers still headed for the gardens, but now there was competition. Wagonettes were waiting to take people to a new event – bicycle racing at the Bat and Ball Grounds.

'We had to lay on eighteen special trains to take them all back to London,' Flossie overheard the station porter saying in the newsagents. 'Packed like sardines, they were.'

Spirits remained high for the Queen's Golden Jubilee on the 20th June, and most people were out celebrating. It was a glorious day at last, with barely a breeze. The jetty was packed with revellers basking in the sunshine, watching the activity on the even more crowded Thames.

'Sorry I'm late,' Flossie gasped, collapsing next to Jess on the old bollard. Nowadays it was Jessie who had to wait for her friend to finish work. 'It was too hot to run all the way. I had to bundle up the dirty linen for the great wash before I could leave.' Loosening the laces on her boots she let out a sigh of relief.

'So how is the miserable Mrs Knight?' Jessie asked. 'I still remember running away from her mansion in Hive Lane when we used to go souling.'

'Oh, she's reasonable enough and the job isn't too arduous. Her new home is a good deal smaller than Hive House and there's only her and their youngest daughter to clean for.'

'Meant to ask you ages ago, are those harpoons still on top of the gates?'

'Yes! Mementos of the Sturge family's dealings in the whaling trade, apparently. I'm supposed to polish them daily.'

'In that case, I reckon we should be glad we're not employed at Buckingham Palace,' Jess said with a laugh. 'I hear there's going to be a banquet tonight to which fifty European kings and princes have been invited. Can you imagine the washing-up?'

Flossie nodded. 'Don't worry, there'll be plenty of that *here* tomorrow. The schools are holding a grand jubilee fete for five thousand children. Sam and Joe's little ones have been practising their singing for days; though it's catching the pig by its tail they're looking forward to the most.'

'You seem to be spending quite a bit of time with Sam's new family,' Jess said tentatively. 'Does that mean you have forgiven him?'

'Well, I can't deny that I am at my happiest in their company. Sam and Lizzie make me feel very welcome, and it's lovely to watch them with their children.'

'Doesn't it make you angry, considering your own childhood?'

'Envious, maybe, but I can't change the past, so I made up my mind some time ago not to look back any more. He may not be my father, but I consider myself part of his family.'

Jess thought her friend very grown-up all of a sudden.

Spotting Annie Devonshire struggling to get onto the slipway, both girls rushed over to offer her a hand. Crumpling with the effort, she had to be hauled back to the bollard. The old woman coughed and spluttered before flopping down, exhausted. Flossie removed her frayed bonnet while Jessie untangled her skirts.

'Thank heavens you girls were here to save me,' she said breathlessly. 'I didn't realise it was quite so hot. I fear my days of climbing up here are near over, but I had to see what was being done in honour of 'Er Majesty on this important day.'

For a while the three of them sat and watched the myriad of small boats flitting about amongst far larger craft on the silver river.

'That's better,' Annie said, on regaining her composure. 'I was in need of a breath of the briny. I was just thinking about when Princess Alexandra arrived from Denmark. It was all these launches coming up on the tide that reminded me.'

Sensing Annie was about to embark on another of her epic reminiscences, Jessie set off in search of Sylvester Lee and his restorative ginger ale. Stories of the past didn't really interest her, unlike Flossie, who was all ears for the venerable lady's memories.

'It must be about twenty years ago now,' Annie began. 'I was sitting under a great big banner near the pier, with *Welcome, thou chosen one* in Danish as well as English on it. Got there before midnight so I'd have the best view. There was a huge stand, loaned by Epsom Racecourse of all places, a floral canopy on golden poles and an arch stretching across Harmer Street, with statues. Couldn't understand it meself, but it was supposed to be Neptune handing over the princess into the care of Britannia. I'd never seen anything so lavish before, nor since, for that matter.'

Flossie nodded, already spellbound.

'The Prince of Wales stayed in his carriage while the top ratepayers handed over their golden tickets to wait on the pier for the *Victoria and Albert* to arrive. When he saw his betrothed standing on deck the prince sprang on board and planted a kiss on her cheek. It brought about the loudest cheer I have ever heard. As they walked back, arm in arm, they were quite close to me. She was wearing a velvet pelisse trimmed with sable and a white bonnet ornamented with roses and lilies of the valley. Oh, Floss, did she look beautiful! Young maidens strewed her path with petals as they approached the royal carriage. Everyone was fluttering their handkerchiefs or waving mottos. The one I remember best said *Welcome to English Hearts and English Homes!* I felt truly proud to be British that day, I can tell you.'

'I wish I had a handsome prince waiting at the pier for *me* one day,' Flossie said with a sigh, thoroughly caught up in the romance of it all.

'He'd have to have studied the Tilbury Ferry timetable first,' Jessie said with a laugh as she returned with the drinks. 'I rather doubt *you'll* be arriving on the royal yacht.'

'At least a young girl can dream,' Floss laughed, pointing an accusatory finger at her friend. Dreaming of romance was all either of them could do, as neither prince, nor knight in shining armour seemed to be coming their way.

Lottie's life, on the other hand, seemed full of romance. Even in the wilds of Canada she had men falling at her feet. Flossie looked forward to reading each episode, but when the next letter fell onto the doormat, it delivered pleasure and pain in equal measures.

1st September 1887

Dearest sister,

I am so, so relieved that you have been able to rebuild a relationship with Sam, whether he be your true father or not, and I am delighted that you feel part of his new family. It cannot have been easy for you.

I have to admit to feelings of envy on learning that he has a new brood looking up to him. I still think of myself as the baby of the Gant family. Lizzie certainly sounds a fine young woman, and completely different from our mother (more of her to follow).

I so very much enjoy reading about the Bailey family and Jess' exploits. You certainly tell some amusing tales, Floss – I loved hearing about Bevan's annual outing. Eight hundred of you on the sands at Margate must have been a sight, and I reeled at the thought of anyone trying to catch a cannonball fired from the Boswell circus canon, even if the prize was twenty-five pounds!

But it was the account of eleven chickens being stolen from the landlord of The Hope that made me laugh out loud. How embarrassed that forbidding woman, Bessie Turner, must have been when the trail of feathers led the police to her house – then to discover that the thief was none other than her lodger! Fancy trying to hide them in a space between the ceiling and the roof!

Without a doubt, I would be feeling very homesick were it not for recently meeting Andrew McPherson – my heart's desire. You will be astonished to hear that he comes from the Island of Lewis! Indeed, very many families from the Scottish Highlands have started arriving in Manitoba, paid for by the British Government. Most experienced dreadful crossings in steerage, many losing their children to the bitter cold on the way, all in search of a new life on the Prairies. Little do they know that their trials are just beginning. Whatever will go wrong in the settlers' lives ultimately comes from bad weather. Even a hardy Scotsman can offer up little defence against it.

I met Andrew when he came to the recruiting depot for the North-West Mounted Police here in Winnipeg. Goodness, he is so tall and handsome and seeing him in full dress uniform takes my breath away. Scarlet tunic, collar and cuffs edged with yellow cord and dark blue pantaloons with a red stripe worn with black riding boots. The white helmet has a brass spike and chain and is worn with matching long white gloves. When he's on horseback with his sabre hanging from his side, my heart is all of a flutter. After an initial period of learning police practices and how to use firearms at Regine in Saskatchewan, my 'Mountie' has now returned to Manitoba, patrolling the American border to deter liquor smugglers. My love has signed up for a term of three years, and in the first, as a constable, he earns fifty cents a day. What's more, with good conduct he gets an additional five cents. With free rations and kit and accommodation in barracks this is indeed a good wage, and will put us in good stead for the future. I can easily wait three years for someone so utterly worth it as my Andrew. I do hope that you will meet someone soon, dearest sister, and be as happy as I am.

Now, to return to the subject of our indefensible mother. It came as no surprise to me when you disclosed her conduct in Ipswich as I already knew her version of the events. I am mystified as to why she considers me her confidante, but I recently received a letter from her new lodgings in Wisbech. It seems she found another new suitor and saw fit to abscond with him before Henry was released from gaol. I haven't written back to her so I assume she still isn't aware of the death of her son Henry, but my darling, I wish I were there to hold you tightly when I break it to you that she now has another son. William George Allen – he's just a few weeks old. The poor child's father had disappeared before he was born, hence he has Mary's maiden name. Her last plaintive letter was nothing more than a plea for me to send her money. I have to say I was sorely tempted, were it not a certainty that it would be spent on gin.

It seems pointless to waste any more ink in correspondence on such a disappointing woman. By the same token, it has caused me great pain to accept that I am the daughter of the profligate Henry Oxer. Indeed, it has made me question whether I will ever return to England. I feel that I should put the past behind me, become a naturalised Canadian citizen and live out my life here with Andrew.

I have a heavy heart, as I have no idea if I shall ever see you again, but I will pray that time will be a great healer and that one day I will.

With deepest love,

Your true sister,

Lottie

Flossie had forbidden herself to dwell on the notion that she might never see Lottie again. It was just too awful to contemplate. Now, seeing those ominous words in print made it impossible to ignore. To be able to come to terms with the past she had had to put all such negative emotions behind her. Free from the acrimony which had previously engulfed her, she had been able to function. Now the idea that she might lose her sister due to the actions of their parents once again forced the floodgates open, allowing the tide of sensations to overwhelm her.

Feeling utterly wretched and looking for someone to blame for their misfortune, she found herself scarcely able to talk to Sam. What was the point, anyway? It had all been said before.

For his part, Sam kept quiet too, hoping the dust would settle. What Flossie couldn't know was that he secretly considered Lottie to be somewhat like her mother, liable to change her mind and her men on a whim. Though he'd cared for both girls as children, knowing that he was definitely not Lottie's father made a profound difference to how he felt about her.

15

'Increasing demand from America,' Sam said, putting on his jacket. 'Surely you don't want me to turn down an offer of overtime? We were pinched enough last winter when there were no orders, and it could just as easily happen again.'

Lizzie stood silently in the doorway, arms folded. She wasn't happy with her husband being out at work so much, but couldn't deny the need for extra money. So precarious was the cement business that one minute Mr Bevan could be laying men off and the next giving them a day off with pay to witness the double wedding of two of his children.

'I'm sorry I can't go with the bairns to see the whale, but Flossie's said she'll take Henrietta and Samuel George for you, and Tom Handley's agreed to row them over.' Leaving a sixpence on the table for Flossie's entrance fee, Sam kissed his wife on the cheek and rushed off to work.

Lizzie was relieved. She'd promised the children they could go, and now at least they weren't going to be disappointed.

'Is it real?' asked a wide-eyed Henrietta a few hours later.

'Yes.' Flossie nodded, barely able to believe it herself. On Tuesday 4th October, a thirty-five-foot whale had swum upriver to Northfleet Hope and become disorientated. By dawn the following morning, as the tide receded, it became stranded on the shore and died. The carcass had been removed and taken to the engineers' yard in Tilbury Dock where it was on display.

As soon as the school bell rang, children on both sides of the river clamoured to see the creature.

'How the dickens did they get it here?' Tom said, scratching his head. 'The sign says it weighs over six tons.'

'Jess'll get a surprise,' Flossie laughed. 'It also says the skeleton has been purchased by the Tilbury Hotel for its front lawn. Hope it doesn't smell by then!'

The New Year began with such a mild January that it seemed destined to be followed by a frightful few months. The wind rattled the doors of Northfleet House until they sprung open and refused to stay shut. No amount of trying could keep the fires alight and the freezing, damp air started to get everyone down. Flossie struggled to see the point of her employer keeping a house of this size. From the windows, she could see hay swirling around the field behind the coachman's and gardener's cottages. The smoke billowing from their chimneys looked far cosier and more appealing than the big house.

Sudden snowstorms and ice were catching people and animals unawares too. By March, Flossie was still battling to get to the shops. The mud-hole, at the bottom of Stonebridge Hill, was frozen solid, depriving the carthorses of a welcome drink of water before tackling the treacherous ascent. *Still*, she thought ruefully, *things can't be as bad as they are for dear Lottie.* Having reluctantly accepted her estrangement from her sister, rarely a day passed when she didn't think of her having to cope with the ferocious weather being reported on the American continent.

News of New York City caught in the grip of a fearful blizzard had just reached our shores. Flossie scanned the stories as she ironed the newspaper each morning before leaving it on a silver platter in the breakfast room. Fifty inches of snow, people stranded for days after their trains crashed, horses frozen solid in their harnesses in the city centre, women in billowing dresses blown into drifts and not discovered for days. In all, four hundred people had perished in one week alone, and 198 ships had been sunk or damaged in the harbour. It was shocking. But it wasn't until Lottie's letter arrived recounting the pathetic tale of the 'Schoolchildren's Blizzard' that the enormity of the tragedy really hit home.

5th March 1888

Dear Flossie,

I must apologise for the tardiness of my letters. I have two unanswered letters from you and we have begun a ferocious new year since I last wrote.

Do you remember how we used to struggle to see out of our frosty bedroom window in The Crick and think that we would never be warm again? The cold and damp were relentless, yet predictable. It will be hard for you to imagine, but the weather here is so very much worse. The temperature can drop dramatically, creating severe conditions in minutes. In fact, we are still recovering from a blizzard tragedy that befell us on January 12th. They are saying that five hundred people have lost their lives throughout the Canadian and American prairies. It is so much more miserable as over one hundred of the victims were children caught out on their way home from school, lost in the white-out. Even in a region so used to blizzards, this one was unprecedented in its violence and suddenness. One moment it was mild with a shining sun, then three minutes later the temperature dropped eighteen degrees.

Hurricane-force winds blew the snow horizontally

and the air was so thick with ice crystals that people could barely breathe. Ice literally webbed their eyelashes and sealed their eyes shut; it got into the weave of their coats, shirts, dresses and underwear until their skin was packed in snow. Farmers who had spent a decade walking the same worn path became disoriented in seconds, many freezing to death in the short distance between their houses and barns. It is so tragic, sister, there is hardly a day that passes without hearing about yet another lost soul discovered through the frozen folds of an apron, a boot, a shock of hair or a naked hand.

It can be so hard living here, I long for the summer and for those precious days when Andrew is on leave. I so enjoy your letters too, dearest sister – you make me feel close despite your being so very far away. Hearing the news of Little Rose from our days at Barnardo's, and of your exploits with the Gant and Ollerenshaw children, is heart-warming and it sounds like you'll be even busier with Lizzie being with child again.

But, goodness, I must admit to feeling somewhat uneasy about the demise of poor old Bruin the Bear. To hear that he had long been replaced by younger bears and kept tucked away from sight was bad enough. But to then discover he'd been put down and a portion of his hindquarters smoked and cured and served up to guests at the Fishing Smack Inn – I didn't know whether to laugh or cry! Will Rosherville Gardens ever be the same?

With deepest love,

Lottie

The news of 'Little Rose' that Flossie had passed on to Lottie came about as a result of a chance glimpse at one of her employer's newspapers. Details of a strike at the Bryant & May match factory in the East End caught her attention because of an image of a young girl marching at the head of a demonstration demanding better conditions for factory workers. Having often wondered what had become of the emaciated matchgirl whom she'd befriended at Barkingside, Flossie drew in breath when she realised it was, indeed, Rose in the picture.

The dismissal of a factory girl at the beginning of July had resulted in another 1,400 refusing to work. This was unheard of amongst unskilled workers, especially women. The management refused to reinstate the employee, but the women held firm. With no pay, a strike fund was quickly organised and distributed whilst fifty girls went to Parliament to express their grievances. Threatened by bad publicity, Bryant & May's directors finally agreed to the girls' demands. Not only was the sacked worker reinstated, but concessions were granted, including the removal of fines being unfairly deducted from their wages.

The strike brought the plight of these thin, pale and undersized girls to public notice. Far from being passive victims of exploitation, they had displayed remarkable solidarity in the face of intimidation. To Flossie, Rose was a heroine. She had stood up for something that mattered, and it came as a huge relief to think that, as a result of their courage, the matchgirls could now enjoy such simple pleasures as being able to eat their meals in a separate room, safe from contamination from phosphorus, the cause of the dreaded 'phossy jaw'.

But there was another story making the headlines that Flossie shared with her sister in her next letter. Keeping women in the forefront of the news – this time for all the wrong reasons – it involved sinister goings-on in Whitechapel and the reports were often so gruesome that they almost caused Flossie to scorch Mrs Knight's newspapers. The murders of several prostitutes had been the main topic of everyone's conversation for several weeks. Two mutilated bodies had been discovered in the street, with their throats cut and abdomens ripped open. The removal of their internal organs had led to speculation that the killer must have had some anatomical or surgical knowledge. Journalists were having a field day, especially after a letter written by someone claiming to be the murderer, and calling himself 'Jack the Ripper', was sent to Fleet Street.

Hysteria really set in when the killer struck again in the early hours of Sunday 30th September. Two more women, Elizabeth Stride and Catherine Eddowes, were murdered within three quarters of a mile of each other. Once again, their bodies had been mutilated.

However, what really took Flossie aback was a letter she spotted in *The Times*, sent by Dr Barnardo of all people. *Only four days before the recent murders*, he wrote, *I visited No. 32 Flower and Dean Street, the house in which the unhappy woman Stride occasionally lodged.* The women, he said, had been frightened by the Whitechapel murders and expressed the fear that some of them might become victims too. On viewing Stride's body, he confirmed that she had been one of the women he had spoken to in the squalid dosshouse.

What on earth was Dr Barnardo doing visiting houses favoured by prostitutes? Flossie wrote to Lottie. After all, it was a far cry from rescuing destitute children. Surely the whole sordid tale couldn't possibly involve their benefactor?

But there was yet another story connecting them to Elizabeth Stride which Flossie knew her sister would find intriguing. 'Long Liz', as she was known, reckoned that she had been on the *Princess Alice* with her husband and children when it went down. Kate Bailey remembered reading the pack of lies she told the papers about how climbing a mast enabled her escape, only to watch her family drown. Long Liz reckoned she'd been kicked in the mouth, which did untold damage and caused all her teeth to fall out. Turned out she was just trying to get charity money from the church.

'Wicked, that was, when so many really deserved it,' Kate had said. 'Not only was there was no damage to her palate, when it came to the post-mortem,' she continued without a hint of sympathy, 'but when the journalists dug deeper, they found out her husband didn't die until six years *after* the *Alice* sunk. So, as far as I'm concerned, she got what was owing to her.'

Flossie left that last part out of her letter. Kate was entitled to her opinion, but no one deserved to die at the hands of a merciless killer.

Come November, the last of the Whitechapel murders was still filling the pages of the newspapers, but Flossie had neither the time nor the inclination to read any more gruesome details. There were more pressing matters to deal with at home. All of Sam's children had contracted whooping cough and there was real concern over the tiny baby Ada Eliza, who had only been brought into the world in August. To avoid *his* children becoming infected, Joe Ollerenshaw managed to find alternative lodgings for his family.

The Gant house became eerily quiet. By day the children had to be kept calm so as not to provoke coughing fits. By night Flossie and Lizzie sat up trying to prevent them from choking. Battling tiredness, Flossie was relieved when Sam returned one day having found the money to buy some tincture of belladonna to help reduce the severity of the coughing fits. One by one the tots slowly recovered, except for the baby. By the end of the month and quite blue with lack of oxygen, Ada passed away. She was barely three months old. *Another tiny coffin*, thought Flossie.

'Why don't you move in here?' Lizzie suggested not long after. 'Now the Ollerenshaws have settled elsewhere, you can have their room. It'll be company for me and the children would love it.'

It didn't take Flossie long to decide. Having a room to herself – even with small children rarely out of it – was a luxury she'd never experienced before. Besides, she could afford to pay a fair rent, having just been offered advancement at Northfleet House which, fortunately, didn't require her to live in. Miss Elizabeth Knight had recently come of age and required a lady's maid from seven in the morning until seven in the evening. Florence Gant was moving up in the world, and ironing newspapers was now definitely beneath her. Not that this lessened her thirst for information. Any chance she could get to read the news was taken, with cuttings of stories sent on to Lottie in Canada. Lottie, of course, was delighted, except perhaps for the rather gruesome report of a relatively unknown Dutch painter cutting off his own ear just before Christmas. *A decidedly queer and miserable way to start the festivities, sister dear*, Lottie remarked by return.

Christmas at Lawn Road was anything but miserable, however. Flossie had bought warm coats from Nottons outfitters for the children, and was as pleased as punch to spot a newly devised board game in a toyshop window nearby. Snakes and Ladders quickly became everyone's favourite game, and when Lizzie read on the box that the idea had been conjured up in India, it became even more exciting.

Listening to little Henrietta squealing with delight when she discovered a straw doll at the end of her bed took Flossie back to the time when she and Lottie had received similar dolls from Sam. My, she thought, how innocent they had been then. She could still remember her own doll vividly, straw escaping from its thin calico casing after being kept hidden under her pillow at Dr Barnardo's. Eventually it was so ragged that it had to be thrown away and, along with it, the last memory of happy times in The Creek.

Now things had turned almost full circle, and for the first time in many a year she felt contented. *I might be living in a different house as part of a different family*, she thought, *but with Sam still at the helm it feels quite normal.* Like so many growing families all around them, there was never enough money to go round, but what he and Lizzie couldn't give their children in terms of possessions, they made up for in love and attention.

Flossie felt their affection enveloping her too, and was moved to tears when, a few weeks into the New Year, on her twentieth birthday, she came home from work to find a gathering of the masses in her honour. There was hardly room to breathe as the Gants, Baileys, Ollerenshaws, Larkins and Annie Devonshire crammed into every nook and cranny of the parlour, kitchen and scullery.

'At least we can save coal money tonight,' Sam quipped. 'All these bodies means plenty of heat to go round.'

Birthdays had always been 'just another day' throughout her childhood. Mary had no time for such things, and it was much the same at Barkingside. At Lawn Road, though, they were considered worthy of celebration. Flossie felt embarrassed to be the centre of attention when gifts were bestowed on her even by the children, and Kate had made an enormous cake.

'Be just my luck to get the thimble in my piece,' Jessie said forlornly. 'I'm destined to be embroidering for the rest of my life.' Pulling a handkerchief out of her sleeve, she dabbed mock tears from her eyes and turned away.

Flossie laughed out loud. '*You'll* never be a spinster, Jessie Larkin,' she said with a giggle. 'You're bound to get the coin. I'm the one that's going to get the thimble.'

Reflecting for a moment on what she had just said, Flossie wondered if she would ever meet a man with whom she could share her dreams and live in her own house like this. Looking around, she smiled at the cement dust on the floorboards, tramped in by numerous hobnailed boots. Opening the front door, she felt the heavily laden, gritty air wafting around her and watched the men from the factories heading off for their evening drink at the pub. A distant foghorn sounded from a passing ship. Suddenly she had an overwhelming sense of happiness. For the first time, she felt truly secure. This was where she belonged.

'It'll be good to get away from the freezing damp for a day,' said Sam, wrapping scarves around his children. 'And it won't cost very much, only a few pennies on the train. The tram and the ferry will be free.'

'Are you sure it's safe, mixing with so many people?' Lizzie said, a note of concern in her voice. She hadn't let her children out during the winter due to a flu epidemic, and now rumours were spreading about an outbreak of typhoid fever in Portland Road. 'Ten children in seven houses, Sam. When the little ones are digging in the brickworks breeze at the end of the road the stench is terrible. There's dead dogs and cats in the heap.'

'I think it's more to do with shallow wells, my love. The water company have been urged to lay down water mains,' Sam reassured her. 'Besides, we can't stay in forever; it's nearly the end of March.'

Lizzie reluctantly agreed and within minutes everyone was suited and booted and off on their new adventure.

'How does the tram move without a horse pulling it?' Henrietta enquired, pulling on her father's arm.

'By electrical traction,' Sam answered matter-of-factly. 'We've got one of the first electric tramways in the world. Only running from The Leather Bottle to Huggens College, but it's a start.'

'What's "electric" mean?' Henrietta responded, totally flummoxed.

'Something that makes horse-power without needing a horse. It makes big things like tramcars move as if by magic.'

The idea of a magic ride pleased Henrietta. Sam silently hoped there wouldn't be too many more questions like that, as he was already out of his depth. By this time they were now at Susannah Cottages, where his eldest daughter collected the Ollerenshaw children. Once assembled, the troupe made their way to the new stop where they watched in awe as the mysterious horseless carriage came round the corner with *Series Electrical Traction System* painted along its side.

'Well, that was a new experience,' Sam said with a laugh as they alighted at the station. 'A glimpse of the future, no doubt about that.'

'Still prefer the old horse,' Flossie mumbled, rearranging her hair after the juddering, stop-and-start ride.

'Oh, I don't know,' contested Lizzie. 'I was on a tram when Strickland upholsterers caught fire. Horse was commandeered by the fire brigade, leaving me and all the other passengers stranded!'

The station platform was crowded with other like-minded travellers, smoke from the oncoming locomotive causing them to cough and splutter. Sam pushed his way on board, grabbing each child as they were passed up to him by Lizzie and Flossie. The tiny ones needed consoling once on a lap as the thundering giant had given them a considerable fright. Every spare handkerchief was needed to wipe their eyes and clean their smutty faces. Thankfully it didn't take long to reach Woolwich Arsenal, the main focus of their day, and soon they were making their way through the busy town.

It was an auspicious occasion. 23rd March 1889 – the day on which the Free Ferry was to be officially declared open. Woolwich town was decorated with flags and bunting. All the streets on the way to the river were lined with volunteers from the local artillery, so Sam found a suitable spot for the family to stand, giving them the best view. Thankfully they didn't have to wait long before a huge procession could be seen in the distance, preceded by mounted police and followed by local traders and associations with their banners and bands. Sam lifted each child, one after the other, onto his shoulders so as to catch a glimpse of the open carriages carrying all the local dignitaries.

Thousands of people surged slowly towards the riverside where the 154-foot-long *Gordon*, a side-loading paddle steamer with shiny black hulls and funnels, was waiting to make its first crossing. After the officials had boarded, the Gant women, skirts lifted well above their ankles and a child perched on their shoulders or balanced underarm, joined the undignified scramble to be amongst the hundreds squeezing through the makeshift turnstile onto the pristine vessel.

Being capable of a speed of eight knots, it didn't take long to reach the North Woolwich side, where the great and the good were met by yet another procession. Before the party recrossed the Thames, Lord Roseberry, leader of the newly formed London County Council, stood atop his carriage to declare the ferry 'open and free forever'.

On the way back the vessel had to stop to let a large ship pass. While this was going on, Sam and Lizzie found time to take the children to the door of the engine room, where they stood and watched the mighty machines power the paddle wheels.

Finding herself alone for a brief moment, Flossie was idly watching the crew going about their business when a young deckhand caught her attention. His features and mannerisms seemed strangely familiar. Trying not to appear *too* interested, she cast her eyes at him again and realised he was Albert Bull's older brother, Stanley, last seen by her when he was working on the Thames pleasure boats. He seemed extremely proficient at his tasks, giving orders to his subordinates, and a quick mental calculation told her that he had to be around twenty-three years of age by now. Although not particularly handsome, there was something about his strong, muscular physique that she found very appealing. *Just as well this ferry is free*, she thought to herself. *I know where Jess and I will be spending our next afternoon off together...*

16

Stanley Bull was leaning nonchalantly against one of the guard rails, smiling broadly at the girls.

'That first weekend the *Gordon* came into operation, we had twenty-five thousand people making the crossing,' he told them as he flicked ash from his penny cigarette over the side of the ferry. 'Word got out that there was going to be a bare-knuckle fight somewhere on the Kent marshes. Londoners came out in droves. When the police stopped it, the contestants rowed across to Essex, so we were full going back as well!'

'My goodness,' Jessie responded coquettishly, running her hands through her long hair as she did so. 'You must have worked really hard. It's a good thing you're so strong.'

Flossie almost choked with embarrassment. She knew Jess was an unashamed flirt, but this really took the cake.

'I've seen a few men smoking those new cigarettes in the hotel where I work,' Jess continued, twisting a stray ringlet around her finger. 'They make you look very manly. What are they called?'

'Woodbines, five a penny,' Stanley confirmed, taking a final puff and casting the stub into the river. 'Listen, I'd better be getting back to work. This is two Sundays in a row I've stopped to talk to you two fair princesses. You'll be getting me the sack.'

Taking Jessie's hand in his, he briefly kissed the back of it before rushing off. 'Bye, Flossie,' he shouted as he disappeared behind one of the churning paddle wheels.

From the look in Jessie's eyes, it was clear she was completely besotted. 'Did you see the way he touched me, Floss?' she said, spinning round on the deck. 'The twinkle in his eye when he smiled at me? Do you really think he likes me?'

'I don't doubt it for a minute, Jess dearest. He only had eyes for you.'

Realising that this sounded a little like sour grapes, she turned and strolled over to the other side of the deck. It was true that she, too, found Stanley attractive, but Jess seemed to be falling head over heels in love with him after just a couple of meetings. So was this a little pang of jealousy? After all, it wasn't as if Jess had *stolen* him from her.

It didn't take Stanley long to seek Jessie out on dry land. Flossie could see that he was proving to be the perfect beau for her friend, and fortunately was happy enough to act as their chaperone when walking out. The three of them often found themselves mulling over their respective upbringings in The Creek and Dock Row, and all the experiences they had shared since childhood.

Flossie had been terribly shocked on learning that Albert Bull had died four years earlier fighting for Queen and country in the Sudan, but now, listening to his older brother describe the circumstances, she was overcome with sadness. It had always been the conscientious and steadfast Albert who could be relied upon to build the children's camp while the others were climbing trees or swinging on ropes, so it was no surprise that he saw it as his duty to join the army as soon as he came of age. Signing up with the Queen's Own Royal West Kent Regiment, he only got in when the infantry lowered their minimum height requirement by three inches to five foot three, acknowledging that men from the urban slums were part of a shrinking generation due to the fall in nutritional standards.

Having proudly accepted his despatch to Khartoum as part of the Gordon Relief Expedition, Albert marched across the desert to the aid of the besieged General Gordon, only to fall at the Battle of Abu Klea, fighting bravely against the Mahdi's forces.

'He never got to see his fellow soldiers in the British Desert Column emerge victorious that day,' Stanley told the girls. 'Probably just as well, though. They arrived two days too late to stop our brave general, and the garrison, from being massacred.'

Flossie shivered at the thought of young Albert dying out there in the African desert. Losing a life to illness or poverty on their own doorstep was somehow understandable, but to die in battle thousands of miles away was unfathomable.

'If Gladstone hadn't delayed the rescue,' Stanley snarled, 'Albert's death might not have been in vain. Our ma's never got over it.'

Jessie stroked Stanley's arm affectionately, aware that his brother's loss had wounded the Bull family very deeply. For all the pride they felt, there was an equal measure of pain to deal with. Flossie turned away with tears in her eyes, flashes of their childhood adventures evoking memories of scrambling around steep-sided disused chalk pits and sitting on jetty walls watching the clippers unfurling their sails in the sunset as they made their way down the estuary towards the open sea.

At the beginning of June, Flossie, Jess and Kate Bailey managed to get the increasingly frail Annie Devonshire onto a tram. She had been saying for ages that she wanted to witness Gravesend's new clock tower being formally dedicated, so the women were determined to get her there. It was obvious to everyone that this was likely to be Annie's last outing and it was only dogged determination that eventually enabled her to straighten her body and lift her eyes to admire the finished fifty-foot tower in all its Portland stone glory.

It had been two years since the foundation stone had been laid at the top of Harmer Street as part of the Queen's jubilee celebrations. Finally, enough money had been raised to complete the building. Annie clapped as the mayor started the clock just before midday, informing the assembled audience that, come evening, the dials would automatically be lit by gaslight, which would turn itself off again in daylight. It seemed nothing short of miraculous.

Flossie was pleased they had made the effort because Annie went steadily downhill after that. Prolonged humidity dampening lungs already clogged with cement dust proved too much for her. The delightful old lady with whom she had loved spending so much time died peacefully in her favourite chair. St. Botolph's was full of townsfolk whose lives she had touched, and because she had led a long, fulfilling life, her funeral service was reflective rather than sad.

After Annie's favourite hymn, which she called *For Those in Peril on the Sea*, Flossie gave the eulogy. Surprising herself for having the courage to stand at the pulpit, she told the congregation how much she had loved hearing Annie's colourful stories and how they had taught her so much history. She regaled them with humorous anecdotes about the visit to the Grand Exhibition at the glittering Crystal Palace, where Annie was more impressed by the shimmering four-ton pink glass fountain than the famous Koh-i-Noor diamond, which she said didn't sparkle nearly enough. And although she had marvelled at the full-sized trees growing inside the palace and the miles of exhibits of every conceivable invention, it was Northfleet's own Portland cement stand that she was most proud of. The only thing that had really niggled her was Robins paying the entry fee for their workers, yet leaving her to find her own shilling.

After a respectful time at the graveside, the congregation made their way back to the riverside and piled into The Huggens Arms. Raising their glasses to a 'stalwart of The Creek', everyone acknowledged that she would be sorely missed.

Lizzie caught sight of Flossie sitting alone in a corner. 'I know it's an odd time to be telling you this,' she whispered, sidling up to her, 'but you look like a bit of good news might not go amiss.'

Flossie looked at her quizzically.

'Sam and me are expecting again. Due next February, I reckon. We've decided if it's a girl, we're going to call her Florence. After her big sister.'

Overwhelmed, Flossie burst into tears.

'I thought you'd be pleased,' laughed Lizzie, giving her a big hug.

'Of course I am,' Flossie spluttered, reaching for her handkerchief. 'I'm so pleased for you both, especially after losing little Ada. What happens if it's a boy?'

'Well, we'll just have to wait for the next one, then, won't we?'

Perhaps Annie's passing had been the signal for new life to begin, Flossie thought as she clinked her glass against Lizzie's.

As summer progressed, the heady, humid weather, which had encouraged an infestation of greenfly, finally began to improve. By the first day of July, it had become pleasantly warm and dry with glorious sunshine and the river was teeming with all kinds of vessels, many adorned with bunting and flags.

'I'm a lot happier today, girls, make no mistake,' declared Tom Handley as he greeted Flossie and Kate on the shore. 'Not only have all those blasted insects stopped getting up my nose, but I'm back getting five bob a body again!'

Flossie smiled at Tom's obvious delight at the return of his gruesome source of income. Two years earlier, Woolwich

County Magistrates had stopped rewarding watermen for bringing dead bodies out of the Thames. Since then decaying corpses had been floating up and downriver on the tides, the stench overwhelming.

'Mind you, it's only to clean up the river while the Shah's here, but I'm not complaining. In fact I might thank him for doing me a good turn if we see him on deck.'

Waiting until the swell of a passing steamer died down, Tom helped Kate, with Flossie tiptoeing gingerly behind, down the slippery jetty. Discarding her bonnet and stuffing it unceremoniously into her bag, Kate hung on to Flossie for grim death, wobbling dangerously as the two women clambered on board after Tom. With the boat tipping and rolling in the swell, they both collapsed with laughter.

'When you two have quite finished we'll get going, shall we?' the skipper groaned, pushing his cap back and rolling his eyes. 'I thought you wanted to see if he's brought his eighty-four wives with him? Can't see it meself, though. He'd have to have a steamer the size of the *Great Eastern* to hold them all, that's fer sure.'

No longer able to keep a straight face himself, Tom joined the women, who were still chuckling, and, with a quick flick of the mooring rope, pushed off from the jetty and picked up his oars.

'Let's be seein' how close we can get then, eh, girls?'

His Royal Highness, Naser al-Din, Shah of Persia, purported to be travelling en masse with his harem, had anchored at Gravesend. While his forty attendants and baggage were being landed and sent on to Victoria Station, he was welcomed aboard the *Duke of Edinburgh* by the Prince of Wales. From there the royal party was scheduled to make its way, amid pomp and ceremony, slowly upriver to the Speaker's Stairs at Westminster. His Majesty's final destination was to be Buckingham Palace, where a suite of rooms had been placed at his disposal, at his own request.

With barely a few feet between the multitude of vessels crowding the water, Flossie began to wish she hadn't been quite so keen to catch a glimpse of the numerous wives of Naser al-Din. There were so many boats that it soon became clear they were in danger of collision. Tom made the sensible decision to turn back, seeking safety at the shoreline, much to Flossie and Kate's relief. As they watched the huge masts of the prince's paddle steamer pass them by, Flossie pointed to two figures on the deck. One was clearly the Prince of Wales, wearing a tricorn hat topped with white plumage; the other, the Shah, his emerald-encrusted fez glittering in the sunlight.

A flotilla of smaller boats containing dignitaries followed close behind, amongst which Flossie spotted Bevan's *Spry*, its brown sails flapping gently in the breeze. Mrs Knight and her daughter could be seen standing proudly on deck in all their finery. Having spent all morning helping Miss Elizabeth prepare her wardrobe for the event, Flossie was thrilled to see that the off-white crêpe de Chine dress matched perfectly with her turban hat, decorated with lilies of the valley. The flat iron had certainly been put to good use that morning, and Flossie's reward was the afternoon off in illustrious company. Whether Elizabeth actually saw her waving as Tom tried to steady the boat by Baltic Wharf, Flossie wasn't sure, though she liked to think she did.

The following day the newspapers confirmed that the Shah's eighty-four wives had remained at home.

'Just as well we didn't get any closer, then,' Kate laughed as she folded her washing. 'Being in a harem isn't all it's cracked up to be, you know. Seems that when he congratulated Mr Gladstone on his golden wedding, the Shah said, "It's better to live with one wife for fifty years than fifty wives for one year!"'

After that, every time Flossie looked up at the London Portland Cement chimney shaft, hastily finished during His Majesty's visit, she had to smile knowing that its nickname, 'the

Shah's hat', came about because the top had been fashioned to look like his fez.

As the heat of the summer intensified, fields and gardens wilted under the power of the scorching sun. The water company turned off their hydrants for a fortnight, with the result that road-watering was curtailed. The still air led to a dense cloud of smoke hanging over Northfleet, affecting people's health. Emotions were already running high amongst those living and working on the River Thames due to the low pay, dangerous dock work and the wretched housing conditions that dockers and their families were being forced to accept. There were fears that all this was causing unrest in the Port of London, and right down to Tilbury.

Social reformer Charles Booth's ongoing research into pauperism in the East End had already showed that at least a third of all families were living in abject poverty. The threat of social unrest frightened politicians. Companies dependent on mass labour feared loss of profits through strikes. It had always been the case that dock companies took on labourers only when they needed them, much of their trade being seasonal. Sugar came from the West Indies, timber from Scandinavia and the Americas, tea and spices from the Far East. It was hard to predict when ships would arrive, and there was often little notice given to dock workers. As the loading and discharging of cargo was highly labour-intensive, demand for men consequently varied from day to day. Employers needed a surplus of men who were always available for work, yet didn't want to pay them when there wasn't any. Most workers in the docks were casual labourers taken on for the day; sometimes only for a few hours. Twice a day there'd be a 'call-on' at each of the docks when labour was hired for short periods. Only the lucky few would be selected. The rest would be sent home without payment.

The success of the matchgirls' strike the previous year had encouraged unskilled workers to form unions and fight for better conditions. In March, the gas workers at Beckton had won an eight-hour day. Now it was the turn of the dockers. On 14th August the men of the West India Dock struck and immediately called for their fellow dockers to join them. A strike committee was formed to handle the dispute, the aim being to demand the docker's tanner – a wage of sixpence an hour and an overtime rate of eight pence an hour – and 'call-ons' reduced to two a day. Men were to be taken on for minimum periods of four hours and the new National Union of Dock Labourers recognised throughout the port.

With no funds, help came when the Amalgamated Stevedores Union joined the strike. Not only did they carry weight, but their work was essential to the running of the docks. As more and more workers joined the strike, the Port of London became paralysed.

'Lightermen and bargemen are out,' Sam told Lizzie and Floss on his return from The Huggens. 'Looks like they want *us* to come out now. There's notices pinned up outside all the cement works, and the ironworks too.'

'But Sam…' Lizzie shot her husband a look of desperation. With three children and another on the way, to have no pay was unthinkable.

'I know, I know. I'm not going to, not yet anyway.'

It was a half-hearted denial and it worried Lizzie immensely.

By the end of the second week, the strike committee was organising mass meetings and had established pickets outside the dock gates. Any men still working were branded 'blacklegs' and faced intimidation if they didn't show support for the cause.

'Only a matter of time now, dearest Lizzie,' Sam warned. 'There's fights breaking out all over the place. Men howling like banshees going from factory to factory, threatening vengeance if we don't join them.'

'But how will we feed our bairns?' pleaded Lizzie. 'The dockers have been getting shilling food tickets, but there's so many on strike now I've heard there's many families starving.'

It was an awful prospect. Flossie was only too aware that her meagre wage wouldn't put enough food on the table for all of them. Up until now she was all for supporting anyone who was trying to improve their lives, but now that the strike was spreading to the cement factories and seemed likely to affect everyone she knew and loved, it was difficult not to wish that it would stay squarely on the other side of the river.

At Northfleet House, Flossie avoided catching the eye of Mrs Knight. She'd overheard snatches of conversations in the drawing room which left her in no doubt as to her opinion of the 130,000 who were now on strike. Trying to keep her emotions in tight check, Flossie spent more time below stairs, out of harm's way. On 26th August, before heading home, she caught sight of the butler's *Evening News and Post* and read:

Dockmen, lightermen, bargemen, cement workers, carmen, ironworkers and even factory girls are coming out. If it goes on a few days longer, all London will be on holiday. The great machine by which five millions of people are fed and clothed will come to a dead stop, and what is to be at the end of it all? The proverbial small spark has kindled a great fire which threatens to envelop the whole metropolis.

Shutting the servants' door, Flossie heard a commotion as she climbed the steps onto the High Street. It was dusk but everyone seemed to be out of their houses, crowding the pavement. Anxious women, huddling in doorways, pushed their prams back and forth, too preoccupied to care that their older children were running amok. Outside The Little Wonder a scuffle had broken out between several inebriated cement workers. It soon became clear that the factories had finally come out in support of the dockers. They had downed tools at three o'clock and headed straight for the alehouses.

Flossie found the journey home slow going and somewhat intimidating. At the top of Samaritan Grove, a crowd had formed. A young man, standing on a soapbox, was addressing them in an impassioned manner. Not wishing to soil her shoes by stepping off the pavement onto the rag stone and flint road surface which was constantly being churned up by the iron wheels of heavy wagons, she decided to wait until enough people lost interest in the speaker to allow her through. From the back, she couldn't see past the sea of caps and bonnets, but something about the man's voice made her want to listen.

'We are driven into a shed, iron-barred from end to end, outside of which a foreman walks up and down with the air of a dealer in a cattle market,' the animated speaker said. 'He picks and chooses from a crowd of men, who, in their eagerness to obtain employment, trample each other underfoot, and where, like beasts, they fight for the chances of a day's work.'

The more he spoke, the more silent the crowd became, hanging on his every word. He seemed to have them in the palm of his hand, ending with a rallying cry for action: 'Friends and fellow workmen, stand firm with us. To earn a decent wage for a decent day's work is all we are asking.'

The audience, including Flossie, burst into spontaneous applause. Desperate to catch sight of this inspiring activist, she squeezed through several rows of people to the front to find herself looking at a tall man, about her age, with soft blue eyes. She laughed as he took a rolled-up cap out of his pocket, plonked it on a mass of unruly blond hair and then pretended to produce a farthing or two from behind the ears of the children who had been sitting there bored. Squeals of laughter followed as some of them tried to copy his antics.

There was something about his presence that she found

immediately captivating. As she continued watching him perform magic tricks for his young audience, it slowly dawned on her who he was.

This charismatic campaigner was none other than Henry Luck.

17

Averting her eyes, Flossie rushed away, desperately hoping she hadn't been recognised. It seemed impossible to believe that the boastful little jester who had so irritated her all those years ago had grown into such an impressive young man. Two evenings later she was back in the High Street, hoping to catch sight of him again. Try as she might, she couldn't get him out of her head.

Hearing a loud commotion outside The Coopers Arms, she approached cautiously and smiled on seeing a mop of blond hair protruding above the crowd. Working her way to the front, she was soon mesmerised by his oratory.

'Ben Tillett, our leader,' Henry Luck told his audience, 'reckons the dock companies are losing money hand over fist, but they say giving in would set a dangerous precedent. They think we'll be defeated through hunger. But, fellow workers, we have to stand firm. The strike *will* continue, trust me. Money has started to pour in from our comrades in Australia and us dockers scent victory.'

Thirty thousand pounds had been raised by Australian dockers and their allies. It arrived at just the right time; ending fears that the strikers and their families would be forced to go without food. Now they were able to sustain a longer strike, the picket lines had been strengthened. On 5th September, the Lord Mayor of London intervened to bring the two sides together, and within two weeks the strike was over. Almost all the strikers' demands had been met. It was an exciting time for the union movement. As a result, twenty thousand Londoners joined the new General Labourers' Union. When Ben Tillett was elected General Secretary, he wasted no time in recruiting the ardent young activist, Henry Luck, to work alongside him.

Flossie watched as Henry stepped down from his soapbox amid applause and started shaking hands with the people just to the left of her. Suddenly it was her turn. With no chance to escape, she braced herself for his handshake. He recognised her instantly.

'Flossie Grant... it really *is* you. I thought I caught sight of you the other day.' His quizzical gaze made her blush.

'Hello, Henry. Yes, it was me,' she stammered, embarrassed at finding herself so unguarded.

'It's truly wonderful to see you again,' he said, still holding her hand. She looked up into his smiling eyes, her cheeks reddening even more.

'I was impressed by your speech,' she muttered.

'You know me, Floss, I've never been afraid of giving people the benefit of my opinion.'

They both laughed and he winked at her before being swamped by other onlookers, eager to congratulate him. Then he was gone.

Squeezing through a gap, she headed for home, her head in a whirl. He had held on to her hand. He never averted his gaze the entire time they were together. The grown-up Henry Luck was so different to the bumptious boy she remembered. Her heart was in a flutter, but whatever she did now, it was important not to appear forward. She must seek him out no more.

'Oh, Jess, he *can't* be interested in me. It's been three weeks, and not a word,' Flossie stuttered as her friend joined her on their seat outside The Elephant's Head. It was milking time at Johnson's dairy farm opposite and it was hard to be heard.

'No,' Jess shouted, putting an arm around Flossie's shoulders, 'that's not it. Stanley says he's left Tilbury docks and gone to London. He was on the ferry. Talked about how he's on a "campaign trail" to get every docker to join the union while the strike is still fresh in their minds.'

The look on Flossie's face was a mixture of elation and dejection. He'd left on a mission, so maybe he just hadn't had time…?

Jessie frowned. 'I'm sorry, Floss. I know you see him in a different light now, but he still sounds like a show-off to me.'

Flossie had to restrain herself from jumping to Henry's defence. If Jess had seen his inspired oration she might not be so quick to judge. Oh well, she comforted herself, at least there was a good reason why he hadn't come looking for her. Lizzie would be relieved too; it was tiring work having to tidy up every time the door knocker went.

It was the first time in Flossie's life that she had felt like this. Taken by surprise at the strength of her feelings for Henry, she felt exasperated over his going before she'd had time to get to know him better. Worse still, she now found it difficult to watch Jess and Stanley embrace. Envy, she had always been taught, was unchristian, yet now she was consumed by it.

One morning a postcard dropped onto the doormat at Northfleet House. For a second Flossie imagined it was from Henry, but she knew it couldn't be. He didn't know where she worked, and anyway, he was gone and had probably forgotten her by now. Sighing, she picked up the card and looked to see to whom it was addressed.

Miss Elizabeth had travelled with an aunt to watch the

closing ceremony of the Exposition Universelle in Paris, and the picture on her card showed the entrance to the fair with well-dressed people passing under a strangely beautiful metal arch. Sneaking a peek at the hastily written message, Flossie was amazed to see that it had been despatched from the top of the Tour Eiffel – *an extraordinary metal structure rising 984 feet into the sky, with a post office at the top!* Having paid five francs for an exhilarating ride in an open 'lift' all the way up, the young lady was overcome by the experience. *It is truly a thing of wonder*, she wrote, *especially at night, when it is lit up by hundreds of gas lamps!*

How Flossie wished she could have been there to witness the spectacle. To holiday in another country sounded so exciting, but was not something a person in her position was likely to do. A day at the seaside on a cement works outing was the nearest she was likely to get to going anywhere exotic!

As 1889 drew to a close with another harsh winter underway, Mrs Knight broke the news that she and her daughter were going to live in London. Northfleet House was simply too big and draughty. Flossie thought it had more to do with finding the young Elizabeth a suitable husband, and imagined that there would be no place for an inexperienced lady's maid in sophisticated London society. She soon perked up, however, when it became clear that they wanted her to go with them, and it took no time at all for Flossie to accept the offer. After all, a diversion to occupy the mind was what everyone was saying she needed.

'Oh, Floss, does that mean we are to be parted again?' Jessie sighed.

'I'll not be far away, and besides, you have Stanley now.'

'You *will* be able to come back for the wedding, won't you? You're my bridesmaid, after all.'

'Of course I will. Besides, I will get more free time, seeing as I'll be living in now.'

'It's going to be such a glorious day. I fear my heart will burst.'

'I wouldn't miss it for the world,' Flossie said, kissing her dearest friend on the cheek.

Flossie waited until after the New Year celebrations to tell everyone she was moving. Sam and Lizzie appeared disappointed, yet she felt they were secretly relieved. Their new baby was due soon and now that Sam's earnings had improved, thanks to the union, they no longer relied so heavily on Flossie's rent money. The children could have their own room.

'You know there'll always be somewhere for you here,' Kate Bailey whispered as she hugged Flossie on her doorstep. 'It seems to be that every time Sam and Lizzie have another bairn, one of mine grows up and leaves home!'

'I know.' Flossie nodded, holding back the tears. 'You've been more of a mother to me than my real one, that's for sure.'

They held each other for what seemed like forever.

'That reminds me,' Kate said, wiping her eyes on her ample apron. 'Have you heard from her of late?'

'No. Nor do I wish to. She's inclined to write to Lottie when she's desperate for money, that's all I know.'

'That's no surprise. Good riddance, I say,' Kate said, shrugging her shoulders.

Flossie didn't think it possible that the winter fog in London could be worse than it was in Northfleet, but it was. Sulphur-laden smoke from tens of thousands of domestic coal fires and factory chimneys clogged the atmosphere, turning yellow, green and brown in the process. The newspapers coined them 'pea-soupers'. Medical experts began to realise that they were responsible for the increasing number of deaths from bronchitis. Even animals suffered. A number of prize cattle at Smithfield choked to death during a particularly dense and suffocating bout that lasted a week.

Much to Flossie's annoyance, the polluted air seeped into their new Kensington home through the doors and windows, coating furniture and clothes with an oily, gritty smut which was the Devil to keep clean. Even the aspidistra on its jardinière withered.

Not being able to see your own feet through the impenetrable filth made getting lost, or being run over by a cart, a genuine hazard. The trusted linklighter urchin who huddled in the porch of 54 Stanhope Gardens was made good use of. Boys such as him earned a few coppers carrying flaming torches to lead people through the darkened streets, though the less honest ones led others down alleyways to be robbed. Flossie made sure she always tipped him after he'd guided her to the post office safely. There were always letters and parcels to post and, besides, writing was the best thing to do on your day off when the sun never seemed to rise. Lottie's letters, in particular, always demanded a swift reply.

16th March 1890

Dearest Flossie,

Goodness, how you have played with my emotions! I have laughed and cried in equal measures reading your last letter. Cement dust in The Crick was bad enough, but the goings-on in 'The Smoke', as you call London, sound dreadful.

Frivolity aside, I must address the sad news of Sam and Lizzie's lost baby. I can only imagine how tragic a stillbirth must be, and all this coming so soon after the death of tiny Ada Eliza. It is truly heart breaking. I also read with sorrow your account of the death of old Annie Devonshire, and that of Albert Bull. Annie was often sitting on the jetty watching the ships as we children, including the reliable Albert, played on the beach below.

On to happier matters... How thrilling that romance is in the air. I couldn't put your letter down until I had read it thrice over for fear of missing anything. So Jess is in love with Stanley Bull, and you, dearest sister, have feelings for Henry Luck. Can this really be after all you said about him when we were children?! I tease you, of course. He certainly sounds like a very different character now. In truth, I felt your frustration when I read that your hopes appeared to have been dashed so quickly. May you be reacquainted with him again soon – perhaps at Jess and Stanley's wedding in May? I would love to imagine you being there together on such a perfect occasion, and I can't wait to hear about what you will all be wearing, what colour was chosen for the bouquets and garlands at the church... Oh, how romantic!

Now to bring us back to earth with a bump. I feel I must impart the latest news I have regarding our mother. Brace yourself for this, my darling. She is once again in Ipswich. Henry Oxer took her back, but only on the condition that she left her child behind. Naturally, we only have her word for that. It is to be assumed that young William George Allen is now in the care of the authorities in Wisbech. Sad that this may be, you and I both know that it's probably the best place for him.

Finally, on to my own unsettling news... My Andrew will have been a Mountie for three years this summer and must decide soon if he wishes to sign up again. There has been civil unrest here in Manitoba and my beloved has been on call for much of the time. It's all to do with the large numbers of immigrants that have moved here from Ontario. The majority of people are now Protestant and resent public funding for the Catholic schools. In their wisdom, the province has passed an Act to create a

*single, non-denominational school system in English only.
Obviously the Catholics are far from happy, and everyone
is wondering whether French will survive as a language
and a culture in Western Canada.*

*All this brings me back to Andrew. As a Catholic
himself he is feeling quite anxious and thinks that we should
move out of the province and start afresh somewhere else.
I shouldn't be getting your hopes up, but I cannot keep
it to myself – we have even pondered whether to move
back to Scotland. Andrew does so miss his family in the
Highlands, as I do you, but I will have to accept whatever
decision my betrothed comes to. Knowing my previously
fickle nature, I am sure you are surprised that my feelings
have remained steadfast. In fact, sister dear, I love him as
much now as I did when we first met.*
*I cannot wait to hear more details of Jessie's wedding, so
please write again soon.*
All my love,
Lottie

As she opened her eyes early one morning, Flossie momentarily
wondered where she was. The sun streaming through the
threadbare curtains quickly brought her to her senses. Shaking
her arm to ward off pins and needles, she realised that the body
next to her had been lying on it, and was still fast asleep. Not
having the heart to disturb the bride-to-be on the morning
of her wedding, Flossie sat up and looked around the room,
wondering if today might be the day she was going to see
Henry Luck again. It seemed like forever since he had held her
hand.

'Pinch me,' Jess said quietly, stretching as she did so. 'Am I
really getting married?'

'Yes,' Flossie whispered into her ear. 'Saturday, 3rd May – the
day you are to become Mrs Stanley Bull.'

Jessie shrieked as she felt her arm being pinched and both girls fell back in a fit of giggles.

William Bailey was waiting patiently outside 7 The Creek with the beautifully groomed Dobbin as Kate festooned his cart with evergreens and blossom. Meanwhile, Jessie's older brother, James Larkin, paced up and down the aisle of St. Botolph's, twisting the white rosette pinned to his left lapel, determined to undertake his usher's duties seriously.

Jessie looked beautiful; her white satin bodice pulled in at the waist and long gathered skirt falling naturally over her hips. 'You look lovely too,' she said, adjusting her bridesmaid's headdress. A ring of flowers, with ribbons hanging delicately from them, framed Flossie's face. 'Thank you for this,' Jess said, smiling as she folded the handkerchief Flossie had given her with her new initials embroidered on it in blue thread. 'I'll tuck it up my sleeve for when I shed a tear.'

'Something old, something new, something borrowed, something blue and a lucky sixpence in your shoe,' Flossie chanted as she lifted Jessie's lace veil before letting it fall over her face.

With one final glance in the mirror, they held hands and carefully descended the perilous stairs in their matching delicate silk shoes. Jane Larkin lovingly handed her daughter a bouquet of sweet-smelling orange blossom and opened the front door.

St. Botolph's bells pealed forth as Dobbin made his way slowly along The Creek and onto Lawn Road. Being uphill most of the way, George Larkin, father of the bride, took pity on the old horse and walked alongside William Bailey. Children jumped over the wall from the chalk pit where they had been playing and followed the cart. Flossie spotted Joe Ollerenshaw's brood amongst the array of dirty faces and waved at them. As they neared Sam and Lizzie's house, Henrietta Gant, flower girl extraordinaire, waited proudly on the doorstep looking as pretty as a picture with her hair in ringlets and pink muslin dress adorned with matching ribbon sash and rose petals. William whisked her up and placed her effortlessly alongside Jessie.

Emerging from the house, Henrietta's two small brothers rushed over to Dobbin and offered up a carrot. Quick as a flash Lizzie appeared, swooping one of them up under each arm. This was not the day for her sons to soil their Sunday best in the muddy gutter. Sam then appeared, carrying Lizzie's bonnet and the boys' caps. Making the finishing touches to their outfits, the Gant family fell in line with the others to follow the cart up to the church. Flossie smiled, thinking how lovely it was that they were all together on such an auspicious occasion.

A hushed silence greeted the bride as she hovered in the arched doorway of St. Botolph's. Once Floss was sure that Jess was completely ready, Henrietta set off bravely down the aisle, dropping petals as she did so. Jess followed, holding on to her father's sturdy arm, followed by Flossie who, as protocol decreed, stared straight ahead, though secretly hoping that somewhere from within the confines of the old church Henry Luck was watching her.

And he was. In fact, he couldn't take his eyes off her. The ceremony seemed to take forever, and the signing of the register even longer. Finally, the wedding party emerged from the vestry and made their way back down the aisle and out into the sunlight. A huge cheer greeted the bride and groom, who laughed happily as they were showered with rice and rose petals.

Standing back, her task accomplished, Flossie cast her eyes around the assembled guests. Through a gap, she caught sight of the man who had been filling her dreams for what seemed like an age. He was leaning against a gravestone with arms folded and a huge grin on his face. Without a thought for her silk shoes, she raised the hem of her gown, stepped onto the mossy grass and walked slowly towards him.

'You look truly beautiful, Florence Grant,' Henry said, taking her hand in his. She blushed at the compliment and they both smiled, knowing that he had deliberately used her childhood surname.

'At least you remember me, Henry Luck,' she said, teasing him with her eyes.

'How could I ever forget *you*, Flossie?'

'Well, you're such a busy man these days…'

Realising that what he was about to say only confirmed that judgement of him, he took hold of both of her hands.

'I'm so glad you came over, I wanted to have you to myself for a few minutes. You see, I'm afraid I cannot stay for the wedding breakfast.'

Flossie's heart sank. The initial euphoria on seeing him suddenly drained away. She looked down and gently withdrew her hands from his.

'It is wonderful to see you again, Henry. I hoped that you would be able to come. It must be difficult with such a demanding job.'

'That's just it,' he replied awkwardly. 'I have to get back to London. There's a May Day procession tomorrow and we're expecting a quarter of a million trade unionists marching to Hyde Park. I'm in the thick of it all, I'm afraid.'

The look of disappointment on Flossie's face was obvious. Henry pursed his lips, knowing that he had handled the situation badly.

'The problem is, you see, Floss, union membership has doubled in this year alone. There are over two million of us now and this march is an opportunity for us to show our solidarity. If it all goes to plan, it'll happen every year.'

Flossie sensed his discomfort, but found herself unable to say anything, which only made the situation worse.

'I felt I had to come and see Stanley and Jessie get married…
for Albert's sake, you understand,' he stammered, taking his cap
out of his pocket and thrusting it on top of his dishevelled hair.

'Of course,' Flossie said quietly. 'I understand.'

'Truth is,' he blurted out suddenly as she started to turn
away, 'I haven't been able to stop thinking about you since our
all-too-brief reacquaintance… and I really wanted to see you
again. I hope you don't object to my forwardness.'

Turning back to face him, she placed a hand on his arm. 'Oh,
Henry, of course not. I was so hoping you would be here. I'm just
sorry you have to leave so soon.'

Relieved, he took both of her hands in his and pulled her
towards him. She closed her eyes as she felt him plant a gentle
kiss on her cheek.

'May I have your permission to call on you then, Miss Grant?
Stanhope Gardens, isn't it? Tradesman's entrance, no doubt…'

Flossie looked up, surprised, and nodded, delighted to still
be in his embrace.

'I promise not to bleat on about the unions next time,' he
laughed, releasing her slowly from his grasp. Winning a tussle
with his pocket watch, he realised that time was now of the
essence. 'Goodness,' he exclaimed, 'it has to be right now if I am
to catch my train.'

With a frantic wave to alert Stanley and Jessie to his
imminent departure, he blew Flossie a kiss and was gone.

Flossie walked slowly back to the wedding party, elated that
Henry had gone to the effort of finding out her address. She
didn't dare think about the kiss. That had to be saved for later,
and besides, Jess and Stanley were about to depart.

The rug from the Larkins' front room was just being laid outside
as the cavalcade of wedding guests made their way along the
High Street a few steps behind the cart. A revived Dobbin
confidently pulled the newly married couple back to The Creek.

The Bailey boys had rounded up two dozen or more assorted kitchen chairs from their neighbours, with a couple of doors placed end to end and covered with Sunday-best sheets, which served as an excellent table.

By the time Jess and Stanley Bull were ready for their wedding breakfast, the women had transformed what few provisions they could muster into a veritable feast. A barrel of ale donated by Robert Scott of The Huggens Arms helped oil the men's throats for their speeches and Sylvester Lee pitched up with his barrel organ to jolly things up. Someone piped a sailor's farewell on a tin whistle as the bride and groom slipped away to the privacy of their own bedroom at the Bull residence in Dock Row – Albert's old room, in fact.

It had been a day neither Jess nor Floss would forget in a hurry.

18

'What race did you say Henry was rowing in?' Lizzie asked Flossie as they struggled to keep hold of the children after paying the sixpenny entry fee to the Terrace Pier and Gardens.

The sheer number of people cramming through the gate was alarming. Flossie had had visions of them sitting on one of the many seats along the promenade where you could get uninterrupted views of the river, but it was no use today. Every seat was already taken. The Gravesend Amateur Rowing Club regatta was a red-letter day on everyone's calendar, and Flossie had an extra-special reason for making it her destination on her afternoon off.

Deciding this was not the moment to answer Lizzie's question, she took charge and battled through the crowds of revellers more intent on hugging the beer stalls than watching the early heats. Eventually – and miraculously without losing a child – they made it to an ice-cream cart pitched near the front. With barely a cloud in the sky, the early September sun was fierce. Flossie tipped Henrietta's bonnet forward to protect her eyes from the intense glare reflecting off the water whilst watching Samuel George, penny in hand, heading towards a boy of similar age selling official programmes.

Lizzie, meanwhile, surveyed the sedate lawn of the Clarendon Royal Hotel, reserved for the exclusive use of subscribers, where corseted ladies in fine hats were peering through binoculars over the heads of the riff-raff to the finishing line below.

'I can see the mayoress' chains glinting in the sun,' she laughed. 'Don't envy her having to wear *them* all day. She'll need some horse liniment for an aching neck tomorrow.'

Flossie smiled, but her own eyes were firmly fixed on the river. Countless boats, overloaded with passengers, had taken up position along the course. Studying the timetable, she realised they had already missed the Fishermen's Scullers Race (first prize: a case of Sunlight soap), but were just in time for Walking the Greasy Bowsprit at twenty past three.

The children laughed hysterically as one barefooted man after another slithered no more than a few inches along a greasy pole before sliding off into the water. Climbing back again, each continued the hopeless pursuit until one was finally declared a sodden winner, with another, a well-deserving runner-up. (First prize: a pig; second prize: a leg of mutton.)

No sooner had the hilarity died down than a display of daytime fireworks filled the sky – much to Alfred's dismay. It was the first time the four-year-old had witnessed pyrotechnics, and only the promise of an immediate penny lick seemed likely to placate him.

The more serious events got underway just before 4 o'clock with a Training Ship Boys Race (first prize: two pounds and ten shillings), and a Four-Oared Amateur Race (first prize: five pounds and five shillings; second: five silver pencil cases; third: five silver-mounted briar pipes).

Then at a quarter past five came the race Flossie was waiting for – the Pair-Oared Amateur Race, rowed on the ebb tide. Having won his earlier heat, Henry was about to row in the final. As the white flag was hoisted on the committee boat, Flossie knew she had little time to squeeze to the front of the crowd before the start. Leaving her family behind, she weaved her way forward, realising that the perfect vantage point would be on the beach. Several men had already breached the barrier, but she was to be the first woman. Grateful for years of practice in The Creek, she lifted her skirts and, casting care aside, made her way expertly across pebbles, seaweed, tar and broken glass to the water's edge. With the finishing line now in view, she barely had time to catch her breath before the starting gun boomed across the water from the Clifton Baths Club House.

Everyone peered into the distance, trying to catch their first glimpse of the sweep boats as they rounded Terrace Pier and then yelling encouragement as soon as they did so. Flossie watched in amazement at how two rowers, each working one oar, could make their small boats appear so totally at home on the heaving river. As the pair in the lead rounded the east flag and emerged from the shadows, Henry's mop of yellow hair shone in the light and his stroke-side reflection danced artfully on the water. Flossie could barely contain her heart's thumping as she observed him in mid-drive, legs pushing, arms extended in the power part of the stroke. He and his upright partner, both strong men, were perfectly harmonious and in time. It seemed they were sure to win, but the second boat was closing in and as they headed for the upper yacht buoy, the exactness of its rowers placed it smoothly and expertly in the lead.

Trailing for what seemed like an age, Henry's dogged determination finally came into play. His chest swelled as he began to dig deeper, encouraging his partner to do the same. The boats were neck and neck right up to the finish. Flossie screamed till she was hoarse and then cried with delight as the bow of Henry's boat passed the finishing line first – by a whisker. As the winning colours were hoisted on the committee boat, the victor, dripping with sweat, headed across the beach. Grabbing Flossie round the waist and spinning her round until her bonnet fell down her back; he squeezed her tightly and planted a kiss on her cheek.

It had been four months since Jess and Stanley's wedding. Union business had kept Henry very busy, but he made sure he took every opportunity to walk out with Flossie on her precious free afternoons. They had talked and laughed, held hands and secretly kissed. Flossie had no doubts about her feelings. Henry Luck was the man for her.

Now, standing next to him as the final of the Free Waterman's Race started, she found it impossible to concentrate. Racing in old-fashioned wager boats, each competitor knew the stakes were high and no one wanted to come second, particularly as the first prize was a pristine boat. Henry jumped up and down frantically, yelling, and when, suddenly, the cheering erupted into tumultuous applause, Flossie realised that she hadn't even noticed who had won.

'J. Jennings,' shouted Henry. 'Good for him. He'll be set up for life with that boat.'

Flossie looked up at him and smiled at his boyish enthusiasm.

With all the events over, it was time for the prize-giving. As the band of the Queen's Westminster Rifles heralded the arrival of the Countess of Darnley, Henry made his way to the Clarendon Hotel's beautifully illuminated lawn while Flossie wended her way back to Lizzie.

Old Tom Handley got a special cheer from the children as he collected his prize for coming second in the Veteran Scullers Race. Lizzie wondered what use he'd make of the cruet that was placed in his huge hands, but reckoned he'd find the 15cwt of coals useful. Soon it was Henry's turn. He stepped forward to receive his prize of a set of binocular glasses, then, after thanking the Countess, turned to the applauding audience and gave a short, theatrical bow. The mischievous glint in his eye was not lost on Flossie.

It was getting late. Lizzie made for home, leaving Henry and Flossie holding hands in the dark during the magnificent display of aquatic fireworks that sparkled and shimmered across the River Thames, transforming it into quite the most magical place.

Walking back through the Fort Gardens, Henry pulled Flossie up the steps of the new bandstand and out of view. As he kissed her passionately, she felt her legs giving way under her.

On 5th November, a telegram from Lottie in Toronto arrived at Stanhope Gardens. Its contents threw Flossie into turmoil. No matter how many times she reread the dozen or so words, she could barely believe what it was saying.

No time to write.
Leave Quebec November 8th on S/S Parisian.
Arrive Liverpool 16th via Londonderry.
Will go to Crick.
Lottie and Andrew McPherson.

Concentrating on Elizabeth Knight's list of chores was almost impossible for the rest of the day, and it was a relief when seven o'clock arrived. Henry had planned for them to celebrate Bonfire Night on Hampstead Heath, and whilst Flossie knew that the event was likely to be spirited, she looked forward to telling him her news.

Meeting at South Kensington, the couple crammed onto an already packed tram. Guy Fawkes Day attracted many thousands of people from all over the metropolis and everyone was out for a good evening. Competing against numerous loud voices, Henry just about got the gist of the telegram's revelation. He was amused by Flossie's undeniable excitement, her cheeks flushing as she gabbled ten to the dozen. Unable to get a word in edgeways, he finally signalled to her that they had reached their stop at The Hare and Hounds Hotel.

On leaving the confined safety of the tram, they quickly found themselves in the middle of a large gang freely discharging firecrackers in the street. People were piling out of the many alehouses to await the procession, most the worst for drink. Henry held on to Flossie's hand tightly as he found a place for them to stand away from carts pulled by boys bearing elaborate 'guys'.

At nine o'clock torchbearers arrived in a blaze of red and green fire, followed by a masquerade of characters including court minstrels, clowns, Spanish cavaliers and brigands. A brass band heralded the arrival of Britannia, behind which everyone surged onto the Heath where an immense fire lit the sky. Bonfire boys clad in every conceivable disguise promenaded with tar barrels before hurling them onto the fire. A great cheer went up as the effigies of Guy Fawkes burnt ferociously.

As the crowd began to drift away, Flossie took advantage of the glow from the embers to show Henry her telegram.

'I will have to make a trip home on Sunday to inform every one of their arrival,' she declared.

'But that's only a week away,' Lizzie said, trying her hardest to think where her guests would sleep.

'Our little Lottie, married,' Kate sighed. 'I long to hear all the details.'

Sam remained silent. With so little information he was inclined to wait until he saw the couple before making any judgement.

'I think she's grown into a sensible young woman,' Flossie whispered, sensing his unease with all the enthusiasm. 'I share your concerns, but I cannot fault the way she has remained true to Andrew these past three years.'

'I hope you are right, my dearest Floss, but I'll reserve judgement until I have seen her for myself,' Sam replied, unconvinced. 'Meanwhile, I'm off to watch our football team.'

Heading off along Stonebridge Road, away from the excited women for a couple of hours, the thought of spending time at the newly formed Northfleet United Club was just what he needed. Not daring to air his suspicions, he feared more than anything that Lottie would be like her mother, having picked a wrong 'un and now looking for money. That, he knew, would break Flossie's heart.

It was only fair, Andrew thought, seeing as they were to spend their married life together in the Highlands, that his new wife should have her way now. So no sooner had they disembarked from their ship than they travelled straight to Northfleet. Cold and tired, Andrew had let Lottie talk non-stop about 'The Crick', but now, standing on the pavement outside Kate Bailey's terraced cottage, he was somewhat bemused as to what had made her so determined. The street looked dismal to him: small dwellings covered in grime and full of runny-nosed children sitting on doorsteps, despite it getting dark. Struggling with their luggage from the station, the surrounding terrain was nothing like he had ever encountered before: massive chalk rocks that had been extensively quarried, leaving huge pits and perilous cliffs; cement factory after cement factory lining the riverside, emitting ear-piercing noises and dust that was already filling his lungs and boots. It was a far cry from the wilderness he was used to in both Manitoba and Scotland.

Kate was expecting the knock on her front door. It was only natural, she thought, that Lottie would come to her first. With tears in her eyes, she beckoned them into her warm and welcoming home.

Once they had some hot food inside them, Andrew soon revived and they all talked well into the night. Reminiscing about the past and discussing the future, both Kate and Lottie were full of questions. Life in Canada, Andrew's family, Sam and Lizzie, Mary and, of course, Flossie.

Kate warmed to Andrew straight away. 'A respectable, responsible young man and a good match for Lottie,' she revealed to a prying Bessie Turner the next day.

Sam thought so too, which allayed his fears and brought him a great sense of relief. He also saw that the Scotsman was strong-minded, something he would need to be with Lottie. Taken aback by how much she looked like her mother in the early days, he was reminded of why he had found Mary so irresistible. Setting his doubts aside, Sam soon fell under the young woman's spell, finding her enthusiasm and optimism admirable and her acceptance of his own failures humbling.

Watching Lottie playing with the children, Lizzie was less enraptured. She was grateful that Kate had offered the newly married couple her front room. It had been easy to accept Flossie back into her family; she was so unlike her mother. But Lottie's similarity was far harder to swallow, bringing back too many painful memories. Looking at herself in the mirror, her body altered by her sixth pregnancy, Lizzie couldn't help feeling jealous of this beautiful young woman who appeared to have stolen Sam's heart just like her mother had. With hormones raging and emotions out of control, she wished Flossie were there to keep Lottie in her place.

'I am returning to university this weekend, Florence,' said Elizabeth Knight. 'There will be no work left here on my account, so I'll speak to my mother to see if she will allow you to have a few days to reacquaint yourself with your sister.'

Flossie tried not to show her excitement. Hannah Knight did not share her daughter's compassion and had little interest in her staff. Miss Elizabeth often talked to Flossie. She knew all about the girls being abandoned at a home for destitute children, and Lottie's transportation to Canada. Flossie occasionally wondered if her interest was more to do with studying the lower classes than genuine concern for them, but she tried not to be churlish. Despite being the same age and having been brought up within yards of each other, there was precious little similarity between Elizabeth's experiences at Hive House, with its ten bedrooms, and Flossie's two-up, two-down in The Creek. John Knight may have been dead ten years, but his widow and daughter never wanted for anything. Elizabeth was intelligent enough to know that they owed their great fortune to the hard toil of those he employed in his cement factory.

Fortunately for Flossie, Miss Knight was also a determined young lady and could be very forceful. She convinced her mother to allow her maid a week off. It was without pay, of course, but as Elizabeth set off for Cambridge she handed Flossie an envelope. *For expenses*, it said on the outside.

Flossie spent the entire train journey to Northfleet trying to remember the young child she had watched marching out of the mighty gates of Dr Barnardo's. Then Lottie had been a bright-eyed, pretty little thing with golden ringlets, adept at getting her own way. There were times, Flossie had to admit, when her tantrums became insufferable, but mostly she was a loving, happy child who needed her older sister's protection. It all seemed such a long time ago, especially as that child was now a married woman.

As she slammed shut the carriage door, Flossie momentarily thought she was hearing things.

'Floss, Flossie? Are you there?' The voice was unmistakable. Emerging through the billowing smoke and steam, Lottie rushed forward and threw her arms around her sister. The two women hugged until neither could breathe, their tears mingling, the years simply melting away. It was a moment Flossie never dreamt would ever happen.

19

Sam stood and stared up at the stars in the cloudless sky. He'd been sent to the coal bunker to scrape out what he could to keep the fire in Kate and William's grate from going out. Doing up his coat buttons to keep out the cold, he took his time gathering his thoughts before returning. He was glad that the 'reunion meal', as Kate kept calling it, was being held at her house. Lizzie was losing her patience – and her temper – with him the nearer she got to giving birth. It had been out of the question to host any celebration at their house. Nevertheless, he was relieved that Flossie was staying at home with them during her week off as she definitely improved his wife's mood.

What he couldn't fathom was why his daughter was walking out with Henry Luck. Remembering Henry as a young boy, Sam had never understood why the likes of Albert Bull and others seemed to hang on his every word. His bragging used to irritate, especially knowing how he came from Dock Row where the cesspits were always overflowing into the back gardens and people chucked their slops out into the street. The Crick certainly wasn't Paradise, but Dock Row was scarcely fit for habitation. Now, his speeches encouraging the workers to join the union annoyed Sam even more. Protecting workers' rights was an admirable cause, but anything that put the backs of the employers up just led to more job losses, and that wasn't something anyone could afford to take a chance on. The factories were already struggling and the writing was on the wall for some of them. But which ones? The idea that Bevan's might be forced to close didn't bear thinking about.

Shrugging his shoulders, determined not to let such bleak thoughts spoil the evening, Sam carried the ancient coal scuttle back into the scullery. He'd just about come to terms with Lottie being married, so if Flossie was heading the same way, he'd better seem pleased for her. He had to admit it was heartening to see both young women happy, and now that they were together again, everyone's day would be brightened up with their chatter and laughter.

It had been decided that Lottie and Andrew would stay until the day after Boxing Day, after which they would set off for the Highlands of Scotland, arriving, weather permitting, in time for Hogmanay. Kate was overjoyed that her kitchen would be full to bursting yet again. Filled with enthusiasm, she couldn't imagine anything putting a dampener on the occasion.

It was Bessie Turner who spotted her first. Scrubbing the doorstep had given her backache, so she was leaning on the windowsill to rest awhile when an unmistakable woman with wild red hair escaping from a faded red chenille bonnet turned the corner of Grove Road and entered The Creek. Scarcely believing her own eyes, Bessie watched, transfixed, as the woman hesitated slightly before entering The Hope.

Knocking the bucket over in her haste to get inside, Bessie shouted for her husband. 'Jacob! She's back, that Mary Grant! Gone in The Hope. Can you believe it? Better not come knocking on our door.'

'She might, if she thinks Sam still lives here,' Jacob replied, a note of trepidation in his voice.

Full of Dutch courage, Mary Oxer was soon staggering down The Creek. Bessie had been keeping an eye out for her and was scraping dust off her window as Mary rapped the door knocker at Kate Bailey's house next door.

'Fancy you having the nerve to show your face down here again, Mary Grant,' Bessie spat, having had plenty of time to practise her words.

Mary turned, momentarily confused. Before she had time to answer, Kate opened the door and gasped.

'My God, Mary, whatever are *you* doing here?' she said, visibly shocked at how ten years of heavy drinking had taken its toll on her old neighbour.

'I've come to see my daughters,' Mary slurred, slumping against the wall.

Kate pulled the dishevelled woman across her threshold, grabbed a chair and helped her into it. 'I can't say I am pleased to see you, Mary,' she continued, shaking her head. 'It's frankly a good thing that Flossie has gone back to London and is not here to witness this.'

Mary shrugged her shoulders. 'It's my Lottie I've really come for. Back from Canada with a husband, I hear. She'll be pleased to see me.'

Kate stared in amazement. Not only would Lottie *not* like what she saw, but Andrew was hardly likely to be impressed by his new mother-in-law. Nor would they take kindly to being asked for money, which was undoubtedly the real reason for the visit.

Bundling Mary and her tatty belongings into the front room to sleep off the drink, Kate wrapped herself up in a thick shawl and hurried off to the factory gates to catch Sam as he left work. *Forewarned is forearmed*, she thought. Lizzie was close to giving birth and she certainly didn't need such a shock.

'I am sorry that you have been involved in this, Kate,' Sam sighed on being told the news, the colour draining from his face as he contemplated the outcome of Mary's visit. 'I shudder to think what damage she's going to cause, and so close to Christmas too.'

They stared at each other silently as dozens of men jostled past them on their way home from work.

'I reckon I'll need to keep Lizzie and her apart, then?' he said with a sheepish look on his face.

'Don't you go looking to me for approval, Samuel Gant,' Kate responded angrily. 'There's a lot that needs putting right here, and seeing as I *am* involved, you're going to get a piece of my mind whether you want it or not. It's not just your wife you need to feel responsible for, it's those girls who thought you were their father. You should have gone looking for them years ago, whether they be yours or not. But you were too weak and feeble. It was easier to put them out of your mind. You're just lucky that they've both turned out well so you don't have nothing bad on your conscience. But mark my words, Mary's after something and Lottie needs protecting.'

Sam hung his head, knowing she was right. He couldn't make amends for his past failings, but he could be strong now and do what was right. He needed to send Mary packing and be quick about it.

The unwelcome visitor slept until midway through the next morning. No one was in, so she made her way to the scullery with an aching head, telling herself it was the harrowing scenes she'd experienced the day before that had left her so tired and drained. Bending forward to splash water on her face, the hairpins falling into the bowl were a reminder that her mane would need taming before it willingly lay flat under her bonnet.

Ablutions complete, and with the house still empty, Mary searched her pockets and then those of the Baileys' meagre clothing hanging over a chair near the range. Finding a few pennies, there was just enough time to see if there'd been any changes at The Huggens before seeking out her daughter.

Downing a large gin, she was just ordering a second when she spotted old Tom Handley at the bar. Greeting him like a long-lost friend, Mary lurched towards him, spilling her drink on his coat sleeve. Alcohol on an empty stomach was hitting the spot with speed.

'I got two letters on the same day, Tom,' she said, trying to mop up with her grubby handkerchief. 'One of them was from my Lottie, of course, telling me she was married. My little girl, married, to a Canadian Mountie from Scotland, who would believe it?' Not waiting for an answer, Mary swayed before carrying on. 'There was good news in the other letter, too, if only my darling girls will help out. You remember my mother, Tom?'

Tom shook his head, wishing he had chosen The Plough for his pint.

'Yes, you do – Fanny, Fanny Allen. She came to The Crick to help me with my confinement when Flossie came into this world. Anyway, she's in Stone House. I went to find her yesterday, on my way down here. Found the poor woman in one of the airing grounds. She barely knew me, Tom. The paupers don't get much looking after in the asylum. Still, praise be she's not in Bedlam. Anyway, they're offering to move her to a new private ward, just being built. I just need to come up with the money.'

Mary looked at her empty glass, and realising that Tom was unlikely to buy her another drink, gathered up her shawl and bonnet and without wasting another word, hurried off, intent on finding bigger fish to fry back at Kate's.

Quarrelling one time too many with her son and his wife, Fanny Allen had left their uncomfortable home and finished up penniless on the streets of Spitalfields. Most of her days were spent slumped semi-conscious in doorways until her drunken, incoherent outbursts resulted in an arrest. Diagnosed with dipsomania, she was committed to the City of London's lunatic asylum at Stone, three miles from Northfleet. Now with the recent changes in the Lunacy Act, the asylum was allowed to take in private patients, for whom better treatment could be exacted for a fee. It was all too obvious what Mary was after.

'Oh, my beautiful little girl, my favourite,' Mary cried, holding on to Lottie tightly. 'How I have longed for this moment when you would return to the bosom of your loving mother.'

Lottie recoiled, sickened by the cloying words and the stale smell of the alehouse that pervaded Mary. Both stood looking at one another for a few seconds until Lottie plucked up the courage to speak.

'It's been too long, Mother. I am not your little girl any more. I had to grow up all too quickly and now I am a wife.' Feeling her resolve weakening and tears welling, she looked desperately at Andrew. The tall, reserved Scotsman who had been watching from the shadows now came forward and stood beside Lottie, holding her hand firmly.

'So this is your man,' Mary slurred. 'How strong and serious he looks. May I kiss the cheek of my son-in-law?'

Andrew bristled, making it quite clear by his stance that her kiss would not be acceptable. He had heard plenty about Mary Oxer, and for two farthings would have thrown her out on her ear forthwith. He hated seeing his Lottie so distressed, especially following a sleepless night worrying about this encounter.

Feigning hurt, Mary slumped into a chair. 'Please, please, don't turn on me,' she wailed. 'I've come all this way for fear that I wouldn't catch a glimpse of my darling daughter before you go to live in Scotland. Surely I must have been forgiven for what I did in the past, mustn't I? I know there's little point bringing it all up again, but I had to straighten things out with my rightful husband, your father. We are back together again now and making the best of it. He would love to see how you've turned out, dearest Lottie.'

Having been so upset at the thought of seeing her mother after all this time, Lottie was surprised that she felt almost nothing but pity for the pathetic creature sobbing before her. There really *wasn't* any point looking into the past again. After all, nothing could be changed. Nothing would make her look upon Henry Oxer as her father, and she certainly had no desire ever to meet him. No, instead she would look forward to her new life with Andrew, with children of her own to love and cherish. She must consider herself extremely fortunate.

'I am only interested in the future,' Lottie declared with a new resolve.

The chill air in the room had a sobering effect on Mary. Her mind whirred. It seemed Henry was right. He had said that he doubted much sympathy, let alone money, would be forthcoming from the newlyweds. Knowing the Scotsmen he'd drunk with in the pubs of Ipswich, they were keen to keep hold of their money, so any nice little nest egg the McPhersons may have brought with them across the Atlantic wasn't likely to be coming her way.

Mary looked up at Andrew's stern, unwavering face, convinced that he had turned her daughter against her. She needed to try another tack. Surely Lottie would want to sponsor her own grandmother's care as a private patient in Stone House? As a pauper patient, the conditions were terrible, and no one should be expected to live like that in their old age.

'If you could just see your way to giving us a shilling a week,' Mary pleaded after giving a graphic description of what she had experienced the day before at Stone, 'and maybe if you could talk to Flossie about giving us the same, especially since I hear she has a beau of her own, your grandmamma will be kept in a separate ward away from the paupers, with bedding rather than straw. She'll get proper food and be able to wear her own clothes, too. Follow your conscience, think of the good you will do,' she finished sanctimoniously.

Andrew had heard and seen enough. Being locked up due to alcoholism was the woman's own fault as far as he was concerned, and it was very likely that Mary would end up the same way. Neither of the girls had ever known their grandmother and Lottie couldn't even remember Mary talking about her. He felt certain that the money – should they be foolish enough to agree – would get no further than the Oxers' pockets. Signalling to Lottie to get her coat, Andrew fixed Mary with a steely glare.

'What do *you* know of conscience, woman?' he snarled.

Mary's face betrayed a mixture of bewilderment and anger. She had done her best to appeal to Lottie's good nature and to please Henry. Slumping into the nearest chair, she covered her face with her hands. Andrew opened the front door and, with his arm round Lottie's shoulders, they both stepped out into The Creek.

Kate looked at the mantle clock. She had arranged for Sam to come straight to her house after the finishing whistle went and time was getting on. They had decided it was best to keep his arrival from Mary as she would surely take herself off to The Huggens and be rendered incapable of making the train.

In the event, she was just finishing a much-needed bowl of stew when the door knocker went. Kate let him in and Mary heard them talking quietly to each other in the hallway. For a second she seemed not to take in who was standing in the kitchen doorway. Then, as if a volcano was erupting, she hurled the bowl, as well as a torrent of abuse, at Sam.

'Get your things together,' Sam shouted, holding his ground. 'You're going back to where you came from. I'm taking you to the train.'

Mary's barrage of obscenities continued unabated. If this was the woman he had been so devastatingly attracted to, there was nothing left of her beauty. An all-too-thin creature in near-rags was all she was now, her grey, lined face ravaged by drink.

If ever she felt remorse for what had gone wrong between them, it was clearly forgotten. Indignation and recrimination were all that she felt now towards her former lover.

Sam could see no point in wasting his breath defending himself. Better to save his energies for getting her to the station. Recognising the old carpet bag he was pushing her things into, he gave an ironic smile. He had filled this before – when she left Ipswich with him, all those years ago.

Cold air filled the room as he opened the front door. Kate hastily wrapped a chunk of bread and cheese and slipped it into Mary's pocket. It was pointless bidding her farewell as the woman's protests drowned out everything. Bundling Mary out and down The Creek, Sam could hear the foghorns on the river. He walked her up College Road, away from the temptations of The Huggens and nowhere near Lawn Road and Lizzie.

Mary was silent by the time they reached the station in near-darkness. Moving under a gas lamp on the platform, Sam looked into her dull eyes.

'I always thought it went wrong for us after our son – the boy you so longed for – died. You took that badly. So tell me, how could you have abandoned your new son, a *healthy* son, in the workhouse?'

Mary's face turned black as thunder. 'What's it got to do with you, Samuel Gant? But since you ask, Henry wouldn't take me back with a child he hadn't fathered.'

'And you have no regrets?'

'No regrets? I had no *choice*. It was the same with Flossie. You left me with no choice then. I couldn't go back to Ipswich with her in tow, so I decided to leave both girls. It was a good place and at least they had each other. I know where my boy, William, is and maybe I'll get him back one day.'

Dumbfounded, Sam stared at her as a huge locomotive shuddered to a halt, enveloping them both in smoke. Straightening the tattered feathers on the top of her crumpled bonnet, Mary plonked it on her head and got on the train without so much as a backwards look.

14th March 1892

Dear Floss,

I still cannot get used to writing to you from the Lowlands of Scotland rather than the Canadian prairies!

It seems hard to believe that we have been back over a year and have been living in Glasgow for eight months. Andrew's parents wanted us to stay in Argyll, but they understood that the move was necessary for him to find work, which fortunately proved true. My love is doing very well as a police constable in Glasgow – said to be the oldest police force in the world – and now that the city's territory has doubled, he is kept very busy. He tries to tell me about it, but to I prefer to remain ignorant about the horrors of Sauchiehall Street on a Saturday night!

We went to see Buffalo Bill's Wild West Show recently. I heard they were making Glasgow their only stop north of the border on their latest tour and I remembered your vivid description of the cowboys and Indians arriving at Tilbury some years back. Andrew marvelled at the marksmanship of the diminutive Annie Oakley, and the Indian attacks on the wagon train were so exciting! Sadly, though, the troupe has been seen far and wide across the city, quite often the worse for drink, and there is still no sign of some of them leaving despite the run having come to an end over six weeks ago. My brave love came home quite exhilarated and full of his exploits one night when he had to apprehend Charging Thunder after he assaulted the show's manager. The Red Indian is currently languishing in Barlinnie Gaol!

Well, sister, it seems you are moving up in the world... Kate told me in her last letter that you no longer look to the Knight family for your employment now that Miss Elizabeth has left university and is studying to be a doctor of medicine. I suppose she has no need of a lady's maid any more. How brave she is to enter what has always been a man's world. So perhaps it is her pioneering spirit that has inspired you, too, to work for the first ever women's trade union? My principled older sister, a campaigner! I am so proud of you. You and Henry are to be commended for your efforts to improve working conditions. Together you make a formidable alliance!

Kate also mentioned that Joe Ollerenshaw is on reduced hours, forcing his wife to take in washing to make ends meet. It's certainly a grim time for all the families in The Crick now that so many of the cement factories are failing. It seems doubly unfair that a shocking number have perished from influenza throughout the winter, particularly the old and the young. It was a great relief to hear that Sam and Lizzie's brood have recovered, especially baby Florence Gertrude. I know there were great concerns for your namesake for a while.

And so, my darling, this leads me on to my own exciting news. I have amazed myself that I have managed to keep it till last.

I am expecting Andrew's child! We are overjoyed, of course, as are the rest of the McPherson clan, and were beginning to think it would never happen. (I have to admit I was somewhat frustrated when I heard that Jess and Stanley are now on to their second child.) I have been quite nauseous of late, but that seems to be passing and we are so looking forward to our long-awaited bundle of joy arriving in August.

*Please write soon, I know you are extremely busy, but
I so love hearing your news. Your life is so different from
my own.*
Your loving sister,
Lottie
PS: I trust your lodgings are comfortable?

Flossie folded Lottie's letter carefully and placed it back in its envelope. Her lodgings in Nevern Road, Earl's Court were indeed comfortable, and from her window she watched the servants disappearing down the steps to the basement entrance of the mansion next door. Less than a year ago she might well have been one of them. Instead, here she was, in secure employment enabling her to pay rent to a professor of mathematics and his wife, who took in boarders. Elizabeth Knight had provided an excellent reference to overcome the landlord's initial reluctance to take in a single woman, Flossie being the only female out of the six lodgers, each with their own room.

Dear Elizabeth – what an influence she had turned out to be. Having filled her lady's maid's head with new – often radical – ideas whilst studying classics at Newnham College, Cambridge, she had made Flossie realise that there was a world out there to which she could contribute rather than simply being in service. At the same time Elizabeth had confided in Flossie her decision to give up classics and leave Cambridge in order to train for a career in medicine. For both women, the course they now chose would require great strength of will and commitment.

Both Elizabeth and Henry were in no doubt that Flossie should apply for the post of campaigner at the Women's Trade Union League. Initially she was afraid she wouldn't be good enough for such a responsible job, but Henry especially gave her the confidence to try. There was a widespread belief, even amongst trade unionists, that letting women work threatened men's jobs. Henry was different, though. He believed that women had the right to choose their own destiny, but knew that emancipation involved struggle.

'I am so proud of you,' he told Flossie on hearing that she had been accepted for the job. 'It takes courage to do something you believe in, but it's hard getting on in this world when you don't have a head start.' That's why she loved him. He was always there to support her.

A bewildered Jess, on the other hand, couldn't understand how her friend was even contemplating such a job. 'You'll be married and laden with a bairn soon,' she said. 'My Stanley wouldn't hear of such a thing if I were to think of doing so.'

Flossie had become used to such comments. Women got married and had children. That was what was expected of them. Jess and Lottie were content with producing children, so why shouldn't she be? Why should she be any different?

But that was the point. She *was* different. Her experiences had made her so. Never forgetting the girls at Dr Barnardo's, from factory worker to matchstick girl, their stories had left a deep impression on her. By joining the Women's Trade Union League, she would be able to do something useful at last. Reading about Emma Paterson, the league's activist founder, Flossie realised how much this courageous woman had achieved during her short lifetime. Forced into the labour market after the death of her father, she became involved in union activities and suffragism at an early age. Her organisation set up over thirty trade unions. From dressmakers and upholsterers to bookbinders and typists, all benefitted from her vision. One of the first female delegates to the Trades Union Congress, she had, early on, pressed for equal pay for women.

But the thing that caught Flossie's eye was Emma's role in setting up the Women's Union Swimming Club in 1878, following the huge death toll in the *Princess Alice* paddle steamer accident on the River Thames. She revealed that because women had limited opportunities to learn how to swim, they would not have known how to save themselves in such an accident. Flossie remembered Henry counting the bodies of women and children as they floated downriver, and the men on Bevan's *Spry* fishing them out of the water. Reading about the accident again sent a shiver down her spine.

20

Flossie had been enjoying an early dinner with Henry at The Gaiety in the Strand when he proposed to her. The restaurant was extremely busy and she could barely hear what he was saying, but the look of adoration in his eyes as he took her hand was unmistakable. Of course she accepted without hesitation, and the pair left the restaurant lost in their own world.

'I have a surprise for you,' Henry said as they strolled up Bow Street.

'*Another* surprise?' Flossie asked playfully.

'I'm full of surprises,' he laughed.

Turning the corner, there, lit up by burning torches, stood the magnificent Theatre Royal, Drury Lane.

'Harry Relph!' Flossie exclaimed on seeing the posters advertising the leading man in the Christmas pantomime. 'Oh, Henry, how wonderful.'

Henry had told Flossie they were going to the music hall, but not that they were going to the Theatre Royal to see a young man they had last encountered tap-dancing on the cellar flap at The Elephant's Head when they were children. Harry Relph had gradually worked his way to stardom. From earning pennies outside Rosherville Pleasure Gardens to pounds appearing in music halls across London, he had become famous touring America as 'Little Tich', as he now called himself, and was back in London performing with Marie Lloyd and Dan Leno in one of Drury Lane's extravagant productions.

Henry and Floss were thoroughly entertained watching Tich in the title role of Humpty Dumpty, where the skills displayed in his new big-boot dance captivated the audience. Standing on the tips of his twenty-eight-inch shoes and leaning at extraordinary angles, he had people crying with laughter. The 'Young Tichborne' had clearly come a long way.

The show provided the perfect end to the perfect day and there was much to discuss as Henry escorted his new fiancée back to her lodgings in Earl's Court. Kissing goodbye, Flossie couldn't have been happier. For the first time, her future seemed to be mapped out with some degree of certainty.

Kate Bailey was in her element when it came to the big day. A summer wedding was the best time for flower-arranging and St. Botolph's looked glorious. She sat in the front row, hoping to take advantage of a few minutes' calm, but it didn't last long. Henry and Edward – his brother and best man – followed by the ushers Stanley Bull and Andrew McPherson, came through the heavy, creaking door and began pacing the nave. Kate could do nothing but smile.

Back in Lawn Road, Lizzie was trying hard to keep the hoard of children in her front room as clean and happy as she could whilst Lottie and Jess battled to flatten Flossie's hair. Given their previous experience, it began well, but getting the veil to stay on was trying their patience. At the same time, in The Creek, William was finishing off the adornment of Dobbin's cart and, with a carrot or two to encourage the old horse, they set off together to collect their precious load.

Flossie looked radiant as William helped her up into her 'carriage'. Getting her attendants in alongside her didn't go quite so well, but after a couple of false starts, Dobbin trotted off, clearly determined not to falter on this most important day.

The church was full of family, friends and colleagues as Sam proudly led his daughter down the aisle. The bridesmaid, twelve-year-old Henrietta Gant, followed behind, glancing back occasionally at the three tiny, but perfect, flower girls: sister-Florence Gertrude, cousin-Agnes McPherson and Jessie's daughter, Mabel Bull.

As Henry and Flossie stood before the altar and said their vows, more than a few tears were shed amongst the congregation. Pronouncing them man and wife, the vicar gave the groom leave to kiss the bride. Against all convention a great cheer greeted the happy couple's embrace. St. Botolph's windows rattled with enthusiastic hymn-singing and as the bride and groom emerged into the sunlit churchyard they were covered in rose petals and rice.

Elizabeth Knight had decided that the best wedding present was a contribution towards the cost of the reception, so Kate and Lizzie had prepared a fantastic spread for everyone back in The Creek. True to form, Henry was the life and soul of the celebrations. Later, spilling out onto the river's edge, Flossie thought her heart would burst as she danced with him in the moonlight.

Having saved up enough money, the newlyweds rented a small cottage in Greenwich, close by the river, so that they could be near enough to regularly visit their families. One day in April 1894, the Gants and the Lucks walked to the old riverside Red Lion public house at the foot of Crete Hall Road. A large residential area had just been cleared in readiness for the construction of another cement factory, and today was the official opening of its deep-water wharf. Projecting 230 feet into the Thames, it, for the first time, allowed vessels to moor and leave even on the lowest tides. Numerous press and shipping men had come to see it.

Sam failed to understand the need for yet more competition when other cement works were struggling, but he and his sons couldn't help but marvel at the vast amount of chalk being loaded into the massive hull of the *Southern Cross*, the first vessel to moor at the wharf.

'Bet you're glad that's not your job today, James?' said Henry's mother, Daisy, as she affectionately squeezed her husband's hand.

Having watched the opening ceremony, everyone was eagerly awaiting the ship's departure for America, but there was a delay. Sam went off to find out why, but as the children were becoming fractious, Lizzie decided she would take little Florence and nine-month-old Maud Eliza home, leaving Flossie in charge of the rest.

'The crew's gone missing,' scoffed Sam on his return. 'Too much free beer on the wharf, it seems. C'mon, chaps, let's down a tankard ourselves in The Red Lion while we wait. There's something I want to ask you, Henry.'

Much to Flossie's irritation, the thirsty men disappeared without giving her a second thought.

'So what do you make of this letter that everyone's talking about?' Sam said between gulps of ale.

Henry had been expecting such questions from him. The union had been involved in several heated meetings about the proposed cement factory lay-offs.

'It's only a matter of time, Sam,' he replied. 'Desperate times call for desperate measures. Not right, I know, but if the cement's being tampered with, it only worsens our bargaining position.'

A circular letter had been sent to all the cement manufacturers on the Thames by a firm of London solicitors.

They pointed out that the adulteration of cement by some works was a scandal which was bringing the trade into disrepute, and suggested that the only way to protect a threatened industry was to amalgamate the various manufacturers. That hadn't gone down well with the workforce, and there was tension in the air.

'But what will happen to all of our jobs?'

Henry shook his head. What he suspected wasn't something he wished to divulge. 'Hopefully the worst is still a long way off,' he said evasively.

Sam stared at him for a moment and then drained his beer. Both men knew the writing was on the wall for Northfleet's cement industry.

Henry blinked as they emerged into the sunlight. A lot of people had already drifted away, but Flossie was still standing there with the children. She motioned for him to join her as something exciting was happening. No fewer than sixteen Trinity House pilots had assembled and were preparing to ease the mighty *Southern Cross* away from the wharf before navigating it out into the estuary. A blast on the horn made the children shriek.

'Should all go smoothly now, then,' Henry said with a guilty laugh.

17th August 1895
Glasgow

Dearest Floss,

I'm afraid this is going to be a short letter. Keeping up with Agnes, at three, and Arthur, who is walking, takes all my time.

Our little family is expanding nicely as I am with child again, dearest sister. Andrew is proving to be an attentive

father and I am turning out to be a fulfilled mother –
which I expect surprises you!

I was pleased to hear that Lizzie has given birth to
Hilda Emily. That's three girls in a row now!

I had to smile when you wrote about the Thames
being obstructed by large ice floes in February and Henry
skating on the canal. Remembering how boisterous he was
as a child, I had visions of the ice cracking beneath him
and you having to pull him out.

One final thing, my darling sister: I have to explain the
scrap of newspaper I have sent you. I received it recently
from our mother. It was her latest attempt at pulling at my
heartstrings to convince me to send her money. All to no
avail, I hasten to add. She obviously felt I should see what
depths her 'beloved' Henry has sunk to, and how all their
money goes on paying fines.

I sincerely hope that we can all be together again this
Christmas and New Year.
All my love,
Lottie

Unfolding the piece of paper from the *Ipswich Journal*, Flossie
read the account without emotion:

10 June. Henry Oxer, described as labourer on tramp,
fined 10 shillings for being drunk and disorderly in Carr
Street. He said he would not go to the police station unless
40 policemen were called. However, he offered no real
resistance.
20 June. A sad story of domestic misery was disclosed
in the progress of an assault case brought against Henry
Oxer, labourer, from 2 Gooding's Court, by his wife. It
seems that on Monday the defendant struck his wife for
not preparing a dinner for him; the woman plaintively

*added that she was unable to procure any comestibles,
for she had no money. It next appeared that for ten years
the couple had been parted several times – fined 10s 6d.*

Screwing up the flimsy scrap, Flossie threw it into the fire and
watched it burn until the blackened fragments rose up from the
grate and disappeared up the chimney.

Mrs Hannah Knight and Elizabeth returned to Northfleet in
November of the following year, 1896, to attend the official
opening of the Knight Almshouses in Perry Street. As founders,
there was much handshaking and polite conversation to
endure but, as soon as she could, Elizabeth slipped away to
meet Flossie by the old Five Ash Windmill close by. Once an
essential feature of the local farming economy, the windmill
had become obsolete as the wheat fields shrank and Perry
Street expanded.

'Seems strange not to see the old sails going round,'
Elizabeth said as they embraced upon meeting. 'It's too cold to
stand still. Let's take a walk around the church; I want to hear
all your news.'

The two women chatted for quite some time. Elizabeth's
experiences at the operating table made Flossie feel quite
queasy, but there was no mistaking her enthusiasm for
medicine. As for her own news, Flossie talked of her life with
Henry, her job, Lottie's and Jessie's growing broods, as well as
Sam and Lizzie's eighth child, baby Ernest William.

'And what about you, my dear? Elizabeth laughed, pulling
open Flossie's coat and staring at the slim figure before her. 'No
additions to your own family yet, I see.'

'Certainly not,' squealed Flossie, quickly closing her coat.
Discussing something that private with her former employer
made her acutely embarrassed.

Thankfully Elizabeth sensed her discomfort and

apologised. Grabbing Flossie's hand, she led her to a nearby bench.

'I'm so proud of what you have become. We women have to stick together, to fight the good fight for our own sex. It makes me so angry that even Mr Gladstone is against giving women the vote.' Picking up her bag from the floor, she pulled out a well-thumbed copy of *The Emancipation of Women and Its Probable Consequences*. Flossie noted that it had been written by a woman.

'He has sent copies of this book to all the female members of the Liberal Party who support our cause. I must read you one passage, then you'll see why we must fight together for women's suffrage.'

Indignantly, Elizabeth began reading: '*If women take the jobs, men will not be able to support wives and families. Hence marriage rates will decrease. And if marriage rates decrease, culture will fail. Additionally, women who work will not be able to serve their husbands as they should, with the consequence that woman's nature will be prevented. Even women doctors ultimately undermine women's sacred role. Rather than trying to serve in more than one capacity, women should remember that the greatest civic role is to bring up their children well, and that the highest moral role is to serve their husbands.*'

Slamming the book shut, she added, 'It seems we are a danger to the welfare of humanity.'

Flossie was at a loss for words. Though she understood Elizabeth's anger, they saw the world differently. If you came from the working classes you had limited expectations about self-improvement, let alone gaining the vote. With the damp air beginning to permeate her clothes, Flossie looked at her pocket watch.

'I have to go,' she said. 'Otherwise I'll miss my tram. I'm so sorry, Elizabeth.'

Kissing each other on the cheek, Elizabeth took hold of

Flossie's arms and said seriously to her, 'You do see that women should have a right to choose which path they take?'

Flossie nodded as thoughts of her mother's life in the slums of Ipswich flashed through her mind. 'Some of us don't have the luxury of choice, though,' she found herself saying.

Elizabeth shrugged. 'Comparisons are odious. I may have had a more privileged upbringing than you, but today we are fighting for the same cause, and together we will win in the end. Look at the progress we have made already.'

As they parted, Flossie found herself thinking that as nearly half the male population were still without the vote, there was a long, long way to go before women could dream of equality.

Over the next three years life got even harder for Sam and Lizzie. Having well and truly outgrown their lodgings in Lawn Road, they moved back to The Creek at number 34. Sam worried constantly about paying the rent without boarders to help them out, but he kept such thoughts to himself. Lizzie blamed the sudden death of Ernest William on their overcrowded conditions, and was making herself ill over it.

The 'summer complaint' – a deadly disease of the hot, moist months – struck the tiniest of children and poor Ernest had only just started crawling. He developed such a high fever that despite his two older brothers being told to run all the way to the chemist for a bottle of Mixture Cholera Infantum, the poor child died within twenty-four hours.

Luckily another boy, Frederick Charles, came along barely a year later, helping Lizzie overcome her grief; then by the autumn of 1899, she gave birth to Herbert Henry.

'I have to go, Lizzie dearest,' Sam said, grabbing his cap. 'Maybe Kate can help you. Send one of the girls next door to ask.' He knew he wasn't popular, leaving Lizzie to fend for herself now that Henrietta had a job as a scullery maid and wasn't home to help.

'Are you ready, son?' he said, checking to see where Samuel Junior was hiding. 'We mustn't be late, this is really important.'

Young Sam, now aged fifteen, had only just been taken on at the new Red Lion Cement Works – the first to use locomotives to haul chalk wagons. He'd been building up his muscles loading and unloading all day long, and was tired. Dragging his feet as his father rushed up Hive Lane, the last thing on his mind was having to be there for the beginning of the meeting. In any case, he'd heard that Red Lion were determined not to join the so-called 'combine', so he didn't think there was any chance he would lose his job. His father, on the other hand, thought amalgamation spelt trouble for everyone and was not surprised to find the Factory Club full to bursting with like-minded individuals.

It was difficult to keep order and the representatives from the proposed Associated Portland Cement Manufacturers looked flustered as they repeatedly tried to put across their argument.

'Rationalisation of the industry is the only way to survive!'

'We can eliminate unnecessary competition.'

'Concentrate on the most efficient works.'

A representative from the General Labourers' Union, who had been drafted in for his local knowledge, spoke for the mob by asking the question that was on everybody's lips: 'But what about people's jobs? Can you give assurances that no one will be put out of work?' It was Henry Luck.

Acknowledging that amalgamation would inevitably cause hardship for some, the cement owners professed that it was the only way to protect the industry from overseas competition.

'We will protect one another. It will be those of you whose employers do *not* join the combine who will be at risk of losing your jobs,' one of them said forcefully.

'You see – the Red Lion works is possibly at more risk,' Sam reminded his bored son.

The meeting ended in rancour. There was little chance of finding common ground between the two sides. Sam Junior disappeared as soon as people started to move, while his father and Henry made their way to The Huggens for a pint. Both men appeared deep in thought. After a while, Sam asked Henry what he made of it all.

'Whether we like it or not,' Henry replied, 'I fear amalgamation may be the only solution to the problems facing the industry right now. There's going to be a lot of unemployment though, Sam. Not all the works will survive, and that will affect everyone else – coopers, bargemen and the like – just as much.'

It wasn't what Sam wanted to hear, but he sensed that Henry was right. 'Hard times ahead, then,' he said, banging his tankard down on the table.

On the 10th of July 1900, Associated Portland Cement Manufacturers was registered as a company. Twenty-four cement companies, owning a total of thirty-five cement plants, were amalgamated, nine of them between Swanscombe and Northfleet.

As Henry had speculated, the amalgamation wasn't popular with riverside tradesmen, who saw the demise of the small firms as a nail in the coffin for their businesses. There was angry talk in the alehouses, though little could be done to halt the lay-offs. The fate of thousands of workers now hung in the balance.

'So, Floss, how did you enjoy Christmas in Scotland?' Jess asked.

'It was beautiful, and so lovely to see the McPhersons in their own home. They made Henry and I feel very welcome.'

'I suppose it makes sense, you going all the way up there. It must be difficult for them to travel right now.'

'Four children and another on the way,' sighed Flossie.

'I can barely get to the shops and back without losing one of these,' Jess laughed, gathering her children around her. 'I'll tell you what, though, let's leave these with my ma and then we can go for a walk – just like old times.'

The two of them strolled to the Undershore, making their way through the alleyways they had roamed as children, before emerging outside the deserted Rosherville Gardens.

'I cannot believe this,' Floss said, pointing at the bill posted on the entrance kiosk. 'It says it's up for auction.'

'It's gone bankrupt,' confirmed Jess. 'Londoners can afford to go to the seaside for the day now, so they're not coming here anymore. Who would think such a magical place would ever close? It seems impossible that we won't see those much longer, either,' she added, pointing to two passing horse-drawn trams. After much debate about the respective merits of gas and electricity, it had finally been agreed by the corporation to use electricity for the tramways and street lighting.

'At least we might be able to get across the road without having to lift our skirts so high,' Flossie laughed.

'So tell me more,' Jess continued. 'Any more news of your mother and that waste of a husband she seems unable to leave?'

'Well, it seems she *has* left him and retrieved her son William from the Wisbech Workhouse. They are living with a widower in Ipswich.'

'Goodness. How old is William?'

'Fourteen, and old enough to earn her some money, no doubt. Henry Oxer is back living with his mother in that disgusting place, Bond Court.'

'It's the end of an era and things will change, my dearest Floss. What with the war in South Africa and the old Queen gone, I suppose we'll be calling ourselves Edwardians from now on.'

There had been several public processions and services in memory of the much-loved Queen Victoria, who had died on

22nd January 1901. No one was sure how her pleasure-seeking son Bertie would fare as King Edward VII.

'Edwardians… how strange that sounds,' Flossie repeated. 'No, we two are definitely Victorians, but our children won't be.'

Jess blinked and gave her a quizzical look. '*Our* children?' she said.

Flossie blushed, aware that her slip of the tongue placed her in an awkward position. Turning to her friend, she looked her straight in the eyes.

'I do have some news of my own, Jess, but I've been waiting to pick the right moment.' Taking her hand, she pressed it against her stomach.

'You're not!' Jess shrieked. 'Florence Luck, you weren't going to tell me, were you?'

'I was, dearest Jess. I just didn't know how. It's such a surprise. We had all but given up hope, especially now I'm almost thirty-two.'

The two women hugged each other, half-laughing and half-crying.

'A baby Luck, at last. Well, I never. About time too! I didn't think it polite to ask.' Jess fumbled for her handkerchief. 'I thought you had no time for children, being so hell-bent on getting every woman in England to join a union?'

'I shan't be able to travel to Scotland next Christmas, that's for sure.' Flossie smiled. 'And there's a bit more news which will surprise you, too. I have given up my job as Henry is so worried about my delicate state. Since he spends all his time here, what with the unemployment over the cement combine and all that, we've decided to move back to Northfleet.'

Jess clapped her hands together in sheer joy. 'Oh, Floss, I am so pleased. How wonderful! About everything, I mean. You know I was only teasing you about the job.'

'I know you were,' laughed Flossie. 'The job *is* important and I certainly intend to continue the fight, but at the moment

I think it's best for me and Baby Luck to leave the campaigning to the likes of Elizabeth Knight. After all, she's in a far better position than me to fight for change.'

Kissing Jess on the cheek, Flossie paused before continuing.

'You know, we've come such a long way, but women like us don't have the choices that women like Elizabeth have, let alone the freedom that men enjoy by not being the child-bearers. That's why for now, I'm going to concentrate my energies on giving my child all the love and security I can.'

'We didn't have a bad childhood here, did we?' Jess asked.

'No,' Flossie replied. 'It could have been a lot worse.'

AUTHOR'S POSTSCRIPT

With no bidders, Rosherville Gardens, the place Londoners went *to spend a happy day*, closed in 1902.

Following the amalgamation of the largest British cement manufacturing companies of the time, Associated Portland Cement Manufacturers Ltd eventually closed down its entire Northfleet works, with the exception of Bevan's. After modernisation in 1925, Bevan's Portland Cement Works became the largest of its kind in Europe.

On Thomas Bevan's death in 1907, his three sons took over the business. For reasons of his own, he bequeathed to his daughter, Mary Pauline, forty thousand pounds on the condition that she did not marry a clergyman. On 24th September that same year, she married the Reverend Ernest Watkins Grubb at Christ Church, Westminster. A newspaper report, entitled *Heiress's Love Match*, described it as *a real love romance.*

Elizabeth Knight, the wealthiest woman doctor of her time, became a prominent campaigner for women's suffrage. She was sent to prison for calling at 10 Downing Street to ask Prime Minister Asquith why he had promised more votes for men, but not for women. She was imprisoned twice more for refusing to pay taxes while supporting the 'No Vote, No Tax' campaign. Dr Knight died in 1931 after being hit by a car in Brighton. Unwilling to go to hospital, she succumbed to internal injuries two weeks later.

Mary and Henry Oxer never got back together after Mary retrieved her son William from the workhouse. Private William George Allen Oxer of the 2nd Battalion, the Suffolk Regiment, was killed in action in Flanders during the Great War. Mary died shortly afterwards.

Andrew and Lottie McPherson remained in Scotland. They lost their beloved son to diphtheria, but went on to have four more girls. Like their mother, they all knew how to get their own way.

After the birth of her only child, a daughter named Emmeline, Flossie never went back to work for the union, though she remained committed to the cause of women's suffrage and continued to support Henry's fight for working people. The Lucks continued to live close to their devoted friends Jessie and Stanley Bull.

Sam and Lizzie Gant carried on producing children. Sam acknowledged having fathered fourteen in all, including the boy born to Mary Oxer. The list, however, did *not* include Flossie.

Maud Eliza Gant, their fourth girl, born in 1893, was my grandmother.

ACKNOWLEDGEMENTS

Special thanks go to Chris Manning and Kevin Scott – members of the Essex Gant family – who helped solve some early mysteries and set me on the right track.

I am also particularly grateful to Ken McGoverin, chairman of the Northfleet History Group, for allowing me access to his personal research on the area's cement industry.

USEFUL SOURCES

Genealogy, Family Trees and Family History Records
(www.ancestry.co.uk).

Medway Archives & Local Studies
(www.medway.gov.uk/libraries).

Gravesham Borough Council
(www.discovergravesham.co.uk).

The Northfleet Harbour Restoration Trust
(www.northfleetharbour.org.uk).

Memories of Northfleet by the Riverside (2010) and *Memories of
Northfleet High Street* (2007), booklets by Alex Pavitt.

The Place to Spend a Happy Day by Lynda Smith, Gravesend
Historical Society, Northfleet Press (2006).

*Rags and Bones: A Social History of a Working-Class Community
in Nineteenth-Century Ipswich* by Frank Grace, Unicorn
Press Publishing Group (2005).

The Children's Blizzard by David Laskin, HarperCollins
Publishers Inc. (2004).

London's Lost Riverscape by Chris Ellmers and Alex Werner,
Penguin Books Ltd (1988).

*For the Sake of the Children: Inside Dr Barnardo's, 120 Years of
Caring for Children* by June Rose, Hodder & Stoughton Ltd
(1987).

History of Gravesend by F. A. Mansfield, reprinted by Rochester Press (1981).

An Historical Walk Through Gravesend and Northfleet by Robert Heath Hiscock, Gravesend Historical Society, Phillimore & Co. Ltd (1976).

The Maiden Tribute of Modern Babylon by W.T. Stead, Pall Mall Gazette (1885).

Victorian London by James Greenwood, Diprose & Bateman (1883).

Street Life in London by John Thomson and Adolphe Smith, Sampson Low, Marston, Searle and Rivington (1877).

A Month at Gravesend 1863 by Elizabeth Jane Brabazon, Kessinger Legacy reprints (2010).

ABOUT THE AUTHOR

Angela Jean Young grew up in Gravesend, Kent. Her family has lived and worked on the River Thames for generations - which is what inspires her writing. Her autobiographical novel *Hollow Victory* (2014) charted a teenager's coming-of-age journey through the Swinging Sixties. Angela worked as a researcher in London's dynamic advertising scene and now concentrates on writing and historical research.